A Rob Wyllie paperback
First published in Great Britain in 2022 by Rob Wyllie Books, Derbyshire, United Kingdom

Copyright @ Rob Wyllie 2022
The right of Rob Wyllie to be identified as the author of this work has been asserted by him in accordance with the Copyright, Design and Patents Act 1988
All rights reserved. No part of this publication may be reproduced, stored in a retrieval system, or transmitted. in any form or by any means, electronic, mechanical, photocopying, recording or otherwise, without the prior permission of the copyright owner.
All the characters in this book are fictitious and any resemblance to actual persons, living or dead, is purely coincidental.
RobWyllie.com

The Maggie Bainbridge Series

A Matter of Disclosure
The Leonardo Murders
The Aphrodite Suicides
The Ardmore Inheritance
Past Sins
Murder on Salisbury Plain
Presumption of Death

The Leonardo Murders

Rob Wyllie

Chapter 1

Two-thirty pm on a late June afternoon, and for once the forecast had proved accurate, the sun splitting an azure-blue sky, its elevation perfect and its alignment about one hundred and ninety degrees off north. Eddie Taylor checked his little light meter, which only confirmed what he could see plainly with his own eyes. Ninety thousand lux. Couldn't be more perfect.

Carefully he removed his kit from the padded leather holdall. High-end digital SLR, super-steady tripod and the ultra-long zoom. Over two grand's worth in the lens alone, but it was his firm belief that a good workman needed the best tools, so it was money well spent. Particularly since he was having to set up nearly five hundred metres away, a distance that the big Canon lens would make short work of. He liked these little catalogue shoots, as he called them. Twelve hundred quid in his back pocket for half an hour's work, and no ghastly bridezillas to deal with like on his routine wedding work. He'd done two or three in the last couple of years, including the nice all-expenses jaunts to Europe. There was that trip down to the Dordogne and then a couple of months ago the Amsterdam job. And they'd sent him business class and put him up in a quality hotel. What was there not to like?

Today's assignment wasn't without risk of course, because understandably the authorities weren't too keen on primary schools being photographed, but he was far enough away not to arouse immediate suspicion, and of course he'd rocked up here in that little white hatchback with the estate agent's logo plastered all over the side. *Knox Brown Gets You Moving.* Up here in Hampstead you couldn't move for the parasites, the district being one area of the capital that was traditionally immune to property-price wobbles. There was so many of them swarming around the place that no-one would give a guy with a camera a second glance.

This was stage one in the surveillance operation. The idea was to get some decent identification shots of the target and to make sure you understood the pick-up routine. Then a bit of discreet tailing, figuring out the route they took home and sussing out one or two places where the snatch could take place with minimal risk of interruption.

It only took a few minutes to get set up, mounting the camera and lens securely on the stand and connecting the cable that operated the remote shutter release. A couple of adjustments and the school gates were sharply in focus. All set, giving him time to reflect that this assignment was a bit of an odd one. The last two or three, it was obvious why those kids had been targeted. With parents in the public eye and the prospect of a big fat juicy ransom, it made perfect sense. But as far as he knew, this kid was a nobody. Still, such musings were above his pay grade. Just do the job and take the money, thank you very much.

Now it was approaching three o'clock, and a gaggle of grown-ups were beginning to mill around the gate, the mums, one or two dads and of course, this being leafy Hampstead, the nannies and au-pairs. Sometimes they got in the way and made it difficult to get a clear shot, but the problem wasn't insurmountable. The key was to shoot as soon as the subject was in sight and not worry too much about the finer points of composition. He stole another glance at the photograph they had sent him, then scanned the scene, eyes struggling to focus in the bright sunlight. He'd had his first brief look at the boy yesterday, but the trouble was, they all looked pretty much the same to him in their neat school uniforms, and the boss wouldn't be happy if he got the wrong one. So it was important to be sure. But *there*, no doubt about it in his mind, that kid was the one. Skinny, tall for his age, smooth pink skin, thick glossy shoulder-length hair and a mischievous smile. He watched as the boy scanned along the pavement, looking for the fat girl who he assumed was his nanny. Yesterday she'd been nearly five minutes late and he wondered if maybe she made a habit of it. But today she was on time, the boy giving a broad smile of recognition before running over and throwing his arms around her. A quick peek at the viewfinder, a squeeze on the shutter release and the shot was in the can. *Result*.

He tossed the camera bag into the back of his hatchback, blipped the lock and casually began to stroll down towards the school. The nanny had got into conversation with a couple of the mums whilst the boy wrestled with a robustly-built younger girl, ending up with him spread-eagled on the pavement as she easily overpowered him. But soon they were on the move, heading south-east down Christchurch Hill at a brisk pace. He kept about fifty metres behind them, close enough to maintain visual contact without causing any suspicion, not that they ever looked back. Besides, the pavement was full of pedestrians at this busy school pickup time. No chance of him arousing alarm even if they did glance round.

After about half a mile the pair swung right onto Pilgrims Lane then left into one of the quiet upmarket residential streets, lined both sides by neat million-pound-plus terraced properties. This was more promising, with nobody about even at this busy period in the day and plenty of access to get a fast motor in and out in an instant. He removed his smartphone from his pocket, noted down the street name then took a few snaps of the general layout. Great, that was probably enough for today. He'd do one more trial sweep tomorrow and then they would be all set.

About half way back to where he had parked his car, he heard the ping of a message coming through on his phone. Mechanically, he removed it from his pocket and gave it a fleeting look. Another enquiry for one of those mum-dad-and-kids portrait jobs, checking his availability for October and requesting a mates-rate price. He thought it was a bit of a cheek given the mother was absolutely minted, but then the enquiry was from an old school pal from his East End days. Good old Roxy Kemp.

She being the actress now known as Melody Montague.

Chapter 2

It had been an early start, necessitating a 5.30am wake-up alarm and a 6.20am departure, leaving Maggie barely enough time for a shower and no time at all for breakfast. She had however left a few minutes' spare to creep quietly into her little son Ollie's bedroom, at first just looking at him and taking in his wonderful beauty, and then slipping over and kissing him on the cheek without disturbing him. It was a good hour before his normal rising time and he was still deeply asleep, and she hoped his dreams were lovely ones, the ones that every six-year old should have. A new toy car, a visit to the seaside, a kick-about with his school-friends in the playground. After all the tragedy of the last twelve months or so, it was what she yearned for more than anything. *Normality*. Her nanny Marta had already been up and about, busying herself in the kitchen whilst waiting for her coffee to brew. She was an absolute treasure, nothing being too much trouble for her and of course Ollie absolutely adored her. Not for the first time Maggie had reflected how lucky it had been that the lovely Polish girl had decided to stay with the family after the momentous events of the last year. Quite simply, that girl had help save her life. Along with of course, her amazing colleague Jimmy Stewart.

He was waiting for her in the tall glass-lined atrium of Addison Redburn's impressive Canary Wharf tower block, wearing a smart blue shirt with a button-down collar, black jeans and his trademark cowboy boots. He was also, she noted with some amusement, sporting an embryonic beard which she thought might suit him. Not that he needed any improvement, the thirty- two year old ex-bomb squad officer already being effortlessly and ridiculously handsome.

'Morning boss,' he said pleasantly. 'Looking forward to our meeting I must say. But just one wee thing on that subject if you don't mind. Can I just ask that we keep these middle-of-the-night jobs to a minimum? I had enough of them when I was in the bloody army.'

'Sorry,' she said, laughing. 'But you know what Asvina's like. Time is money and all that. And she's the client so she gives the orders.'

Maggie's great friend Asvina Rani was the go-to family law solicitor for London's great and good, with a particular specialisation in high-profile marital disputes involving high net worth individuals. Movers and shakers was how her friend described her client base. A-list actors, billionaire businessmen and high-profile politicians, if you were in that bracket and found yourself in a spot of relationship difficulty, Asvina Rani was the woman you turned to. Her charge-rates were eye-wateringly steep but her results were always impressive so most were happy to pay the price. Her PA Mary had come down to reception to meet them and soon a high-speed elevator was rocketing them up to the twenty-third floor, epicentre of Addison's lucrative family law operation. On arrival, the pretty PA led them over to a huge glass-windowed office, knocking once before pushing open the door and announcing their presence in a broad Cockney accent.

'Miss Bainbridge and Mr Stewart from Bainbridge Associates.' It was delivered with a comical formality, as if they were arriving guests at a Regency ball.

'Thank you Mary,' Asvina said, laughing. She came over to Maggie and gave her a hug. 'It's so nice to see you again.' She ended the embrace and extended a hand to Jimmy. 'And you too of course Jimmy. Sorry for the early start but my schedule's absolutely wall-to-wall today.'

Her friend was immaculately turned out as ever, elegant in a black knitted dress set off by a string of pearls that were obviously expensive. Tall and slim and with a silky jet-black mane that extended almost to her waist, Maggie reflected not for the first time that Asvina could easily be mistaken for a super-model.

'Wall-to-wall?' Maggie said, grinning. 'So just a normal Asvina day then. And as for the early start, Jimmy was just saying to me how much he loved an early rise. Reminds him of the army, that's what he said.'

He laughed. 'Aye it does, but not in a good way. But at least it's summer, so it's not quite so bad at this time of the year. The army used to ship us off to Norway in bloody December and drag us out of bed at three in the morning.'

'Sounds ghastly,' Asvina said, giving a mock grimace. 'Anyway, if you don't mind, shall we get started?'

Maggie nodded. 'Please do. So is it another divorce case?'

'Well sort of,' her friend said. 'There are actually two related matters, one relatively simple, the other rather more complicated I fear.'

'Sounds intriguing,' Jimmy said. 'And we like complicated, don't we Maggie?'

'Absolutely,' she agreed. 'Pray tell us more Asvina.'

'Ok. So our client is a Miss Roxy Kemp. She's an actress and rather better known by her stage name. She's someone you will definitely have heard of. I'm talking about Melody Montague.'

'What, the soap star from Bow Road?' Jimmy said, surprised. 'She's bloody huge. Everybody's heard of her.'

'Yes, she is a big star,' Asvina said, 'although I think she would prefer to be described as an iconic actor rather than a mere soap star.'

'How long has she been in the show?' Maggie said, then answered her own question. 'It must be getting on for thirty years now I'd guess.'

Asvina nodded. 'Twenty eight years in fact. She started when she was just in her early twenties and has been in it from the very first episode. She's a real East Ender too, brought up within earshot of the mythical Bow Bells, although whether they still peel or even still exist I'm not sure. But yes, I think that's why the producers fell in love with her. She's so authentic.'

'You seem to know a lot about her,' Jimmy said. 'Didn't take you for a Bow Road fan somehow.'

'Basic research,' Asvina said, laughing. 'She was so perfect for the role of Patty West. In real life her father was a docker and her two older brothers are a bit dodgy if the tabloids are to be believed. And here we are, twenty-eight years on. You could say the show has been her life, but it's been very lucrative for her too. She's done very well out of it.'

'Attractive woman,' Jimmy said. 'I suppose that's not done her career any harm either.'

Maggie smiled to herself. More than simple attractiveness, it was surely her raw sexuality that had been the driving force of Montague's successful career, being blessed with a Bardot-like sultry look that she guessed had been an absolute gift to the show's scriptwriters. Maggie wasn't an avid fan of the show, but she knew the actress's character Patty West had been through at least four marriages and dozens of affairs too. It was as if when they were stuck for a juicy plot line they just wheeled in a new toy-boy hunk and had him jumping into bed with her. She wondered if Montague's private life was similarly exotic.

'So what's the mission?' she asked. 'What do you want us to do?'

'Well, let's cover the simple one first,' Asvina said. 'Melody's decree nisi from her first husband has just come through and now she wants to marry the new man in her life.'

'She was married to Patrick Hunt wasn't she?' Maggie said. 'And he was in Bow Road at one time I think?'

Asvina nodded. 'Yes he was. In fact they met on the show and married more than fifteen years ago. Although he's not been in it for a few years now.'

'Quite a long marriage then by show business standards,' Jimmy said. 'So what happened?'

Asvina shrugged. 'A mixture of things I suppose. Patrick's career took a bit of a temporary downturn when he was written out of the show about five years ago and so I think there was some jealousy introduced into the relationship then. They didn't have children either and I think she wanted them very much. And then she met Benjamin David on the programme and fell head over heels in love. Or at least that's how she describes it.'

'I can see how that might happen,' Maggie said, laughing. 'Actually he looks a bit like you Jimmy. Quite hunky and he's trying to grow a beard too, although with a bit more success.'

'Ha-bloody-ha,' he said. 'But I'll take it as a compliment. If it was.'

She grinned. 'It was. But Asvina, he must be what, nearly twenty years younger than her?'

Asvina laughed. 'Yes he is, lucky woman. But she's not completely lost her senses over it. That's why she's engaged us, to put together a pre-nuptial agreement. Which is what I need you two to sort out. Because as you can imagine, there's a wide disparity in the value of assets they will be bringing into the marriage.'

Maggie nodded. 'Yes, I guess she is much wealthier than him?'

Asvina gave a wry smile. 'Yes, by a factor of about ten. So you can see why she wants the pre-nuptial in place before she ties the knot. Obviously, she wants to protect her assets.'

Maggie saw Jimmy trying to suppress a giggle and gave him a sharp look.

'You men,' she said, the tone affectionate. 'But yes, I can understand that if she is the wealthier partner. But this one seems pretty straightforward I'd guess. Which makes me worry the other matter is going to be anything but.'

Her friend gave her a rueful look. 'You could say that. *That* one concerns a pre-nuptial agreement too but yes, it's anything but straightforward. It's the one that Melody and Patrick signed more than fifteen years ago.'

'So what's the difficulty with that one?' Maggie asked.

'The difficulty is that Melody's copy of the agreement has gone missing and her recollection of its contents is quite different to that contained in the actual copy her husband has.'

'But surely her solicitors would have kept a copy too?' Jimmy said. 'Even if she didn't.'

Asvina nodded. 'And therein lies the nub of the problem. Because not only has he mislaid the document but the solicitor in question, one Blake McCartney, is currently in HMP Pentonville serving a five year sentence for money-laundering offences.'

'Bloomin' heck,' Maggie said. 'That's awkward. But I assume he was involved in drawing up the agreement in the first place, so what's he got to say about it?'

'He's been pretty useless I'm afraid,' Asvina said. 'It was fifteen years ago and he says he can't remember anything. His excuse is he's done hundreds of the things over the years and he can't be expected to remember the details of every one of them.'

Maggie sighed. 'Yeah, well I suppose that's plausible. I can't remember cases I did five years ago never mind fifteen. But I guess the document must have been witnessed. Have they been contacted and asked what their take on the matter is?'

'Equally unhelpful I'm afraid. One has since died and the other is corroborating Patrick Hunt's version. So you can see the difficulty. But you'll be able to hear the full story when you meet with Melody. And I've arranged something rather special for that.'

Maggie and Jimmy exchanged a quizzical look. 'And what's that?' they said, almost simultaneously.

Asvina smiled. 'You'll be meeting her on the set of Bow Road. And you two had better be very careful because they're always on the lookout for good-looking extras.'

Chapter 3

DI Frank Stewart launched one final kick at the ancient vending machine before issuing a heart-felt *bollocks*. Despondently, he shuffled back down the dank corridor of Atlee House to his ancient battered desk. Boy, how he had been looking forward to that mid-morning Mars Bar, but now he was to be disappointed - again. He resolved that this was the last time he was going to risk a two-pound coin in that damn machine. No bloody Mars Bar and no bloody change either.

That was the problem with working in poverty-spec Department 12B. It had the crappiest building, the crappiest equipment and the crappiest detectives, who quite naturally were assigned the crappiest cases. Present company excepted of course. Frank had been banished to this god-forsaken outpost of the Metropolitan Police not for being crap but because of an unfortunate incident involving his then senior officer. An incident that involved a push, a punch, a torrent of colourful Glaswegian invective and resulted in six stitches above the eye for the huge pile of twatness that was Detective Chief Superintendent Colin Barker. Only the general agreement at the most senior levels of the force that Barker fully deserved it had saved Frank from instant dismissal from the job he loved. Instead, he was sent into semi-permanent exile amongst the has-beens and never-had-beens that occupied Atlee House.

Nonetheless, Department 12B did perform a useful function, being the dumping ground for cases that couldn't find a natural home elsewhere in the Met. Or cases that the brass would rather see swept under the carpet. Cases like the Jamie Grant abduction. Almost two years to the day since the wee toddler had been snatched in broad daylight as he was being wheeled home from nursery by his child-minder. The fact that he was the son of the soap actor Charles Grant guaranteed maximum publicity for the case, but it hindered rather than helped the investigation, generating a ton of false sightings that swamped the murder team. The case had been a disaster from start to finish, not helped by it being under the command of the aforementioned Barker. Eventually when it became clear that there wasn't going to be a happy ending, the Assistant Commissioner quietly shut it down and shunted it off to Atlee House, telling the press it had been put in the hands of a specialist team. That had made Frank smile. Specialist team? It was obvious that the AC had never met any of the brain-dead losers who called themselves his colleagues.

Before heading to the vending facilities, he'd given the empty buff folder sitting in the middle of his desk an appraising look. So far, all he'd managed to do was stick a white label on the front of the folder and scribble the name of the case on it. *Operation Shark.* He wasn't sure why, but he liked to give all his investigations a code name. This one hadn't taken long to come up with and he didn't really know why he picked it, it just sounded sort-of, well, *solid.* He had a hunch that this investigation was going to turn into something big and he didn't want it saddled with a rubbish name.

On his return, he was pleased to see Eleanor Campbell waiting at his desk. He liked the quirky government forensic officer, and he thought she liked him too. Not romantically of course, in either direction, absolutely not, and that wasn't just because of the age gap - he was forty-two but looked about fifty on a good day, and she, he wasn't quite sure, probably thirty-two or thirty-three, but looked about sixteen. No, the gap in years might have been no more than ten, but culturally it was wider that the Grand Canyon. Beside which, there was the spectre of Maggie Bainbridge hovering over him. Very definitely out of his league, that was what he believed, but at least she was about his age. He was seeing her in a couple of days with his brother Jimmy, and was very much looking forward to it. Particularly since he had spent the last few days thinking of little else.

'Well hello wee Eleanor,' he said brightly. 'Ready to go then?'

She nodded enthusiastically, which was very much unlike her. 'Yeah, can't wait.'

He looked at her suspiciously before remembering. Eleanor had a new toy and this was the first time she would have a chance to test it in the field. The woman was a sucker for new technology, especially the shady stuff she seemed to have no trouble procuring from her mates at the Government Communications labs up in Cheltenham. She wouldn't tell him what this one was all about, except she was helping the GCHQ geeks with something called a beta testing programme. She'd explained it once, but he still had no idea what it meant.

'Are we like walking then?' she asked.

'No way,' Frank replied, grimacing. 'It must be nearly four miles. No, we'll take a squad car and stick the blue lights on.' He could tell from her expression that she wasn't sure if he was joking or not. He wasn't.

'I've googled it,' she said in a serious tone. 'It's only two point four miles.'

'Exactly. Too far to walk. Come on, we better get our arses in gear or we'll miss the start.'

He grabbed the keys of an Astra from the board and they headed out to the car park behind the building. Atlee House was located just off the Uxbridge Road and ordinarily it wouldn't take much more than five or ten minutes to get to Speakers' Corner, especially on a Saturday. But today was different. The calendar was approaching midsummer, and with the sun blazing down from a crystal blue sky it was the perfect day to get the crowds out for the biggest protest rally of the season so far. *Stars Against Fascism.* Frank laughed to himself at the colossal self-regard of some of those so-called celebs. But maybe they believed in it all, who was he to say?

The traffic was nose-to-tail along the Bayswater Road, which confirmed he'd made the right decision with regard to mode of transport. Flicking on the blue flashing lights, he pulled out from behind a bus and cruised down the wrong side of the road, giving an occasional burst on the siren to warn oncoming vehicles. Glancing over into the park, he could see his mates in the riot squad were already there in force, a dozen or more lightly-armoured minibuses parked up and ready for any argy-bargy, should it arise. Which as far as Frank was concerned, was a one-hundred-percent certainty.

As he had expected, the entrance to West Carriage Drive was closed, guarded by a pair of sour-faced constables who were unarmed but in riot gear.

'What do you want?' one of them barked as he pulled the Astra up in front of a temporary barrier that had been erected.

He flashed his warrant card. 'DI Stewart. Department 12B.'

The constable gave his mate an uncertain look, not sure if he should have heard of it or not. Frank kept schtum, hoping to avoid long and tedious explanations as to why he was here. It seemed to work.

'Yeah, all right sir,' the constable said, his voice betraying doubt as to whether he was doing the right thing, 'on you go.'

Frank gave him a nod of acknowledgement and threaded the car through the narrow gap that had been opened up for them. He drove on for two or three hundred yards then pulled over onto the grass verge.

'We'll just dump it here Eleanor,' he said, 'and then take a wee stroll over towards the stage, so we can get a good view.'

She muttered something under her breath, her attention fully given to her smart-phone. Looking at her, he saw she was wearing a perplexed expression.

'What did you say?'

'Their stuff is always pretty buggy but I can't get it to boot up. I might have to check the release notes.'

He shrugged, uncomprehending. 'Aye, well I'm sure you'll figure it out. Come on, let's go.'

They got out of the car and began walking towards the large stage, she still head-down and swiping a finger furiously across her screen. Taking in the scene, he struggled to estimate the size of the crowd that had assembled. Six, maybe seven thousand at the most, still decent but nothing like the half a million the organisers had claimed were going to turn up. That figure had made Frank chuckle. *Bow Road* and *Accident & Emergency* were popular soaps, he knew that, and some of the actors were household names, but it wasn't as if they had the draw of an Angelina Jolie or a Beyoncé.

There was quite a broad demographic from the age perspective, but much less so from a socio-economic viewpoint. Alongside the placards and banners, the protestors had come armed with tartan travel rugs, wicker picnic baskets and a seemingly inexhaustible supply of prosecco. For this was almost without exception a nice middle-class day out, attendance seen almost as a duty by the comfortably-off and comfortably-smug Islington set. But they weren't the only group driven to attend by a sense of duty, which explained the heavy presence of the riot squad boys. Because whenever the virtue-signalling left came out to play, the right-wing bully boys came out too. Right now, there was definitely a bit of a party atmosphere, but he didn't expect that to last. As they snaked their way through the crowds, he looked again at Eleanor. This time she was smiling.

'Sorted?' he asked, feigning interest.

'Yeah, think so.' She held the phone out in front of her at arm's length and began to scan the horizon. 'Yeah, sorted. Look.' She thrust the phone into his face.

'What am I looking at?'

'Facial rec linked to the PNC. It's awesome.'

'And it's also illegal.' He'd got to know more than he really needed or wanted to know about facial recognition technology as a result of a recent and very prominent case, and he hoped he'd heard the last of it. But apparently not.

'You can like tell in an instant if someone's got a criminal record. It does real-time interrogation of the Police National Computer. With sixty-four-bit encryption.'

'Good to know,' Frank said, 'but just be careful who you point it at around here, will you? Every second one of them is a human-rights lawyer and they would go ape-shit if they got a sniff of what you're doing.'

'It's only like a test,' she said defensively.

'Whatever.' It was one of her favourite expressions, and he liked to shoot it back to her whenever he could just to wind her up. This time, she scowled but said nothing.

A moderately well-known indie rock band were just closing their set with their sole hit, the lead singer having peppered the six-song performance with obligatory anti-Tory rants. Frank, something of a music buff, knew the guy's background. Public school, Durham Uni, old money. But he didn't hold it against him.

'Great song this,' he shouted to no-one in particular. He saw that Eleanor had her phone focussed on the vocalist.

'He's got a drugs bust,' she said, her tone smug, 'back in twenty-twelve.'

'Put the bloody thing away,' he said. 'You've proved it works, so that's a tick in the box. Let's just enjoy the speeches.'

The speeches. Because that's why they were here, and to hear one speech in particular. Operation Shark's Charles Grant, the left-wing activist nicknamed the Pound-Shop Martin Luther King by his enemies in the press. He'd need to do some research to find out how he'd come by the name, but he knew that they hadn't meant it as a compliment. But before Grant, it seemed there was to be a warm-up act.

'Ladies and Gentlemen, thank *you* for coming. Stars against fascism!' Frank recognised the compère as Paul somebody-or other, a comedian familiar to millions from his appearances on TV panel shows, and known for his left-of-centre politics. Then again, everyone on these shows had left-of-centre politics. It was mandatory and more important than actually being funny.

'Ladies and gentlemen, may I introduce to the stage, Mr Benjamin David and Ms. Allegra David.' As the two actors walked on from the wings, the crowd, seemingly reluctant to divert attention from their picnics, gave a ripple of polite applause. Frank didn't follow the soaps, but he vaguely knew of Benjamin. Played the randy GP in Bow Road, the one lucky not to be struck off when caught with his trousers down. His sister he was pretty sure he hadn't seen before but there was no doubting she was easy on the eye.

'Thanks Paul,' Benjamin said, waving to the crowd. 'Are you all right!' This time, the response from the audience was more enthusiastic, a loud *yes* followed by laughter. Alongside him, his sister beamed a smile and raised her hands in salute. It seemed in fact that it was she who would be the first to speak.

'We're here today, united in our great cause. The fight against fascism, the fight against the rise of global right-wing extremism.'

'Fuck off.'

Frank heard the shout, and knew instinctively that it was all about to kick off. To the left of the stage, a group of men had gathered, slurping from bottles of lager and directing single-finger gestures towards the platform.

'Commie twats.'

'As I said, we're gathered here today, united in the fight against fascism.' Allegra had evidently decided not only to ignore the hecklers, but to confront them too. That was going to prove to be a mistake. She pointed at the group. 'And if we ever needed evidence as to how important it is for us to win this fight, you can see it here. Right here in front of you. Fascist scum.'

Frank guessed she'd used these words plenty of times on her Twitter feed, but she was about to find out it was a whole order of magnitude more dangerous to use them in the real world. There was a horrified gasp from the crowd as a bottle smashed onto the stage just in front of the actress. But this bottle wasn't filled with beer.

'Christ, bloody molotovs,' Frank barked, as a sheet of flame shot up from the stage. Where the bloody hell were the riot boys when they needed them? Especially when he could guess what was coming next. He ran to the front of the stage and gestured to the actors.

'Get off the bloody stage now,' he screamed, then howled in pain as something hard struck him on the back of the head. In front of him, he saw that Benjamin David had been hit too, a stream of blood flowing down his face from where the sharpened coin had sliced into his forehead. Spinning round, he saw that Eleanor had her phone focussed on the ring-leader, and was shouting out a name to him.

But Frank didn't need the help of GCHQ's fancy beta software to recognise who stood just thirty feet from him, his face contorted with hatred. *Darren Venables*. The man known as D-V to his devoted following, and the self-proclaimed leader of the White British League.

That was all he flipping needed. The WBL was a banned organisation and here was their leader blatantly committing common assault in Hyde Park and not giving a monkey's who witnessed it. So much for Frank's hope of a quiet day out. He knew he should wait for the riot boys to get here, but they didn't seem to be in any hurry. And the thing was, he didn't want the scumbag getting away with it. So he checked in his back pocket for his handcuffs, then made the decision.

In for a penny, in for a pound.

Chapter 4

A few years earlier, Bow Road had migrated from its Hertfordshire studios to a purpose-build sound stage built on some vacant land left over from London's 2012 Olympics, and it was here that Asvina had arranged for them to meet with their latest client. Jimmy had seemed quite excited by the prospect, although whether it was because of the assignation with the attractive actress or the prospect of being an extra on Britain's most popular soap she was not quite sure. This time the start time was somewhat more civilised, but 9am still seemed rather early for an actress, engaged as she was in a famously late-night profession. Later Maggie would learn that the world of soap-opera production was far from glamorous, involving regular sixteen-hour days, the gruelling timetable being necessary to churn out the three episodes a week the network demanded. As she pushed open the entrance door that led into a small reception area, she saw that once again he'd got there before her, perhaps further evidence of how much he was looking forward to the meeting.

'Morning Jimmy,' she said, smiling and tapping her watch. 'Very punctual I must say.'

'Army,' he said, his tone apologetic. 'They were always telling us we mustn't be late for the war. It becomes a habit.'

A uniformed commissionaire wearing a stern expression looked them up and down then said, 'Are youse visitors?'

Maggie recognised the Liverpool accent and smiled.

'Yes. Maggie Bainbridge and Jimmy Stewart. We're here to see Miss Montague. She's expecting us.'

He eyed them suspiciously, then after a short pause said, 'Ok, I'll call the production office. And don't move an inch, ok?'

It wasn't exactly welcoming but then Maggie supposed the studios were constantly inundated by fans desperate to meet their heroes. The guy had most likely learned to be suspicious through past and probably bitter experience. Perhaps once he'd turned his back for a moment and an uncontrollable hoard had rampaged over the set, autograph books turned to a blank page. Whatever the history, it was clear they were going nowhere until he'd confirmed their credentials. He took a phone from a pocket, punched in a number then gave their names to someone. They waited in silence for over a minute, the phone pressed against his ear, until finally he nodded and said, 'OK, that's fine.'

'Looks like we're in,' Jimmy whispered.

'Lucy will take youse through,' the commissionaire said, his manner a little less frosty. He picked up a couple of laminated A4 sheets from a pile on the reception desk and handed one to each of them.

'These are the on-set rules,' he said, and this time he might actually have been smiling. 'Follow them to the letter or I'll chuck you out.'

'That won't be necessary Gerry,' a female voice said. They looked over to see a young woman in jeans and t-shirt emerging through the double doors which according to the sign above them led to the sound stage area. She wore glasses and carried a clip-board which gave her an air of quiet efficiency. 'Lucy Roberts, senior production assistant. Please, follow me.'

The doors led through to a cavernous open space, the size of one of these giant warehouses Maggie had seen popping up alongside the motorway on her trips up north to visit her parents in Yorkshire. But the contents of this warehouse were way more impressive than anything Amazon could muster. To her delight and surprise, she recognised the iconic locations of Bow Road, familiar to millions of viewers and recreated here in glorious three dimensions, expertly constructed in timber, plaster and paint. The corner shop, the pub, the West family's front room, even Melody Montague's bedroom with its black silk sheets, they were all there.

'Bloody hell,' Jimmy said, open-mouthed. 'This is impressive, isn't it?'

'Yes, our set guys are amazing,' Lucy said. 'Super-talented.'

'But there doesn't seem to be any filming going on at the moment,' Maggie said.

'That's right,' Lucy said, nodding. 'From 9 to 10 we have script reviews or the leading actors are in make-up. Melody will be heading there after your meeting, but she's in her dressing room at the moment. It's just over here.'

'So you're the super-sleuths then?' Melody said, looking up from her dressing table after Lucy had delivered them to the small room. The tone was pleasant enough although Maggie thought she detected a slight edge. 'I hope you're as good as Asvina Rani says you are. Because she's charging me enough for the privilege.'

Jimmy smiled. 'We aim to please Miss Montague. Or is it Miss Kemp? Which do you prefer?' Maggie noticed the look on the actress's face as she caught proper sight of Jimmy, a look she'd seen a dozen times, in fact more or less every time a woman encountered her colleague for the first time. Often she'd thought that he would make a fine leading man, one of these strong silent types from the golden Hollywood era, a Cary Grant or a Glenn Ford. Or even of course, a Jimmy Stewart. *That* Jimmy Stewart.

As to Melody Montague, she looked a few years older than she did on television, but then, Maggie reflected, what woman doesn't look older without their war paint? But even in a shapeless grey t-shirt dress she still radiated a powerful sexuality, with a wide mouth, large doe eyes and ample breasts. Maggie wondered if Jimmy had noticed. Somehow she doubted he would be immune to her charms, even with the near twenty-year age difference.

'Well you could certainly please *me*,' Montague said, slipping effortlessly into the lascivious tone favoured by her character Patty West. And this was the woman supposedly head over heels in love with her younger co-star. 'And as to your question, I'm Melody Montague now, one-hundred percent. I couldn't be anything else, could I? That's how my public know me.'

Maggie wondered in fact if that was true. She considered it more likely that her public would know her as her character Patty West. For nearly twenty eight years the show's fans had followed every twist and turn in Patty's car crash of a life, and the more desperate her situation seemed to be, the more they loved her. But now as both actress and character slipped into late middle age, the gossip around the show was that Patty's role was to be scaled down as the producers sought a new younger demographic. Maggie wondered how Melody might be feeling about that. She doubted her reaction would be welcoming. But that subject would have to wait for later.

'This will just be a quick introductory session if that's ok,' Maggie explained. 'Today we'll sketch out what we need from you to prepare the pre-nuptial agreement for you and Mr David. That matter we expect to be pretty straightforward.'

'He's not in the shooting schedule today,' Montague said, 'otherwise you could meet him. He's lovely.'

Maggie smiled. 'That's not a problem. In fact if you two are in agreement about everything we probably don't need to see him at all.' Slipping into a schoolgirl tone she said, 'Although from my point of view it would be nice to meet him, because he is rather dishy.'

Montague giggled. 'Yes, he is rather, isn't he? We're so much in love and we're *so* looking forward to building a little family together.'

That caused Maggie to remember what Asvina had said about the actress's first marriage and the fact that there had been no children. She supposed it might be a sensitive subject and decided it might be wise to steer clear of it for now. Instead she said,

'What we would really like to do today if you don't mind is to hear your side of the story with regard to the pre-nuptial agreement with your former husband Mr Hunt. Would that be ok?'

Montague shrugged. 'There's nothing to tell. Patrick is a lying swine and somehow he's got Charles Grant to lie with him.'

Jimmy gave her a surprised look. 'Charles Grant. The guy whose son was kidnapped?'

'Yeah, him,' she replied coldly. 'He was in Bow Road at the time and just happened to be kicking around the set when we needed someone to witness the pre-nup. They of course know very well what the primary residence clause said. Both of them.'

'Primary residence clause?' Jimmy said. 'What was that all about?'

'I love my home and I've spent a fortune over the years doing it up. So the clause said that in the event we split, I got to keep the house. Simple as that.'

'But that's not what your former husband's copy says I take it?' Maggie said.

'No it isn't,' Melody said with undisguised bitterness. '*It* says that the house should be sold and the proceeds split fifty-fifty. As if I would have ever agreed to *that*.'

'So are you suggesting their copy is a forgery?' Jimmy said.

She gave him a dismissive look. 'Well of course it's a bloody forgery. What else could it be?'

Well it could be that it's you that's lying, Maggie thought, given that neither you nor your solicitor seem to be able to produce any evidence to the contrary. But that was another thought best kept to herself for now.

'So as I understand it, your solicitor has lost your copy, is that right?' she said. 'And you didn't keep a copy yourself?' She hadn't meant it to sound admonishing but wasn't sure she had succeeded. But Montague didn't seem to take offence.

'Hell no,' she said, smiling. 'I don't do any of that sort of stuff. I leave all that paperwork to my brothers. They run the family firm and look after all my business affairs.'

Jimmy frowned. 'And they didn't keep a copy either?' It was an obvious question, one that Maggie was about to ask herself.

'No, why should they?' the actress replied sharply. 'That's why they've been using Blake McCartney's firm for all these years. Although not now of course.'

'Yes now he's in prison I believe.' Jimmy said. 'Why's that?'

'I'm not exactly sure,' she said, sounding evasive. 'Some technicality over money transfers from overseas. I think that's what it was.'

Maggie smiled to herself. It was obviously a bit more than a technicality if it had landed him a five-year prison sentence. She remembered what Asvina had said about the questionable business activities of the Kemp brothers and wondered if there had been a connection. It seemed likely, but once again she found herself deciding that this was a line of questioning probably best avoided for now. Instead she said,

'And I'm led to believe he can't remember the details of the agreement.'

Montague gave a bitter laugh. 'No he can't. He's always been bloody useless that man.'

And yet it seemed he had been the long-term legal representative of the Kemp brother's business empire, Maggie thought. Maybe that wasn't such a surprise, given the rumours surrounding the legitimacy of their activities. It was always handy to have a tame lawyer on your side if you operated on the wrong side of the law.

'Well perhaps we'll go and see him, see if we can jog his memory,' she said. 'And of course we'll also need to speak with your ex and with Charles Grant too.'

'Well good luck with that,' the actress said. 'They're a pair of liars.'

It occurred to Maggie to ask why her ex-husband might want to engage in this huge deception, but then of course it was obvious. It had to be all about the money, it frequently was. And it seemed like Jimmy was thinking along the same lines.

'I know it's vulgar to ask,' he said, 'but how much are we talking about? How much is your house worth, in round figures?'

Montague gave a self-satisfied smile. 'I'm having a new wing built at the moment. A huge west-facing entertainment space looking out onto the garden, and we're going into the basement too, for a gym and servants' quarters. When that's finished we're probably talking about seven or eight, maybe more.'

'Million do you mean?' Maggie said, the words shooting out before she could check herself. Of course she meant millions. The house was in Richmond-on-Thames, that much Maggie knew, and you'd pay a hundred grand for a parking space in that neck of the woods. And servants' quarters for goodness sake? Asvina had said the actress had done well out of the show, but now she could see they had seriously underestimated the wealth of this woman. It was little wonder Patrick Hunt wanted to get his hands on some of it. And of course it had been his home for fifteen years, so it would be natural for him to have an emotional connection to the place too.

'Yes millions,' Montague said, giving a little laugh. 'I bought it twenty years ago and prices have gone crazy since then. It's been a very good investment.'

'So I guess it's your forever home then,' Jimmy said, rather guilelessly Maggie thought. But it seemed to have touched a nerve.

'Of *course*,' Montague said with a hint of annoyance. 'And it's just as well, because it looks like I may be spending more time there in the future.'

Maggie gave her a quizzical look. 'Why would that be, if you don't mind me asking?'

'The writers want an affair between Sharon and Benjamin. That's the plot line they want to major on for the autumn season.'

'Who's Sharon?' Jimmy asked. 'Forgive me, but I don't really follow Bow Road too closely.'

Maggie gave an inward grimace. *Great Jimmy, tell our new big client that you don't watch her show*. But Montague just smiled.

'Don't worry Jimmy, I don't think you're in our demographic.'

'What, too young?' he asked. 'Or too male?'

Montague smiled again. 'Too posh. Ours is a working class show and we're proud of it.'

Jimmy laughed. 'I've been called a lot of things in my time but never posh. I'm a wee Glasgow boy through and through.'

But Melody was right, Maggie thought. Lovely Jimmy was a Glasgow boy alright but his father was a leading lawyer up there and he himself had taken a law degree at that city's ancient university before becoming an army officer. So maybe not posh, but he was definitely middle class.

'Well, I forgive you,' Montague said, shooting him a smile that Maggie thought was just a little too familiar. 'Sharon is Sharon Trent. She's new and she's bloody young and bloody beautiful and the writers want her to get her claws into my Benjamin.'

'But it's just a story, isn't it?' Jimmy said, evidently trying to be sympathetic. 'You actors are always kissing one another on screen. It's just acting, isn't it?'

'You think so?' she said, not hiding her bitterness. 'Well Jimmy, you watch tonight's episode and then tell me how you would feel after you'd kissed bloody Sharon Trent.'

Maggie wondered if Melody was upset because the producers were forcing her fiancé into the arms of this beautiful young temptress or because it would mean that her own character Patty West would being relegated in the pecking order. She suspected it might be a bit of both.

'So your comment about spending more time in your beautiful home,' Maggie said. 'What do you mean by that?'

'I might just walk out,' she said, with a hint of petulance. 'And then they'll see that Bow Road is *nothing* without Patty West.' It was said with force, but somehow to Maggie it didn't ring true.

'But won't you miss it terribly?' she asked. 'After all, it's been your life for nearly thirty years.'

'I won't miss it all,' Montague said fiercely. *Who is she trying to convince*, Maggie thought. *Me or herself?* 'Benjamin and I plan to have four or five children,' the actress continued, 'and I will be perfectly content looking after them in my beautiful home.'

I doubt that very much, Maggie thought. As she had suspected, this was a development that Melody would not welcome, whatever she might say. For a moment, it crossed her mind that it would make the perfect plot-line for the show, the fading Patty West usurped by this young and beautiful temptress, her hopes of a perfect future with a younger man ripped from her grasp. Perhaps that's what Bow Road's writers had in mind, to have West so shattered by events that she would turn crazy and try to do something terrible to her new rival? An acid attack or a face-slashing or even murder, that would certainly bring in the viewers. But then something darker crossed Maggie's mind. What if, to coin a phrase, life should imitate art? She had only known Melody Montague for a matter of minutes yet already she could see how much the prospect of her new life with Benjamin David meant to her, and as she approached fifty years old and with the powerful desire to have a clutch of children, time wasn't on her side. Perhaps the actress was only imagining that this Sharon Trent woman might turn the head of her new love, but if that should happen to come true, then what would she do? *Hell hath no fury like a woman scorned.* A cliché of course, but history was not short of examples that proved the truth of the maxim.

'The show wouldn't be the show without you,' Jimmy said, giving a sympathetic smile. 'I'm sure it won't come to that.'

Montague shrugged. 'We'll see. But I don't care. I just want you to sort out my pre-nup. That's all I'm thinking about at the moment.'

They were interrupted by the reappearance of Lucy Roberts, still carrying her clipboard and looking vaguely harassed.

'Excuse me Melody, but you're needed in make-up. Your first scene is shooting at ten-fifteen. With Sharon. It's the pub confrontation scene.'

Jimmy gave Maggie a knowing look, as if to say *that's something I'd like to witness*. They had to assume the live sound-stage was off-limits to visitors and so they'd need to wait like everyone else to watch it when it was broadcast in a week or two. But she would still check the internet news sites later that evening just in case.

Actress Montague murders love rival in on-set spat. Now that *would* make the headlines.

Chapter 5

It was Thursday, Frank's favourite day of the working week and in fact since his weekends were normally a desert of nothingness, it was his favourite day of the week full-stop. Because this was the day he met up in the Old King's Head pub for his post-work drink with his wee brother Jimmy and her boss Maggie Bainbridge. Much to his surprise, he had found himself thinking of her rather a lot in the past week or two, and the phenomenon was beginning to perplex him. The fact was, since the disastrous humiliation caused by his non-marriage many years earlier - the exact number of years he did not like to focus on - relationships with women had not been allowed to become a priority in his life. Actually, the truth was that he feared another rejection so much that a relationship never even made it to the long-list of his priorities never mind making any kind of short-list. But now there was Maggie Bainbridge, and from time to time he was allowing himself to think thoughts that he had tried to suppress for a long long time. Yes, it was going to be very nice to see her again that evening. But now, it was time to deal with the matter in hand.

'So Jones, have you managed to plot out the route they took that day? And did you managed to confirm the timings?'

He was outside a nursery in Wimbledon with detective constable Sean Jones, one of Department 12B's newest additions to their stock of half-wits and rejects. He was young, not much older than twenty-five Frank thought, and so he must have done something off-the-scale bad to already have been shunted off to his department. But the lad was keen enough, which was an unusual but welcome attribute amongst his cohorts. They were here to stage a reconstruction of the Grant snatching, or at least to walk the route the boy and the Australian au pair had taken on that fateful day. Frank wasn't exactly sure why he was doing it or whether it would do any good, but he had always found that he needed to be able to clearly picture a crime scene in his head before the detective juices would start flowing. Although whether the technique would bear fruit on this occasion remained to be seen.

The nondescript single-story building was located on the main Kingston Road, making normal conversation difficult above the noise of the traffic.

'Sure sir,' the DC bellowed. 'I spoke to one of the staff who were in that day. The au-pair arrived at about four-thirty and picked up Jamie as normal. And from there it would be about a twenty-five to thirty minute walk to the Grant's place, just over a mile. She would have the push-chair of course, he wouldn't be walking the whole way.'

Frank nodded. 'How old was he again. Eighteen months old wasn't it?'

'That's right sir.'

'And they did the same walk every day?'

'That's right sir,' Jones said again. 'Exactly the same. The boy had been in that nursery since he was nine months old and the routine never changed. Parents both worked, if you can call that ponsy acting stuff the father did actual work. The wife was in publishing. No idea what anyone actually does in that sort of place but her office was up in Holborn.'

Frank noted the use of the past tense when Jones talked about the wife - Yvonne he thought her name was. The disappearance of her wee boy had broken her and broken the marriage too, hardly surprising really. Of course he didn't have children himself but you didn't need to to know that such a terrible event would be well-nigh impossible to recover from.

'Charles Grant's a very popular actor,' he said, 'and I'm sure they all work very hard.'

'But that isn't why his little boy was snatched, was it sir? It was because he's very committed to progressive politics.'

Frank shrugged. 'That was the theory, but since they never got anyone for it, that's all it is, a theory. Anyway, enough of the jawing. Let's get moving, shall we?'

'Are taking the car sir?' Jones said with a sudden terseness. 'Because I think you'll find all this walking isn't in my terms and conditions.'

And then Frank remembered something his boss Jill Smart has said about the boy. *He's big in the federation.* A union activist. *Bloody marvellous.*

'You haven't got any terms or conditions pal,' Frank said sardonically. 'In fact, you're just hanging on to your job by the skin of your teeth and that's something worth remembering. So no, we walk.'

Jones didn't look happy, but evidently had decided to comply at least for now. 'So what exactly is it we are looking for?' Frank noticed the absence of a *sir* but decided to let it go for now.

'No idea,' Frank said, quite truthfully. 'Inspiration I suppose. See if anything strikes us as we wander round.'

Although that wasn't quite true, he thought. This snatch had been carefully planned and that would have meant there had to have been a surveillance operation by person or persons unknown. Wee Jamie and the au-pair would have been followed, probably on more than one occasion, allowing the abductors to consider a number of possible snatch locations en-route before settling on Merton Hall Road.

The first part of the route took them along Wilton Crescent, and then after about fifty or so metres they turned left into Henfield Road. Rows of modern-ish terraced homes with big picture windows and close to the road. Further along, an extended row of flats, three or four floors high. Too much chance of being observed along here so that would have been quickly ruled out.

About a quarter of a mile on, the route turned right onto Merton Hall Road. Quiet, leafy, tree-lined, with expensive homes hidden behind neatly-trimmed hedges. Yes, this would be a good place, with a high chance of pulling off the snatch without being observed. The Grants had lived in an exclusive cul-de-sac right at the end of the street, nearly three-quarters a mile ahead, giving plenty of options for the precise location of the abduction.

'Look sir, they've got all this traffic-calming stuff with the speed-bumps and inshots and what-not,' Jones said, pointing along the road. 'You wouldn't want to wind your motor through too many of them if you wanted a swift getaway.'

'Aye, you're right Jones,' Frank said, nodding. 'But there's that side street off on the right before you get to the end. They could have nipped along it and avoided all of this I suppose.'

Yes, that would have been an equally good possibility and they would almost certainly have given it careful consideration before finally opting for the location where the crime took place. So someone had obviously been on the ground in the days before the snatch, weighing everything up, maybe taking photographs or even a wee video, making sure nothing was left to chance. *A professional job.*

And then eventually they reached the location of the snatch. As he observed the scene, Frank ran through the events of that day in his mind. According to the account of the au-pair Lydia Davis, a large blue SUV drew up - she thought it was a BMW but she wasn't sure - and two men got out. Next thing, one of the men ran over to her and started to attack her. She was violently coshed, suffering a fractured skull which kept her in hospital for nearly eight weeks afterwards. She passed out at the scene and remembered nothing more about it.

The police assumption was that the toddler was bundled into the vehicle and then driven off somewhere. An ANPR camera positioned at the junction with Kingston Road recorded no sign of a car meeting the description, leading them to assume they'd gone in the opposite direction, probably turning onto Dundonald Road before heading northwards.

A passer-by had witnessed the incident at a distance but was not able to provide any reliable information other than she thought the SUV was on a 62 plate but wouldn't swear to it, and that it was the younger man of the two who had been driving. There was only one other reported witness, a Mrs Molly Peters, who apparently was in her front garden about fifty yards away and saw it happening, but at eighty-four, her eyesight was poor and she was unable to provide a reliable description of the perpetrators or identify the car. However, she said she did overhear some of their shouted conversation. She was sure they were both Londoners from their accents, and that one of them might have called the other Henry.

And that was all they had. There was an appeal for any sightings of a BMW on a 62 plate, and a sketchy photo-fit from the au-pair's brief sight of her assailant was splashed all over the media for a while, but no member of the public came forward with a credible identification of the man called Henry. From time to time the police had issued positive statements saying they were following up some encouraging line of enquiry or other, but everyone knew that it was the first few days that were critical in an abduction if the victim was to be saved. And during that crucial period they had found nothing.

But then, unexpectedly, came the ransom demand. It was never revealed how much the kidnappers asked for, but the press speculation was that it was around a quarter of a million pounds, and that the money was put up by Brightside, the producers of Bow Road. What was known was that the money was handed over but the toddler wasn't. A disaster for the reputation of the Met and a tragedy for his parents.

As the months passed, the assumption grew that Jamie Grant had been murdered and in all probability his body would never be found. So almost two years to the day that he was taken, the case was shunted off to Department 12B. And now here they were, standing on the exact spot where it had happened.

'You can see why they picked here sir,' Jones was saying. 'Just thirty yards from that road. An easy getaway. Well at least as easy as you could expect in these parts.'

Aye, he was right, Frank thought. Bundle the kid into the back of the car and then slam the pedal down, spin into Dundonald Road and you were away.

'Aye, you're right,' he said. 'But does it help us? I'm not sure.'

But when he thought about it afterwards, he felt a lot more hopeful. That scene would have had to have been carefully surveyed by the villains, because you wouldn't want to turn into that Dundonald Road and then find your path was blocked with parked cars strewn all over the place. So they would have taken snaps from every angle just to make sure. Because this had been a professional job and nothing would have been taken for granted.

So the question was, who had taken these pictures and had anyone seen them doing it? There was no question about it, they needed to do another door-to-door, this time focussing on a week or so before the snatch. *Did you see anyone acting suspiciously or anything else that didn't seem quite right?* A long shot of course, given it had happened more than two years ago, but it still needed to be done.

But not to worry. That would be a nice wee job for Ronnie French, the Met's laziest detective constable. He might not be as thorough as PC Jones, but at least he wasn't going to go on strike half way through.

***

Service in the Old King's Head was exactly as normal this Thursday evening, that was to say, diabolical. After unfruitfully waving his twenty-pond note in the nose of the bored-looking bar staff for what he reckoned was at least five minutes, Frank was just wondering whether to get out his warrant card when Jimmy appeared alongside him. Immediately the pretty barmaid with the purple spiky hair-do shot him a smile and said, 'What can I get you?' He was forced to watch ignominiously as his brother effortlessly took delivery of two pints of Doom Bar and a large chardonnay, then proffered his debit card to effect contactless payment.

'Nae bother,' Jimmy said, giving a smug smile as he picked up their drinks. 'Nice girl that.'

Frank shook his head. 'I should have them all bloody arrested. I could you know. Behaviour likely to cause a public affray.'

They had made their way back over to where Maggie was sitting, at a little table in a dingy corner of the packed pub.

'I heard that,' she said, laughing. 'Of course I've been away from the legal trade for a while now but is that really an offence?'

Frank shrugged. 'Probably not, but it bloody well should be.'

'Well thank you for the drink anyway,' Maggie said, raising her glass. 'Cheers.'

'Aye cheers,' Jimmy said. 'But did you see what he did there Maggie? Kidding on he couldn't get served so he could get out of paying. He's a devious sod, my brother.' It was said with obvious affection, Frank responding with a huge grin.

'Well actually I hadn't thought of that, but I'll certainly remember it for the future. It's a cunning plan, no doubt about it. But anyway, what's happening with you guys? What's your latest case all about?'

Maggie smiled. 'We're in show business now. You know, Melody Montague, the Bow Road star? We've got a couple of pre-nuptial issues to sort out for her.'

'Oh aye, I know her. She's one fit bird alright.' The words just slipped out before he knew what he was saying, and he hastily attempted a retreat. 'Sorry, sorry, just a figure of speech. Attractive woman, that's what I should have said.'

Maggie laughed, evidently not offended. 'I'll tell her what you said. She'll be flattered I'm sure.'

'And she's invited us to a big awards ceremony at the O2,' Jimmy said. 'The National Soap Awards. It's a big do apparently.'

Frank grinned. 'I'm jealous, it's just my kind of thing.'

'What, because of the free drinks do you mean?' Jimmy said. 'Anyway, what about you? What are you up to?'

He took a sip from his pint then said, 'So strangely enough, there's a bit of a connection. Remember the Jamie Grant abduction from a few years back? Well now it's been passed down to our wee department as a cold case.'

'Yes his dad Charles was in Bow Road wasn't he?' Maggie said. 'He's in that A&E hospital drama now. But weirdly enough, he was actually a witness to one of Melody's pre-nuptial agreements.'

'What's he like?' Jimmy asked. 'I know he's a bit of a revolutionary isn't he? A sort of Islington Fidel Castro.'

Frank gave him a wry look, pointing to the bruise under his eye. 'And don't I know it.'

'I didn't want to ask,' Maggie said. 'It looks painful. Actually, you look as if you've done twelve rounds with Tyson Fury.'

'Aye, and it feels like it. I was at that anti-fascist rally at the weekend and got mixed up in a bit of a punch-up. Hence this.' He decided he wouldn't mention the three stitches in the back of his head.

'I read about that,' Jimmy said. 'They arrested that far-right guy didn't they? Darren Venables.'

Frank grimaced. 'Aye, *they* did. And don't I know it.'

Maggie looked at him, wide-eyed. 'So that was *you*?'

'Can't deny it. Wish I hadn't though. He's pretty handy with his fists. But no worries, it just comes with the job. But as for Charlie-boy, I don't know what he's like because he won't talk to us. He wrote something in the Guardian the other day saying we're the oppressors of the state orthodoxy or some such bollocks, and on top of that we're bloody useless too. Which to be fair we were when his wee lad was abducted.'

And it was true, Frank thought. It hadn't been the Met's finest hour, but that's what happened when you promoted idiots like Detective Chief Superintendent Colin Barker way above their level of competence. So when it was announced that the case was moving to Department 12B, Grant had taken to the media to say it was nothing but a police arse-covering exercise and he would have nothing to do with it. The trouble was, he was right, in a way. But what sort of father would put his political credo ahead of doing anything that might resolve what had happened to your young son?

'Anyway, enough shop-talk,' he said, smiling. 'I think it's time I had another go at that bar. Now it *is* my round.'

'No, it must be mine,' Maggie said, getting up from her seat. 'Tell you what, why don't we go together? Double our chances of success.'

And unexpectedly, he felt his heart skip a beat.

Chapter 6

It was a distinctly weird feeling, Maggie thought, as she skipped through the front door of the Old King's Head, conveniently held open for her by her colleague Jimmy Stewart. This was the pub which was now firmly established as the Thursday-night meeting venue for the three of them, a get-together that had quickly embedded itself as the highlight of her week. But this was a working Monday, the twelve o'clock meeting time nestled in that strange no-man's land between morning and afternoon, and unlike on Thursdays, the place was virtually deserted. She suspected that was why the actor Patrick Hunt had chosen it for their meeting, because it must be a pain being recognised everywhere you went. But what was most weird about it wasn't the impending arrival of the famous *Accident & Emergency* star, but the absence of Frank from the party. Somehow it just didn't seem quite right for them to be here without him, as if it was some kind of vague betrayal. And it seemed that Jimmy was thinking about his brother too.

'At least we won't have any problem getting served,' he said, laughing. 'Even Frank might manage it this morning.'

'Do you think so?' she said, screwing up her nose. 'He does seem to make heavy weather of it.' The thought of it made her smile, as she pictured him desperately waving a bank note in a barmaid's direction to no avail. 'Anyway, I think I'll just have a cup of tea. Keep my mind sharp and all that.'

He grinned. 'Good plan. But maybe I'll wait and see what Mr Hunt wants first. I might just grab a wee pint if he decides on something alcoholic. Just to show empathy you understand.'

'Yeah *right*,' she said. And at that precise moment Patrick Hunt appeared through the doors, pausing for a moment as he scanned the bar-room for a pair that might meet the description she had given him. *Jimmy's a tall good-looking guy with longish hair and I'm a pretty nondescript forty-something woman.* The description had evidently been accurate, since he almost immediately raised a hand in recognition and walked straight over to them. Or maybe it was because they were the only two people in the bar.

'Miss Bainbridge and Mr Stewart I assume?' he said, extending a hand in her direction. 'I'm Patrick Hunt.' As if half the folks in the UK didn't know that already, she thought. But his manner was polite, although she did find herself wondering if he did the introduction thing for effect, as a sort of false modesty. He was tall, maybe even an inch taller than Jimmy, which made him six-three, broad-shouldered and with greying hair that he wore quite long and swept back into a centre parting. In black jeans and a matching black polo-neck, there was something of a James Bond look about him, and she found herself wondering if in his younger days he had ever been a contender for the role. In her opinion he was certainly good-looking enough, but she suspected that in the eyes of the movie industry executives who decided these things, he was probably just a little bit small time. *Accident & Emergency* was a popular soap and not far behind *Bow Road* as far as viewing figures were concerned, but it was a fact that soap stars seldom made the transition to the big screen.

'Please, we're Maggie and Jimmy,' she said, smiling, 'and thank you so much for agreeing to meet us.'

'Sure, no problem,' he said distractedly, his eyes already focussed on the pretty young woman who was single-handedly minding the bar. Evidently, he knew her.

'Louise, Shiraz please, the usual,' he said, shooting her a smile. 'And for you two?'

'Eh, a pint of Doom Bar please Patrick,' Jimmy said. 'That would be great.'

'And I'll have a Sauvignon Blanc please,' Maggie said, ignoring her colleague's chastising look. 'But just a small one.'

To her amusement, it was not a glass of Shiraz but a bottle and an empty glass that Louise the barmaid placed on a circular tray, sliding it over to Hunt before turning her back to get their drinks.

'I often pop in here for a lunchtime snifter on a Monday,' Hunt said unapologetically. 'We film the atmosphere shots just round the corner at the Royal Free. Using a real hospital gives the show an authentic feel and of course it's very handy for this place.'

He filled his glass to the brim, raised it up and with a hearty *bottom's up*, almost drained it in one gulp.

'That's better,' he said as he unscrewed the bottle-top and began refilling. 'So what's all this nonsense about Melody disputing our pre-nup? That's why you're here, isn't it?'

Maggie nodded. 'That's right. And yes, she has quite a different understanding about the terms of that agreement.'

Hunt gave a smirk. 'Except she hasn't actually got a copy, and *my* copy couldn't be clearer. I get half the house, end of story.'

'She doesn't think so,' Jimmy said, quite sternly. '*That's* why we're here. To sort it all out.'

'Nothing to be sorted,' Hunt said sharply. 'It's all perfectly clear, in black and white.'

Well at least we haven't wasted too much time with small-talk, Maggie thought. But why had he come here today? Why had he agreed so readily to her proposal of a meeting if it was all so clear-cut? She knew he had a copy of the pre-nuptial agreement, and conveniently Charles Grant, one of the original witnesses, had a copy too. So what did Patrick Hunt have to be concerned about, that was the question that was going through her mind. Whatever it was, she was pleased she had taken the time to prepare properly for the meeting. *Well, sort of.*

'Yes, it is unfortunate that her solicitor has misplaced his copy,' she said. 'But Melody is adamant that the agreement was quite specific when it came to the primary residence. And just so you are clear, she is willing to go to court to prove it.'

'Prove it?' Hunt said. 'How in hell's name is she going to prove it?'

Maggie smiled. 'Well for a start, we'll call her solicitor to the witness stand. Right now Mr McCartney is saying he can't remember anything about it, but that may change once he has time to focus on it properly. And of course, his copy may turn up. In fact, as part of the preparation for our meeting, Jimmy and I have been in contact with his practice. I was surprised to find it was still in business after his little difficulty with the police but it seems that his erstwhile trainee Paula Rogers has taken up the reins very nicely.'

For the first time in their meeting, Maggie observed a chink of uncertainty in Hunt's demeanour.

'I doubt if that will do any good,' he said, narrowing his eyes. 'I don't know what you expect to achieve by that.' The tone was sceptical but somehow questioning too.

Maggie smiled. 'As I understand it, Mr McCartney ran a rather chaotic business, especially when it came to paperwork. Miss Rogers has apparently a completely different approach and we are reasonably confident that somewhere in the dark recesses of what her former employer laughingly called his filing system she will uncover some if not all of the correspondence between the parties that led to the final agreement. Because these agreements don't just materialise out of the ether, I'm sure you understand that. There's a lot of to-ing and fro-ing before they're finalised.'

She caught first Jimmy's look of surprise and then a smirk as he evidently cottoned on to where she was going with this.

'She won't find anything,' Hunt said, sounding defensive. 'And even if she does, it's the final agreement that's the important thing, isn't it?'

'Ordinarily yes,' Maggie said. 'But if the preparatory notes and correspondence between the parties tell a different story as to the intentions of the pre-nup, then there's every chance a court may question the provenance of the document it is being asked to rule on. Especially if one of the parties is disputing its authenticity.'

'What the hell does that mean?' Hunt said, momentarily losing his cool. 'Can't you lawyers use plain English?'

Jimmy smiled. 'The judge might conclude it's a fake. That what she means.'

'It's not a bloody fake,' Hunt barked, 'and I've got a witness to prove it.'

Maggie shrugged. 'That's a complication, I admit. As is the unfortunate death of the other witness to the agreement.'

'Yes, poor Sabrina,' Hunt said, 'I was devastated when I heard of her death. Such a nice kid.' The smooth demeanour had been instantly restored, but then Maggie thought, it's hardly surprising he can do this. He is an actor after all.

'So did you keep in touch?' Jimmy said, sounding mildly surprised. 'Because it was more than fifteen years ago since she witnessed your pre-nup. As I understand it, she was just a young production assistant that happened to be on set that day. I wouldn't have thought she moved in your circles.'

Hunt looked momentarily uncomfortable. 'Of course I didn't keep in touch. But I read about her death on social media. She still worked in the industry and news gets around. It's very sad.'

'Aye, sad thing all together,' Jimmy said. 'A hit and run wasn't it? And they've never got anybody for it, as far as I know.'

'We'll get in touch with her family,' Maggie said before Hunt could make any comment. 'I've got an address and a phone number for them so it won't be difficult. Because maybe she kept a copy. Unlikely I know, but it's possible.'

'I doubt it very much,' Hunt said. 'Why should she have done that?'

'You're probably right,' Maggie said, unconcerned, 'but actually none of that is directly relevant to why we asked for this meeting.'

Hunt gave her a suspicious look. 'So what does that mean?'

'We hoped we might be able to come to some sort of agreement. A compromise if you will. Because Melody recognises the difficulties of the situation and might be willing to consider a small re-allocation of the non-property assets.'

She saw Jimmy giving her a sharp look which she met with a gentle shrug. Ok, so they hadn't *exactly* discussed that with their client, but they had been engaged by her to reach a settlement and in Maggie's experience no settlement was ever reached without a bit of give and take. Convincing Melody of the sense of that strategy would be something they could worry about later. But it might not come to that, because it seemed convincing Hunt was going to be a lot more difficult than anything they would face with their client.

'No way,' he said, not troubling to disguise the bitterness. 'Do you think I can be bought with a few grand? So I'm going to finish my wine now and you can trot off back to Melody and give her two messages from me. First, I'm so bloody glad we didn't have kids together. And secondly, tell her I'll see her in court. Bring it on.'

***

Afterwards, back at their little Riverside House office, they had time to reflect on how the meeting had gone. Jimmy had been both mildly amused and slightly censorious about Maggie's stretching of the truth. Yes, they had established that a Miss Paula Rogers had taken over the legal practice of Blake McCartney, but whether she ran a tighter ship that her former boss was still to be established since they had not yet made contact with her. Secondly, they had no idea whether the dead witness Sabrina Fellini had any family in London since they had not yet done any digging into that situation either.

But the fact was Hunt had turned up, leaving Maggie to conclude that he had only done that because he was anxious to find out how much they knew. What was also evident was that he was clearly still bitter about the break-up, however much he tried to disguise it. And then another thought struck her. Melody and Patrick Hunt had been separated nearly three years but it seemed that at first there had been no urgency to get the divorce process underway. Perhaps one or both parties had hoped for a reconciliation, or perhaps Melody had hoped for one last night of passion that would give her the child she craved. Maybe that explained Hunt's bitter comment about being glad they didn't have kids together, a barb designed to cause maximum hurt. Whatever the case, it had taken almost two years for proceedings to get underway, leading to the emergence of the issue with the pre-nuptial agreement.

And that was about the same time, Maggie realised, that poor Sabrina had died under the wheels of that car.

Chapter 7

The dress code on the invitation had been a bit enigmatic. *Dress to Impress*. What the heck did that mean in these luvvie circles? It wouldn't have mattered what Jimmy had chosen of course, because he always looked amazing straight out of the box. For Maggie, the process had been rather more stressful, but in the end she had decided you couldn't go too far wrong with a little black dress. Even if it was about a couple of inches too short and half a size too small. A pair of shoes three inches higher than her normal wear had completed the transformation. A little bit too tarty? You couldn't be too tarty in this company. And besides, a couple of complimentary proseccos into the evening, she no longer gave a monkey's what anybody thought of her appearance. Scanning the packed room, she spotted her colleague in conversation with Melody. Evidently Jimmy had interpreted the code as black tie, and was looking sensational in his elegant dinner suit and spotted bow-tie.

She shook her glass in the air to draw his attention, drizzling herself with sticky warm fizz in the process. *Bugger*. She wandered over to them, draining her glass on the short journey.

'Evening Jimmy,' she said mischievously. 'Hope I'm not interrupting anything.' But then she realised from their expressions that something wasn't right.

'What is it?' she said.' Has something happened?'

'It's Benjamin,' Melody said, her voice dripping with anxiety. 'He's not here, and he's not answering his phone or messages. And he's due to present an award, and he's up for one himself.'

'I'm sure it will be fine.' It was the sort of thing you said, the automatic response, Maggie thought. But surely, it *would* be fine. A dead battery on your phone, your car getting a puncture or your train breaking down, there were lots of reasons as to why life didn't always go to schedule.

'When did you last see him?' Maggie asked.

'Last night,' she said. 'We had dinner in the West End and then he went home. He wanted an early night because of this event. And he was completely ok then.'

'It'll be fine I'm sure,' Jimmy said. 'He'll be here soon.'

Melody looked at him uncertainly. 'I hope you're right. Anyway I have to get back-stage. I need to run over my acceptance speech with the producers, make sure I thank everyone who should be thanked.'

'Her acceptance speech?' Jimmy said after she had gone. 'Does that mean the results are known in advance and all of that hand-over-your-mouth-in-surprise stuff is fake?'

Maggie shrugged. 'I guess so. Actually, Melody did say they'd had a full rehearsal yesterday, so yes, it probably is all faked. But hey, isn't that Charles Grant over there? Maybe we can ask him about the Hunt-Montague pre-nup while we're here.'

'Aye, it is him,' Jimmy said. 'And I think that might be Sharon Trent he's with, you know, the new love rival. Come on, I think we can wander over and introduce ourselves.'

'Mr Grant, Miss Trent, sorry if we're interrupting anything,' Maggie said brightly, conscious that she'd used the same phrase just a few minutes earlier, 'but we wondered if we might arrange to have a *very* quick word with you Mr Grant. It's to do with the pre-nuptial agreement that you witnessed for Melody Montague and Patrick Hunt. I'm Maggie Bainbridge by the way and this is my colleague Jimmy Stewart. Patrick might have mentioned we're working for Melody.'

Grant looked at them with suspicion.

'He didn't,' he said, unsmiling.

Maggie nodded. 'Ah, ok then. So we're working with Melody's divorce lawyer, Asvina Rani. There's an issue on the pre-nuptial agreement she signed with her first husband Patrick Hunt and we've been asked to get to the bottom of it.'

The answer seemed to relax him a bit. 'Ah yes, I've heard about the problem. I'm not sure if I can help but I'll give you a couple of minutes. Any questions, just fire away. You don't mind Sharon, do you?'

The actress gave a bored shrug. 'Sure. Go for it Charles.'

Maggie smiled sweetly. 'Just a simple question Mr Grant. We just wanted to know whether you remembered being a witness to the agreement? According to Melody it was signed on the set of Bow Road. The old set in Hertfordshire, I mean. Although it was fifteen years ago so it would be understandable if you don't remember.'

He fired back the answer without hesitation. 'Yes, I remember, quite clearly.'

'Ah good,' Maggie said. 'And do you remember any of the contents of the agreement or perhaps Mr McCartney, Melody's lawyer, explained them to you at the time?' She was already pretty sure what his answer would be, but she wanted to ask the question anyway to see how he would react.

'Well as it happens I did take the precaution of requesting a copy,' he said smoothly. 'Quite prescient don't you think, given how troublesome it's become lately?'

'So you know some of the details then?' Jimmy asked him.

Grant smiled. 'Yes, as I mentioned, Patrick contacted me a couple of weeks ago and explained the situation. About the disagreement.'

'And asked if you had kept a copy?' Maggie asked.

'Exactly. And fortunately, I had.'

'And why did you do that?' Jimmy said, with a mild frown. 'Why did you keep a copy?'

Maggie smiled to herself. That was the question she was about to ask but her colleague had got there first. He was doing rather well, developing very nicely into a first-class investigator.

Grant shrugged. 'I don't know. I guessed it was an important document so I thought I'd better keep one, that's all.'

'So you'll know that Melody is disputing Patrick's version of the document with regard to what happens to the family home. The primary residence as it's described in the contract,' Maggie said.

He shrugged again. 'I know it's something like that. But I've not really looked at the full details.'

'This is all very intriguing,' Sharon Trent said, who had been listening with an exaggeratedly uninterested expression on her face.

'So do tell Jimmy, what's this all about exactly? Has Melody made the whole thing up? It sounds rather like it to me.'

Maggie noticed the look the actress was giving Jimmy and smiled to herself. Another one snared in his web, and as usual, he didn't know a thing about it.

'Well there's obviously been a mix-up,' Maggie replied, smiling. 'But hopefully we can get it all straightened out.'

Trent smiled. 'Very well. So I guess there's nothing I can add to the proceedings.' She turned to Jimmy and smiled at him, at the same time rummaging in her clutch bag.

'Jimmy, hand please,' she said.

Maggie, puzzled, saw that the actress was holding a slim gold ballpoint pen in her hand.

'Give me your *hand* please,' Trent repeated, reacting to Jimmy's surprised look. She took his hand in hers and carefully wrote what Maggie assumed was her phone number on the back of it, followed by her name, in a delicate and precise script.

'*Call me*. Now if you don't mind darling Charles, I'll leave you to your dull old document.'

Maggie watched with a mixture of anger and astonishment as Trent walked away. Poor poor Charles Grant. The man had lost his son and his marriage and now seemed to be investing his hopes of the future in this, this *brazen hussy*. She couldn't see the relationship turning out well, no matter how you looked at it. Then she noticed that Grant was giving her a curious look. And then he spoke.

'I remember you of course, from the Alzahrani case. The most hated woman in Britain. Quite a label and quite a business that was. A terrible thing altogether.'

'Yes, that was me I'm afraid,' she said quietly. It was an odd change of subject from Grant, given what had happened in the last minute. But it appeared that he had already forgotten his apparent humiliation.

'It seems a lifetime ago now,' she said, 'but it's nearly two years. The same time your little boy was taken. I remember it. I'm afraid it rather pushed your little Jamie's case off the front pages. I'm sorry about that. I can't even think how awful it must be for you, living with it every day. Not knowing what's happened to him.'

A terrible sadness came to his eyes as he continued.

'You might have heard they've just closed the case. They don't say it in so many words of course, but they've taken the original team off it so it amounts to the same thing. Now it's with some hopeless backroom team.'

Jimmy gave Maggie a half-smile. 'They never let these things go Mr Grant. The file always stays open. And I know a little bit about the team they've put it with. They're good guys, really they are.'

'I'm not so sure Mr Stewart,' Grant said with a hint of cynicism, 'but I appreciate your concern. Both of you.'

Suddenly he said, 'Would you take on the case?' Maggie thought she heard the words clearly enough, but was sure she must have been mistaken.

'I'm sorry?'

'You two are private investigators I'm given to believe? So I'd like you to take on the case. Find Jamie for me. I'll pay well.'

It was Jimmy who answered first, raising his hands apologetically, his surprise at the request evident. 'Well, just a minute Mr Grant. We don't do that sort of stuff I'm afraid. I mean divorces and fraud and the like... but we don't do criminal work. I'm not sure we're even allowed to. Don't you need a licence?'

Maggie shook her head. 'No, that's not necessary here in the UK, but really Mr Grant, we're not the right choice for this. There are plenty of firms who are way more qualified than us. Most of them ex-policemen with years of investigative work under their belts. You'd fare much better with one of them.' And of course she knew that the abduction was now in the hands of Frank's Department 12B. If they took it on, it would be awkward to say the least.

He leaned across and placed his hand over hers. 'Look, I've been badly let down by the police. The man they had running it was a fool, and as soon as it started to look embarrassing on the statistics, they couldn't wait to push it into their cold-cases file. It's all very convenient for them because they get to close a live case and then it disappears into a black hole that no-one cares about.' There was a quiet desperation in his voice, the pain seeping out of him like blood from a deep wound. A wound that she knew would never heal until his son was found. *Dead or alive.*

'You see, I need someone I can trust, and already I feel I can trust you. I don't know why I feel that way, but I always go with my gut.'

She placed her free hand over his, clasping it tight. 'Mr Grant, we *can't* take this on in any formal capacity. As I've told you, we don't have any skills or experience in matters of this type. We'd be taking your money under false pretences if we were to accept.'

'The police were bloody useless,' he said bitterly. 'Please, I really need this. Please.'

Maggie could feel her resolve wavering. No matter how you looked at it, he would effectively be placing his future happiness in their hands. Of course she couldn't take this on, no matter how sorry she felt for him. That would be crazy. But she remembered how at her absolute lowest moment Jimmy Stewart had come along, quite out of the blue, and literally saved her life. Without his intervention, delivered by the fates without any warning, she did not know how she could have carried on. And now she recognised a fellow human in exactly the same position as she had been back then. Charles Grant needed her help and not just to find out what happened to his son. He needed help to simply carry on with life.

She leaned over, whispering so that Jimmy wouldn't hear.

'We'll do it.'

'I can't thank you enough,' Grant said, his voice wavering. 'You're my only hope now.'

'We won't let you down Charles, trust me.'

Behind her, Jimmy had caught on to what was happening and was whistling that tune he loved so much. The theme to *Mission Impossible.*

***

In recognition of their nobody status, they had been allocated seats towards the rear of the auditorium, tucked away on the far left.

Maggie couldn't quite explain it, but she was feeling more than a little jumpy. Had she been able to be honest with herself of course, she could have pinpointed at least one reason for her discomfort. It was Jimmy and his encounters with Sharon Trent and Miss Melody-bloody-Montague. Jealousy was such a destructive emotion, but it was easier to recognise than do something about. But then she realised it wasn't exactly jealousy, more a sense of possessiveness, or in fact when she thought about it again, a sense of protectiveness. In her mind he was *her* Jimmy, no-one else's, and at this point in her life, she didn't want any other woman taking him away from her. Not that it was likely of course, because right now Jimmy's over-riding desire in life was making up again with his wife Flora. So far, he'd got nowhere with that.

She looked at him, and it was clear from his dour expression he wasn't enjoying the evening at all. And then she remembered. *Astrid Sorenson, the Swedish country singer*. The woman who had destroyed his marriage. Of course, he would have been to quite a few of these events as a plus-one with the beautiful singer. A do like this one couldn't help but bring back painful memories. She knew he didn't like to talk about everything that had happened, and she didn't like to pry. But one day perhaps she would ask him all about it.

On entry they had been given a glossy programme laying out the running order for the evening. She groaned when she saw there were to be twenty-seven separate awards. And of course the big two, the only ones anybody was actually interested in, were scheduled right at the end. *Best Actress* and *Best Actor*, those were the ones that were most coveted. Before that, there was a pile of tedium to sit through. *Agony*.

The event was being broadcast as-live to the nation's soap fans, of which there were many millions. As-live meant that there was time to cut and re-shoot any cock-ups or beep out any profanities that crept into the acceptance speeches. The stage was flanked by two large video screens on which the proceedings were being displayed. Several cameras raked the audience, all the better to capture the obviously-faked reactions when an artist either received an award, or in a ratio of three to one, was overlooked. And now two hours into the proceedings she was rapidly losing the will to live. All throughout the evening, bored celebrities had been slipping out to the bar when they were sure the cameras weren't on them, like escaping prisoners of war trying to avoid the camp searchlights. But now one by one they were beginning to dribble back to their seats in anticipation of the main awards.

'It's best actress now,' said Jimmy, studying his programme whilst stifling a yawn, 'and I see that both Sharon Trent and our Melody are up for it.'

The presenters were now announcing the nominees, the video screens running short excerpts from presumably what was regarded as their best work. Shakespeare it wasn't, but there was no shortage of entertaining if over-the-top drama on display. Mercifully, the director had kept it short.

'And to present the award, one of Britain's best-loved actors. From Accident & Emergency, please welcome Mr Nice Guy himself, Charles Grant!' The young presenters turned to applaud as Grant bounded on from stage left. He might have been Mr Nice Guy in the popular hospital drama, but the less than tumultuous response he received from the audience tended to underline his real-life reputation as the humourless revolutionary. Not that he had been anything but pleasant to them.

'Thank you, thank you,' he mouthed, waving a hand above his head.

'Do we still think they tell him in advance who's won it?' whispered Jimmy. 'Because he does look very pleased with himself.'

'What, does that mean it must be Sharon?' Maggie asked.

She didn't have to wait for his answer, as Grant tore open the envelope and without looking at the card, pointed triumphantly to where his girlfriend sat. 'And the winner is -of course - the delectable Miss... Sharon... Trent!'

The cameras caught her as she placed both hands over her mouth in faked astonishment. Maggie thought she might even have seen a tear. How did they do it, that crying to order? She supposed they must learn how at drama school. Naturally the director wanted reaction shots from the unlucky losers. Two out of the three managed the obligatory forced smiles and half-hearted applause, but not Melody Montague. Back in the control room, the director let out an expletive and screamed a panicky command. 'Cut, cut, stop the frigging broadcast! Christ, does she want to get me fired?' Simultaneously, the audience let out a sharp gasp followed by waves of laughter. That's what happens when a famous actress is caught giving the one-finger salute to camera.

The director was now on-stage, apologising for the delay and explaining that they would have to re-shoot the scene. The audience, experienced thesps who knew how these things worked, were already slinking out to the bar.

It was ten minutes before the director returned to the microphone and requested everyone took their seats for the retake. Out in the bar, production assistants ushered reluctant drinkers back into the auditorium. The retake passed without further incident, and soon it was time for best actor, the pinnacle award of the evening.

'Whoa, do you see this?' Jimmy said. 'It's only our Melody who's due to be presenting this one. It's best actor, and her new man is nominated.'

But it was clear that something wasn't right. Melody had slipped in a costume change in preparation for her presenting duties, and now she wore a glittery gold mini-dress that was tighter, shorter and more revealing than her earlier outfit, an effect that Maggie would have believed impossible if she wasn't seeing it with her own eyes. Just as well Jimmy's brother Frank isn't here she thought, or he would have a flipping heart-attack. But Melody's face wore a look of deep concern, and all over the stage, producers and assistant producers and directors and camera guys and soundmen stared at clip-boards or scratched their heads, evidently at a loss of what to do.

'He's not turned up,' Jimmy said. 'Benjamin's not turned up.'

Later, Maggie would remember the utter confusion of the moment as the terrible news spread through the crew and then reached Melody Montague herself. The news that Benjamin David had been found in the emergency stairwell, lying in a pool of blood, his head battered in. Alongside the body lay his severed left hand, and on the back of that hand was scrawled a message that the police would find completely unfathomable.

Leonardo

Chapter 8

The scene-of-crime team had worked swiftly and efficiently and within six hours the body had been cleared for release to the forensic pathology lab. According to the interim case report Frank had got his hands on, it hadn't taken much examination to determine the cause of death. A severe blow to the back of the head from a blunt instrument, provenance unknown. Establishing the time of death had been more imprecise, but the non-committal pathologist had given an estimate of about mid-day, just about the time the actors were gathering for the final camera placement run-throughs.

Of course, with the victim being so well-known, identification was a mere formality, but it was a formality that had to be observed nonetheless. Ordinarily, it would be the responsibility of the next of kin, and his younger sister Allegra had been the obvious choice, but she was so consumed with grief that she couldn't face it. As a result, the task fell to his activist friend and fellow actor Charles Grant.

But the big question that Frank was wrestling with was why the hell the Met in its infinite wisdom had decided to allocate the case to the frigging walking disaster that was DCS Colin Barker. He wasn't even remotely half-competent and he was a total prat and a nasty piece of work to boot. Such were the views Frank was expressing to Ronnie French as they waited in the stuffy press room at Paddington Green police station with the assembled media. DC Ronnie French, one of the most useless of the Department 12B squad, an accolade which took some earning in that ocean of uselessness, was his normal reliably cynical self. Meaning he agreed with ever word his guv'nor said on matters Barker-related. Generally speaking, Frank wouldn't have let Frenchie within a million miles of one of his cases, but he'd recently been on the end of a mild bollocking from Jill Smart about his aversion to working as a team. She was right, he bloody hated working with anybody, but such was his respect for his gaffer he was prepared to give it a try. *Reluctantly*. And the thing was, an interesting idea had come to him concerning the terrible murder of Benjamin

David and he felt duty-bound to share it with the official investigating team. Which is why he was here in this bloody press room, awaiting the arrival of the star of the show.

'What I can't understand guv,' Frenchie was saying in his trademark laconic tones, 'is why he's still in a job after all his screw-ups?'

'Said it before Frenchie, that's what always happens. Same as in every organisation. Guys like that get promoted to their level of incompetence. Peter's Principle, that's what they used to call it after some guy who wrote a book. Everyone knows they're rubbish, but no-one's got the balls to do anything about it. Seen it time and time again. But hold that thought, because here's a live appearance from the monumental arse in question.'

Barker waddled on to the platform, taking his place behind a wooden lectern. He was tall, but seriously overweight, with a prominent double chin and heavy jowls. In his younger days, he evidently had been quite good-looking. That, in Frank's jaundiced view, could have been the only reason for his inexplicable career trajectory. Behind him trailed Heather Green, a pretty black PC whom Frank knew and rated, and who Barker introduced as his personal assistant. For him, she was there to look nice, tick the diversity box and operate the PowerPoint. That was the sort of guy Barker was.

'Personal assistant?' Frank said bitterly. 'It's a bloody assistance dog that he needs. Deaf dumb and blind doesn't even begin to describe it.'

The chatter in the room gradually died away as Barker cleared his throat in preparation to speak.

'Well, good morning ladies and gentlemen.' It was two-thirty in the afternoon. *Genius.*

Yash Patel of the *Chronicle* had sat through too many turgid Barker press-conferences and was evidently in no mood to suffer any more than was absolutely necessary. As was his way, he cut to the chase.

'D'you have any suspects, Chief Inspector? Do you have a motive? Are Melody Montague or his sister Allegra suspects? It's usually those closest to the victim, isn't that true? In ninety-three percent of the time it's a partner or a close family member, that's what the statistics say, isn't that true?'

Barker studiously ignored the intervention and ploughed on in his droning voice whilst Frank provided a whispered running commentary. Yes, it was his intention to question everyone who had attended the awards ceremony and to trace everyone who had entered or left the building in the time window between Benjamin David's last sighting and the discovery of the body twenty-four hours later. *'Aye, so that's narrowed it down to about ten thousand suspects.'* No, they did not yet have a motive but they were working on a number of lines of enquiry. *'They hadn't a damn clue and that's not going to improve with you in charge.'* Everyone was a suspect at this stage and nothing was being ruled out. *'That's not even a cliché.'* It was a complex case but he expected swiftly to bring the investigation to a successful conclusion. *'That'll be the first time.'*

This time he said it loud enough for everyone present to hear. Muted laughter rippled round the room, and up on the stage, PC Green struggled to stifle a career-limiting giggle. Barker furrowed his brow and scanned the room, having evidently recognised Frank's voice, but did not react.

'But to conclude, we do have one very interesting piece of evidence that I would like to share with you. Heather, could you do the honours please.'

The PC clicked her mouse, bringing up the next slide. There were gasps of surprise from the grizzled journalists as they began to make sense of the image.

'So is that the victim's hand?' asked one. 'Bloomin' hell.'

'Leonardo? Do you know what that means Chief Inspector? Is that who did it? It wasn't Di Caprio was it?' That drew a laugh, Patel giving a mock bow to the assembled hacks.

Frank was staring at the screen in disbelief. *God's sake, why the hell has he let that out? What a complete numpty.*

Barker gave a complacent smile. 'I don't think Mr Di Caprio is in town, but yes, we have a number of theories about its significance.

However you will forgive me when I say we are not able to disclose these at this moment in time.'

Frank gave an audible sigh, deciding that he just couldn't let this go. He got up and strode to the front of the platform, and ignoring the angry stare of Barker, began to address the assembled hacks.

'Look ladies and gents, I think we've had a wee bit of an IT malfunction here, we didn't mean to show you these pictures.' He gestured to the young PC and immediately she understood, replacing the images with a blank screen. 'And folks, we don't want to read anything about this in your papers or see it on your telly reports. I know I can rely on your co-operation.' *As if,* he thought. Still, the fourth estate wasn't entirely without honour so he could hope for the best.

He shot Barker a serene smile. 'Sorry about that sir, just thought it was worth mentioning in passing. Back to you sir.' If looks could kill, Frank would already be dead, buried and probably cremated too.

Now Patel was on his feet. 'This must mean that the murder was pre-meditated, doesn't it? And that the killer was trying to leave someone a message or a warning of some kind. Are you following that line of enquiry Chief Inspector?'

Barker looked at him contemptuously. 'Yes, thank you Mr Patel, we had thought of that, funnily enough. So, if there are no more questions...' There were plenty of questions waiting to be asked, but evidently he did not intend to answer any of them. Instead he gathered up his papers, curtly thanked everyone for attending and made to leave. Less than six minutes from start to finish.

'What, is that all we're getting?' shouted an indignant Patel, a siren voice above the general mutterings of discontent. 'That's a total disgrace.'

'Come on Frenchie,' Frank said, 'let's grab the idiot before he leaves. I don't suppose he'll listen to us, but we can try at least.' They pushed their way through the throng of departing reporters to the podium.

'Excuse me sir, do you have a minute?'

It appeared Barker had not forgiven Frank's earlier intervention.

'What sort of stunt was that Stewart? I thought they'd stuck you out to grass but here you still are, getting on everybody's tits as usual.'

'Just trying to be helpful sir, that's all. Many hands make light work and all of that. I thought it might be prudent to keep the details of the MO to ourselves for now, don't you agree?'

If he did, he wasn't going to admit it. 'If I needed any help Stewart, you're the last person I would ask. Now I don't know why you're here, but whatever it is, I haven't got time for it. In case you haven't noticed, I'm working on a very high-profile murder case.'

'High-profile? Of course sir. You wouldn't work on any other kind, would you sir? But this won't take a minute sir, I promise you. You might remember my private investigator pals Maggie Bainbridge and Jimmy Stewart? Bainbridge Associates, that's their firm. They're working on a case that has a connection to the deceased. So we thought we'd better let you know the details, just in case it's relevant.'

'Well come on, what's the connection?' Barker said sourly, 'I haven't got all day.'

Frank smiled sweetly. 'I got Detective Constable French to write it all down in his wee notebook. Come on Frenchie, spill the beans.'

'Right then sir,' French began, furrowing his brow as he evidently struggled to read his own handwriting. 'Those Bainbridge geezers are working on a couple of pre-nuptial agreement things. For that Melody Montague, the soap actress. I'm sure you've heard of her. She's that sexy-looking old bird with the big chest. Very high-profile sir. Right up your street sir.'

Frank smiled to himself. Ronnie French might be fat, lazy and a complete waste of space, but he didn't give a monkeys about anybody, no matter what their rank. However it seemed that Barker had not tuned in to the not-very-veiled insult.

'So? What the hell has this got to do with my murder case?'

'Well as I understand it sir,' French drawled, 'there's a mega dispute about dosh in the first matter. A shed load. And Miss

Montague was anxious not to make the same mistake again in her upcoming marriage to the deceased.'

'Aye, more than six million quid,' Frank said, 'and that sort of sum is normally enough to raise the blood pressure don't you think? So we were wondering if perhaps this murder might have been an act of revenge, aimed at ruining Miss Montague's life by killing her fiancé. It's a credible theory, don't you agree?'

Barker gave him a withering look. 'Stewart, do you think I give a shit about your half-arsed theories? You and your bunch of *cast-offs?*' He spat the word out, not bothering to hide his contempt.

It didn't seem to bother Ronnie either, self-awareness not being a concept familiar to him. He simply flicked over a page and carried on.

'A Mr Patrick Hunt is the former husband. He's an actor too, and he, according to Miss Bainbridge, is a very bitter man. Me and my guv'nor think he has prime suspect written all over him.'

'Oh you do, do you?' Barker said, making no attempt to hide his sarcasm. 'Well at least that saves me a job. I can scrub him off the list right away.'

'As I said, Miss Bainbridge reported that Patrick Hunt is off-the-scale bitter,' Frank said, giving a shrug, 'but it's your shout sir. I would follow it up if I was you, that's all I'm saying.'

But he could see that Barker wasn't listening. Arrogant and stupid in equal measures, it was only a matter of time before this case slipped down the drain like all his others. Ok, if that's the way he wanted to play it, sod him. As for motive, Barker wouldn't recognise a motive if it was carved in stone and inserted up his back passage.

But that didn't matter. Because Department 12B had the remit to look at any case it damn well liked and when he got back to the office, he was going to get out another wee buff folder and stick a white label on the front. Then all he had to do was come up with a name.

Chapter 9

Go safely, go dancing, go running home, into the wind's breath and the hands of the star maker. They had stood silently, heads bowed and immersed in their own thoughts as the celebrant committed the body of Benjamin David to be incinerated to dust. They hadn't known him of course but it was Melody's wish that they should attend. Not many people liked a funeral, especially when the deceased had been taken before their time, but for Maggie and Jimmy it was the funerals they had missed that caused them almost unbearable pain.

She hadn't attended the ceremony for her husband Phillip. In fact no-one had attended the simple committal, such was the total ruin of his reputation, and she was glad of that because he deserved nothing better. And how could she go, after he had betrayed her in so many ways? His infidelity with that bitch from the office and his terrible betrayal of everything she held dear. Worst of all, one day she would have to explain everything to her beloved son Ollie and she simply had no idea how she would ever be able to do that.

For Jimmy it was the agonising loss of the comrades-in-arms, the men and women under his command who had become his closest friends, great guys felled by an indiscriminate sniper or blown to bits by an improvised explosive device when barely into their twenties. They gathered and tidied their mangled bodies as best they could before flying them home to Brize Norton or Northalt into the care of bewildered relatives, accompanied by a personal letter of condolence that he always took the trouble to write. *Your son or brother or husband or daughter was a brave soldier, taken too young in the service of their country.* That was always the gist of it, but he tried wherever he could to make it more personal by mentioning a small act of kindness or a humorous incident that he had shared with their loved one. He could never attend the funerals even if he had wanted to, and in truth he wasn't sure whether he did or not. But it didn't need him turning up at a freezing cold graveside in his dress uniform to show the respect he had for these men and women, for that was now fundamental to who he was, and he knew it would always be so.

A function room in a local golf club had been hired for the wake, and the small team of waiters and waitresses were now clearing away the remains of the buffet lunch. The mood was sombre because this was not a celebration of a long life well lived, but of a man in the prime of his life whose time on this earth had been cruelly and violently cut short. As well as family, the room was packed wall-to-wall with well-known faces from the world of entertainment. In particular, it seemed the entire cast of Bow Road had turned out to show their respects to their colleague, whom Maggie suspected had been just as popular with them as with his legion of fans. Although that hadn't prevented him being brutally murdered.

Melody Montague was sitting quietly in a corner, holding the hand of a handsome woman of about sixty whom Maggie had learned was Benjamin David's recently-widowed mother. What a ghastly injustice she thought, to have your child taken from you so young and so soon after you lost your husband. Maggie didn't know the woman of course, but she supposed that any religious faith she had had would now lie in tatters. And now she had to survive the agony of a second funeral.

Throughout the ceremony Melody Montague had been inconsolable, but now she simply looked sad and defeated. It was less than a month since she was telling the press how she was crazily madly in love, more than she had ever been before in her life, and how she was looking forward so much to building a little family with Benjamin. Now for the first time, Maggie felt sorry for her. She walked over and sat down beside her.

'I'm sorry for your loss Melody, I really don't know what else to say.'

The actress reached over and took her hand. 'Thank you Maggie. It's still not really sunk in yet. I look around this room and I expect to see him with a beer in his hand, laughing and joking like he always does. I mean, like he always did.' She struggled to stifle a sob.

'It will get better in time,' Maggie said. 'I know everybody tells you that, but it's true.' Yes, but what they didn't tell you was how *much* time it took. Sometimes it was months, sometimes it was years and sometimes it was never. But everything she knew about Melody suggested that she was a survivor, and that sooner rather than later she would bounce back from this terrible event in her life.

They had now been joined by Jimmy, who gave a nod of condolence and said that he too was sorry for her loss.

'Thank you Jimmy,' Melody said, forcing a half-smile, 'but who would want to kill Benjamin, that's what I don't understand? Everybody loved him.'

'I'm sure the police are covering every angle,' Maggie said. 'It takes time.'

'Yes, I'm sure you're right,' Melody answered distractedly. Maggie looked up to see she was staring at Charles Grant and Sharon Trent, who were standing alone in the middle of the room, he with his arm clasped tightly around her waist, she sipping on a glass of wine.

'Look at them,' she said, with some bitterness. 'It's not fair, is it?' Maggie assumed she was referring to Charles seemingly finding some consolation after the abduction of his son and the consequent breakup of his marriage. Although if she was writing a book about the happiness of the human condition, she wasn't sure she would select Charles Grant as Exhibit A. But at least there seemed to be some progress in the quest to figure out what had happened to his little boy, even if it was Frank who was making all the running.

'I suppose we all have to move on, don't we?' As soon as she said it, she recognised how stupid and badly chosen it sounded. Melody had just cremated her soul mate for goodness sake and here was she talking about moving on. But to her surprise, she seemed to agree with her.

'Yes, you're right Maggie. We do, no matter how hard it seems.' Maggie couldn't help noticing the look the actress shot in her colleague's direction, a quite involuntary response to the sheer force of manhood that was Jimmy Stewart. And it wasn't hard to deduce what Melody was thinking. With men like him around, perhaps there would always be something to live for.

She squeezed her hand. 'That's a brave thing to say Melody, and I hope we can help you a little. Let's try and get the pre-nup matter with Patrick all tidied up so you can at least forget about that.' And if that sounded at first inappropriate, she remembered how grateful she had been to Asvina at the time of her greatest distress for helping her get her affairs in order.

'Yes that would be good,' Melody answered, without much conviction. 'But honestly, I don't care about that damn house now. I don't care at all.'

***

It wouldn't be wrong to say that the atmosphere in the office had been frosty since Maggie had agreed to take on the Grant case. Even Elsa, the sweet office administrator cum secretary they shared with the ten other businesses that occupied their Fleet Street premises, had projected an uncharacteristic coldness in her presence. Uncharacteristic because although she was deeply infatuated with Jimmy, she bore no grudge against her employer, whom she regarded as too old to be a rival for his affections. The infatuation was unrequited, Maggie had always assumed, although it occurred to her it had taken the pair of them rather a long time to fetch three skinny lattes from the nearby Starbucks. Frosty atmosphere or not, she had made a promise to Charles Grant and she intended to fulfil it.

Her thoughts were interrupted by the return of her colleagues, bursting back into the tiny office. It was obvious from their smirks that they had been sharing some private joke, a joke they did not seem keen to share with her. Elsa banged the coffee down on Maggie's desk with such force that warm liquid spilt out from under the plastic lid and down the side of the cup. Maggie smiled brightly at her and said 'Thanks Elsa,' deciding the best strategy was to ignore the elephant in the room. The secretary gave her a haughty look before walking out, slamming the door behind her.

Jimmy laughed. 'Don't worry, she'll soon get over it, and yes I know, I shouldn't have told her what I thought about us taking on the case. She's just a bit protective towards me, goodness knows why. I think I remind her of her dad.'

Maggie gave a wry smile. Jimmy Stewart, at thirty-two years of age, still either oblivious or indifferent to the stupid effect he had on women. Of all ages too, from school-girly Elsas to high-mileage man-eaters like Melody Montague. Goodness, even her mum fancied him. But she thought she had worked out the real reason for his reticence. Because the one time in his life he had succumbed, to the attractions of the beautiful temptress Astrid Sorenson, it had wrecked his marriage and his life with it. He never talked about it, but she knew. She knew his only goal in life was to get back together with his beloved Flora. But at least he seemed to have returned to the office in a sunnier mood than when he left, which was a relief. Particularly since she would now need to tell him about the quite extraordinary development that had occurred in his short absence, a development that she feared he may not see in a positive light.

He smiled at her as he sat down at his desk. 'Got anywhere yet? With our Charles Grant case I mean? Because I've been thinking about it when I was out.'

Our Charles Grant case. That was more like it. Maybe breaking the news about Miss Allegra David might not prove so difficult after all.

She returned his smile. 'Only got the bare facts about the abduction and the investigation. But before that, have you seen this?' She pointed to her screen, an article from the online edition of the Chronicle. *Grieving Allegra hits out at police on murdered brother's case.*

Maggie watched as Jimmy read the article.

'God, that's going to raise Frank's blood pressure isn't it?' he said. '*The police are a right-wing construct of the fascist state and unfit for purpose.* That's the same kind of line that our Charles Grant's been using, isn't it?'

'Well they're mates, or at least political bed-fellows,' Maggie said, 'So maybe not so surprising.'

Jimmy shrugged. 'But she's saying she will not be supporting them in their hunt for her brother's killer. Bloody hell. Talk about putting your principles centre stage.'

'Yeah, and pretty unwise in my opinion,' Maggie said. 'But the Davids are -or were in Benjamin's case- pretty much defined by their left-wing politics. Perhaps she thinks she is honouring his memory.'

Maggie gave him a weak smile. 'Speaking of Allegra...actually, she phoned me when you were out.'

'What?'

'She called me. She'd heard about us from Charles and wondered if we could help her with her brother's case too.' She would have liked to have gently drip-fed the subject into the conversation, but realised it would probably be better if she just came straight out with it. Jimmy's reaction was exactly as she had expected. Or perhaps worse.

'What, are you mental?' he said, giving her an incredulous look, his voice so raised that everyone in the building would likely hear it. 'This is a bloody live murder case, not some stupid wee divorce. And her brother's hardly been dead a couple of days.'

'I know,' she said defensively, 'and she doesn't want us to exactly work on the murder. It's just she had found something out in the days before she died and wondered if we could speak to her about it. To help her decide whether to tell the police or not. To decide if it's important.'

Jimmy shook his head. 'Do you actually hear what you're saying? I mean, I'd need to look up one of my old textbooks, but I'm pretty sure we'd be breaking about a dozen laws with this.'

'I know. But she sounded so desperate.'

'But not desperate enough to junk her stupid politics I take it,' he said, his tone thick with cynicism. 'I mean, *a right-wing construct of a fascist police state*? Who writes her scripts?'

'I know,' she said again. 'Maybe you're right. Maybe we should give it a wide berth.'

That seemed to calm him down a little, for he gave a wry smile and said. 'Well you're the boss, but I think I've made my feelings plain.'

'And thank you for that,' she said with a relieved sigh. 'I'll really think it through carefully, honestly I will.' And she meant it too, because the last thing she wanted was anything to mess up the fine working relationship she had with Jimmy.

'Anyway, to Charles Grant,' she said after a pause. 'I suppose we should be focussing on him since he's our client. The problem is there's not a huge amount to go on. Sadly.'

'Yeah, that's what I thought,' Jimmy said, the last few seconds seemingly forgotten. 'But I guess we have to go back to basics, you know, the old motive, method and opportunity thing. I know it sounds like a cliché but I think it still holds true.'

She nodded. 'Yes, you're right, I did kind of think about that myself. I mean the method and opportunity bit is simple and straightforward, isn't it? Drive up in a fast car, take them by surprise as they're walking back from the nursery and whisk the kid away.'

'And the motive,' Jimmy said. 'Money. Simple as that, surely? A quarter a million a pop's not to be sniffed at. Find a rich celebrity, track their kid's daily routine, and then grab them. Not hard, is it?'

But then it struck her. Was the explanation really as simple as that?

'Jimmy, what if there was more to it? What if there was a deeper motive?'

'I'm sorry, I don't get where you're coming from.'

She wrinkled her nose. 'You see, the thing that's odd about this crime is that it's not repeatable. Organised criminals are no different from legitimate businesses in that they need a reliable business model that they can use again and again, one that always delivers results. But don't you see what the problem with this one is?'

He nodded. 'Aye, I do. If you take the cash, but don't deliver the goods, then that's it. The next time you do one, you're not going to get your ransom money.'

'Exactly Jimmy. So maybe we have to look at another angle. What if this was a one-off, and the primary motive was to hurt the Grants and the money was just an added bonus?'

'Could be,' Jimmy said. 'We know a bit about Charles but do we know anything about the wife?'

'Only that she was politically active like he is. I think she worked as an editor for a publishing house but she was also a Labour councillor if I recall correctly.'

'It would be nice to speak to her,' Jimmy said, 'but maybe that would be one for Frank. Help him to feel involved in our investigation.'

She laughed. 'If he's still speaking to us, that is.'

'I've just had a thought,' Jimmy said. 'Charles spoke at that anti-fascist rally a week or two ago didn't he?'

Maggie nodded. 'Yeah, that's his thing. He's very passionate about it. Even more so than the Davids I think. I mean, if that's actually possible.'

'So maybe that's an angle worth exploring?'

'Ok, let's give it a try.'

Punching in *Charles Grant Activist* returned over a hundred thousand results. Photographs, videos, chat magazine gossip, fan sites, his Wikipedia profile, the sheer weight of information threatened to overwhelm them before they got started. But tucked away, three or four pages down the search, was a headline that simultaneously caught the interest of both.

Activist Grant quits social media after soap star spat.

They looked at one another quizzically. 'Yeah, go for it,' Jimmy said in answer to her unspoken question.

Maggie clicked the link and screwed up her eyes to focus on the article. 'Ah, *that's* interesting. So maybe this goes some way to explaining his reputation as a difficult man.'

'Aye, it seems like it.'

Reading on, it seemed to have started with an inflammatory tweet from Grant postulating that many of his fellow celebrities were guilty of nothing more than virtue-signalling and publicity-seeking when it came to broadcasting their support for what he called *his* progressive causes. Surprisingly from Maggie's point of view, he had, without naming names, called out some of his fellow actors as being guilty of this crime. Less surprisingly, it had generated a virulent response from some of those unnamed colleagues, who clearly knew whom he had been referring to. Including, most directly, Benjamin David.

'Do you see this?' Maggie said, wide-eyed. 'Somewhat blunt and to the point, don't you think?'

'Yeah, you could say that,' Jimmy laughed. *'Eff off you conceited twat. Power to the people.* Do you think David was being ironic with that last bit?'

'Yes maybe, but it soon gets pretty nasty. And it went on for days and days.'

'Aye,' Jimmy nodded, 'so not surprisingly our boy Charlie decides to take a break from on-line life.'

Maggie laughed. 'Yes, but not for long.'

She pointed to another of the search results. 'Did you know he has a monthly opinion column in the *Guardian*? I didn't.'

'So he's just a normal lefty thesp then. Move along, nothing to see here. Ah, but wait a wee minute...' Another search result had evidently caught his eye. He clicked the link to explore it further.

'Look at this one, do you see the headline? *We ignore the rise of the far-right at our peril.* And look, here's another. *Far-right apologists pedalling fake news.* My, he is the right little socialist warrior, isn't he? Not that there's anything wrong with that of course,' he added.

He needn't have bothered apologising on her account, since she didn't do politics, her scumbag former husband making her immune to all that. But then as she quickly scanned the first article, something struck her.

'You see, in this one, he talks about the dogs' abuse he gets from what he calls far-right trolls. He mentions one particular person, who apparently goes by the handle of da Vinci.'

'Da Vinci? Like in the Dan Brown book?'

'Yes, the same.'

'And we are assuming it is a guy?'

'What, with a username like da Vinci? Maggie said. 'Well, I suppose you're right, it doesn't have to be a guy.'

Jimmy had clicked on the Twitter link and was scrolling down through some of Grant's posting history.

'I tell you what, he's not scared to share his opinions, is he? Look, here he is, laying into the Catholic church. Half the responses have been moderated out, but I can imagine they wouldn't be very complimentary.'

Maggie read on. 'Yeah, and now he's accusing the Tories of being evil bastards - that's his actual words - only interested in enriching themselves by exploiting the poor and disadvantaged.'

Jimmy laughed. 'See what I mean? The socialist warrior right enough. And he doesn't seem to care who he upsets in the process. But you don't think this could have anything to do with the abduction, do you?'

'I don't know,' Maggie said, 'but as you say, he does seem to have upset a lot of people. Come on, let's keep looking.'

He nodded, punching in a few more search terms.

'So that's interesting,' Jimmy said, pointing at the screen. 'This is him just a few days before wee Jamie's abduction, calling out the far-right again.'

'Yeah, and look, here's this da Vinci back too. It's really nasty, some of this stuff.'

'Too right,' Jimmy said. 'I don't understand why people do it. But our Charles seems to be addicted to it, doesn't he?'

Maggie nodded. 'Yeah, he does seem to be. But come on, let's see if there's anything else around that time.'

Jimmy modified the search to include the child's name and the month of the abduction. It took some time to find it, the single Twitter posting buried several pages down in the search. Under the hashtag *#GrantAbduction*, it had been posted two days after the event and was as brief as it was brutal.

Commie bastards always get what they deserve.

But this time, the troller wasn't hiding his identity behind a stupid handle. The author being the man known to his followers simply as D-V.

Chapter 10

Jimmy checked the map on his phone again to make sure he had got it right. Yep, 8 Harbledown Road, Parsons Green. It was another one of Maggie's hospital passes and so he wasn't exactly looking forward to this mission. But it had to be done. Go and talk to Allegra David and see if she'll tell you what her brother had been worried about before he was murdered. It was crazy, he knew that, but that was her orders, and Captain Jimmy Stewart always obeyed orders.

Almost all of the properties in the street had been converted into flats, most configured with one dwelling on the ground floor and one above. The street exuded prosperity, every house smart and well-maintained, their elaborately-carved window surrounds pristine and whitewashed, front doors glossy with shiny brass letterboxes and handles. Not surprising when you wouldn't get any change from a million quid, even for the rare one-bedroom attic conversion.

Number 8 however turned out to be the exception, but in a good way, an end-of-terrace still in its original two-storey layout and with a two-car parking space alongside its end wall, currently occupied by a Range-Rover sporting a current-year plate. A hundred-grand car and a two-million-pound pad. Nice, but perhaps not so unexpected given the family background of Allegra Elizabeth and Benjamin Franklin David. New money, that's what they used to call it, the David family having built an industrial dynasty out of ships and armaments starting in the early nineteenth century. They might not be titled, but the family wealth ran to half a street in Mayfair and a couple of country estates. Compared to what they had grown up with, Allegra and Benjamin were slumming it in Parsons Green.

Jimmy had tried to call in advance to make an appointment, but Allegra it seemed wasn't taking calls. Hardly surprising after the murder of her brother, when even thicko DCI Colin Barker would know that it was generally those closest to the victim who were the prime suspect in ninety percent of cases. And if he didn't before, Yash Patel of the *Chronicle* had brought him up to speed with that particular statistic. In all events, Allegra was probably already sick and tired of answering questions, and on top of that, it would surely only be a matter of time before the media ended their self-imposed and brief period of respect for the bereaved actress. Then it would be open season on her life and her relationships and everything in between. Not something to be envied.

He closed the picket gate behind him on its clasp and pressed the bell. From somewhere inside, he could hear the faintest of rings. Good, at least it was working. He waited a few seconds and tried again. This time, he heard nothing. So what, probably the battery had taken its last dying breath, they didn't last long. Not a problem. He reached for the brass knocker and then stopped dead, puzzled. His action had caused the door to open a fraction, and a further light push revealed that it had been left on the latch. Odd.

'Miss David? Miss David?' Cautiously, he opened the door and went into the narrow hallway.

'Miss David?' A door on the left led to a small tastefully-decorated sitting room, where effort had obviously been made to retain as much period detail as possible, the centrepiece being a fine tiled fireplace and oak surround. Half a dozen sympathy cards were displayed on the mantelpiece, and several more were arranged haphazardly on a small coffee table. Jimmy could only imagine Allegra's present emotional state, trying to come to terms with the murder of her brother, although that assumed that they had actually got on. Suddenly it occurred to him that it wasn't outside the bounds of possibility that Allegra David had done it and that he could now be in the home of a killer. He hadn't thought of that before entering the house, and he realised with some annoyance how careless he had become since he left the army. You probably weren't going to fall foul of a booby-trap in SW6, but it was sloppy nonetheless.

He returned to the hallway and continued his search of the ground floor. A door was located directly opposite that of the lounge. He tried the handle but it appeared to be locked. It wasn't unusual for these old houses to have locks on the internal doors, and in any case he assumed it was only a cupboard. Something to look at a bit later.

As was the fashion, the original back parlour and kitchen had been knocked together and extended out into the garden, with full-width bi-fold glass doors drenching light into the room. Jimmy wasn't a student of interior design but he guessed that the stunning top-end kitchen would have cost as much as his own tiny Clapham pad. Of course there was twin Belfast sinks, an island unit the size of a football pitch and, naturally, an Aga. Further proof that the David siblings enjoyed a money-no-object lifestyle, and he was certain it wasn't paid for by their parts in a crappy soap. And now of course the house would be hers alone, although that would no doubt have happened anyway once her brother had married Melody Montague and moved into her impressive Richmond home. Nonetheless, it made him think.

With no particular objective in mind other than nosiness, he started opening all the cupboards. On these Helmand house sweeps you always did a search, and on a good day you might find a stash of ammunition or some bomb-making chemicals, forlornly hidden just as the front door was kicked in. That wasn't going to happen here, but you never knew. And half way around, his half-hunch proved accurate.

In the centre of the island unit was fitted an elaborate waste-bin system. He gave the handle a gentle tug and the unit slid open as in slow-motion. Two large-capacity nylon bins were suspended from a cradle, and the first, clearly designated by the actress for paper waste recycling, was stuffed to capacity with used kitchen-roll. *Used, blood-stained kitchen roll.*

'Miss David!' Now Jimmy's call was more urgent, worried. Looking down, he saw the faintest spots of blood on the white wood floor. Dropping to his knees to get a closer look, he noticed an effort had clearly been made to scrub off the spillage but the trail was still discernible. A trail that he, still on his knees, was able to follow back out in to the hallway and up to the locked door. He jumped up and pulled on the handle again but it wasn't going to move, and since it opened outwards, it couldn't be burst open by putting a shoulder to it. Rushing back to the kitchen, he grabbed a short broad-bladed knife and returned with it to the cupboard.

Examining the lock, Jimmy saw it was of a sturdy mortis design and his improvised tool was unlikely to be strong enough to prise it open. However the hinge-bearing edge of the door showed more promise. These, in contrast to the mortis, were of flimsy construction and soon began to yield as he jammed the blade of the knife between the hinge plate and the door. Within a few seconds he had prised the top hinge free of the architrave and not much later the lower one was also freed. Carefully, he let the door topple out of its frame, and releasing it from the lock, rested it against the wall.

To his surprise, he saw that rather than concealing a cupboard, the door led to a steep stairway disappearing down into the darkness. He hadn't considered that these homes would have cellars, but this clearly was what it was. He felt along the wall for a light-switch, but in vain. He took his phone from the back pocket of his jeans and fired up the searchlight app, aiming the penetrating beam down the dank stairwell.

Jimmy edged his way downwards, one step at a time, in trepidation of what he might discover in the gloom. Before he had even made it half-way his fears were realised. Clearly visible at the bottom of the stairs, the body of Allegra David lay in a crumpled heap, congealing blood still creeping from a head-wound. He jumped down the last few steps and gently placed his fingers on the jugular, feeling for a pulse. It didn't bear thinking about, the number of times he'd had to do this, and you always knew when it was hopeless. Like in this case. Allegra's body was already cold and her beautiful face was betraying the first signs of rigor mortis. Jimmy guessed she had been dead four or five hours. Nothing could be done for her now.

The emergency services' operator was quite insistent. Polite but firm. An ambulance was on its way, but it was very important to be sure that the injured party was dead. She knew it was a difficult thing to ask, but could Jimmy please feel for a pulse once again? If there was even the slightest chance that the casualty was clinging to life, maybe some emergency first aid could be administered, winning precious minutes before the paramedics arrived. Jimmy didn't like to tell her that he'd seen dozens of dead bodies and he knew quite well what death looked like, thank you very much.

'Ok, hang on a minute please.' He was only going through the motions, but he understood why it had to be done. In Helmand of course, he had seen many separated body parts. Too many, the ghastly images still causing him regular nightmares, and he didn't expect them to fade away any time soon. But this was different. God, how had he missed it? He knew why. The understandable desire to nowadays keep as far away from death as was humanly possible.

At least he knew there was no point in taking Allegra's pulse now. He shined his phone torch on to the back of the severed hand to read the spidery message that was written on it.

Leonardo

Chapter 11

Frank had spotted them across the crowded lounge, and aware what his brother had just been through, waved to indicate that he was going to the bar before joining them. A few minutes later, he appeared with two pints and a large chardonnay for Maggie. And then noticed that Jimmy had already been hitting the single malts.

'Sorry bruv, didn't realise you were on the fire water, although I'm glad I didn't notice 'cos pints are a lot cheaper. But anyway, how are you feeling? I heard you've been in the wars. Aye, sorry, maybe not the best turn of phrase but you know what I mean. Hope you're ok.'

'Yeah, no bother, I'm fine,' Jimmy said. 'But it's not something you want to see every day, I can tell you that.'

'What, the hand? I'm with you there pal. A bit grizzly to say the least. Anyway, I heard you've been put through the wringer by my best mate big fat Colin. I suppose he thinks you did it, am I right?'

Jimmy smiled. 'Not exactly, but he did make it clear in his normal pompous manner, and I quote, that I would remain a suspect until my alibi was fully checked out and verified. He even asked me if I had a current passport and was planning to leave the country any time soon.'

'What?' Frank said, amused. 'He must have learned that line from the cop shows.'

'Yeah, it did make me smile. But obviously, his main interest was in finding out why I'd gone to Allegra's in the first place.'

'Oh aye?' Frank said sharply. 'And why *did* you go there?'

He raised an eyebrow as Maggie intervened. 'That's a bit awkward Frank I'm afraid. The thing is, she had asked us to help her. With her brother's murder case.'

'What, am I hearing right? Help with her brother's murder case? Bloody hell.' He didn't mean to sound so aggressive, but it was impossible to help himself. What the hell was she thinking of, getting involved in a brand-new murder? 'You can't do that Maggie, you should know that.'

'I know that now. I'm sorry.' Frank heard the words, but he wasn't sure of how much she meant it. That was the thing about the lovely Maggie Bainbridge. He hadn't known her very long, but it was long enough to know she ploughed her own furrow. But this was different. This could get her and his brother into a heap of trouble, and surely both of them had had enough of *that* over the last couple of years. There was no doubt about it, he would have to keep a close eye on her, if only for her own good. Lost in his thoughts, he suddenly realised his brother was speaking.

'The whole scene was bloody awful,' Jimmy said. 'And I guess you heard about that thing scribbled on her severed hand?'

'Leonardo?' Frank said. 'Yeah, I heard. Look, I haven't told you this before, but this MO is exactly the same as the Benjamin David killing. Exactly the same. The right hand chopped off, the Leonardo thing, the lot.'

Jimmy frowned. 'Right hand, did you say? It wasn't Allegra's right hand, it was her left hand. I'm one hundred percent sure about that.'

'So do you have any idea what it means?' Maggie asked. He was pleased to note she was sounding rather more contrite. 'You know, the Leonardo thing.'

'Absolutely no idea,' he said. 'But the good news is my mate DI Pete Burnside and his wee team have been moved onto the case to boost the numbers so we might start to see sense emerging from Paddington Green for once.'

Maggie nodded. 'I know this will sound crazy, but it just came to Jimmy and me that there might be something linking Allegra and Benjamin's murder to the Jamie Grant abduction. Especially now you've told us that Benjamin David was killed in the same way as his sister.'

Frank raised an eyebrow. 'How so?'

'Well, we found out that Charles Grant was very active on social media in the months leading up to little Jamie's abduction. Some of his postings were very provocative. He made a lot of enemies, virtual ones at least.'

'Is that right?' Frank said, interested.

'Yes it is. Anyway, Jimmy and I had this idea that if the abduction was some sort of a revenge attack, then maybe online would be a good place to look for suspects.'

'What, you think someone got upset just because he twittered or whatever you call it?'

Maggie nodded. 'Well, why not? Some of the stuff is really vicious and personal, you should see it. And as it happens, there was one name in particular who seemed to have it in for him in a big way.'

'Yeah,' Jimmy agreed, 'some weirdo going under the name of da Vinci. Don't you see? Leonardo is that odd message left behind by the murderer, and da Vinci is the handle of the person who's been harassing Charles Grant big-time. I mean, it's got to be more than a coincidence, hasn't it?'

'Leonardo da Vinci, eh?' Frank said, giving a half-smile. 'Aye, I've heard of the guy. And as you say, quite a coincidence.'

'There is something else too,' Maggie said. 'You know of course that the David siblings and Grant were friends who all shared the same politics? So we were thinking that maybe the abduction and murder of Jamie Grant wasn't about the money at all. That it was actually designed to *hurt* them, a kind of punishment for their political views. The Grants had their son murdered and the Davids were killed themselves. So was it some sort of revenge, you know, someone trying to teach them a lesson?'

'We don't know for certain that the wee lad's been murdered,' Frank said, although he knew that he was clutching at straws with that one. 'And actually, we don't know that Grant and the David siblings were friends either. That's still to be established.' He hadn't meant it to sound condescending, but it did.

'And we thought it might be a good idea if you could talk to the boy's mother too,' Maggie said. 'Charles Grant's wife I mean. They're separated now, I guess the strain of the abduction and everything caused that.'

That had been job number one on the wee list that he had slipped into the *Shark* folder. But, anxious to avoid offending her, he decided on a diplomatic answer. That didn't mean that they weren't still bloody amateurs though.

'Aye, that might be a good idea Maggie,' he said, hoping the sarcasm he felt hadn't crept into his voice. 'I'll maybe get one of my guys to look her up.' It was good to remind them that he was the professional and he had the full resources of the Metropolitan Police at his beck and call. But then suddenly a troubling thought came to him, one that he dearly hoped would turn out to be misplaced.

'So Maggie,' he said, narrowing his eyes, 'why all this interest in Charles Grant anyway? You and the boy wonder here seem to know everything about him.' It only took one look at her to see that he was right.

'I meant to tell you,' she said, not looking him in the eye. 'I should have told you before.'

'What Maggie means is *we* meant to tell you,' Jimmy said, shuffling uncomfortably. '*We* should have told you before.'

'Aye, very gallant,' Frank said, shaking his head. 'So what exactly have you failed to tell me? What?'

She spoke so quietly that he could hardly hear her. 'We've accepted an assignment from Charles. To try and find out what happened to his son.'

'Bloody hell!' He made no attempt to hide his anger and astonishment. 'Bloody hell,' he said again, unable to think of anything more eloquent.

'He doesn't trust the police,' Jimmy said.

'No I don't suppose he's allowed to,' Frank said sarcastically. 'That wouldn't go down well with his wee bunch of followers, would it? So he thought you pair of amateurs would do a better job? Give me strength.'

'But he won't cooperate with you or any of your guys Frank,' Maggie said. 'That's what he told us. He feels badly let down by the original investigation team.' Her tone was soft, as if she was trying to hold out an olive branch. But right now, he wasn't in the mood to accept the offer. Shrugging he said,

'Aye maybe not, but that doesn't mean you two should go tramping around an official police enquiry. Because look what bloody happened when you got mixed up with Allegra David. Five minutes later, she gets bloody murdered.' He wondered if he had been unduly harsh on them, but no, he hadn't been. This was police business and they had no right to be interfering. But when he thought about it, none of this social media stuff about Grant had come up in the original enquiry and it was something that would have to be dug into. And that might prove difficult if the guy wouldn't talk to them. He gave a long sigh then said,

'Ok, well maybe it would be a *wee bit* useful if you two reprobates kept a line of communication into Grant. But just remember, we're dealing with a double killing here, and a missing wee boy who's probably been murdered too. There's dangerous people out there so please don't be doing anything stupid. No bloody heroics, do you understand?'

'I understand Frank,' Maggie said, perhaps a little too readily. *Aye make sure you bloody do* was what he wanted to say, but he doubted it would do any good. They would do what they wanted to do, which probably meant they would continue to be a pair of interfering little so-and-sos. *Well, what the hell*. Maybe they could be useful to his enquiry, just as long as they didn't get themselves into any physical danger. For that he had to rely on the street-savvy of his brother, because let's face it, if you could survive three tours of duty in Afghanistan, you'd probably be ok with the mean-streets of London. He gave them a sardonic look as he stood up to leave.

'Well just be careful, ok? Anyway, I've got some bad guys to catch. Must dash.' He always liked to say that, even though there wasn't much bad-guy catching going on in Department 12B at the moment. And with that, he was off.

***

An hour later and back at his Atlee House desk, Frank had managed to calm down a bit and was able to admit to himself that the meeting had proved useful, serving to clarify a few things in his mind. Of course it had to be ninety-nine percent certain that Allegra David was killed by the same person who killed her brother Benjamin. Both had been bludgeoned to death with a blunt instrument, both had a hand severed and the same baffling message written on it. But in one case, it was the right hand that had been cut off, in the other it was the left. Was that significant? He had no idea, but he had managed to stop the media publishing any details of the MO, so few people knew that it was the brother's *right* hand that had been removed. It might be nothing, but it might prove to be something in the future.

But who did it and why? Were they killed to be silenced, or was it indeed revenge as Maggie and Jimmy thought? Or was it some other reason altogether? There were so many questions, and until he had some answers, they wouldn't get very far. He wasn't concerned about this state of affairs because he knew that cases like this always started slowly and messily. With a few promising lines of enquiry already in the bag, that was enough for him at this stage.

As for the link to the Jamie Grant affair, there was no denying that the Leonardo and da Vinci thing was rather bizarre. The problem was, there was more than a two-year gap between the wee kid's abduction and the David murders, which made him seriously question if there actually *was* a connection. He wasn't ruling it out, but for now he was going to work on the assumption that it was simply a coincidence.

Besides, tomorrow morning he had that conference call scheduled with the guys from Lyon in France, when he might find out if his crazy hunch with regard to the abduction had any substance to it. If it did, and in truth he had no expectations of the outcome, they would be looking at a whole different ball game. Then, Operation Shark would be up and running with a vengeance.

Chapter 12

It was going to be a good day. Frank's mood was sunny and optimistic as he carefully peeled back the wrapper of his Mars Bar and took a healthy bite. He wasn't generally in favour of early starts, but the call with Interpol was scheduled for seven-thirty and he would have gladly come in at two in the morning for that had it been necessary. The chocolate bar wouldn't last long but it didn't matter, because there smiling up at him from the meeting room table was a second one. Total calories, six hundred and forty, more than enough to power him through the rest of the morning, and what's more, he'd finally got his revenge on Atlee House's frigging vending machine. In had gone a two-pound coin and out had come *two* bars, even though he had only selected one. Then after a short symphony of whirrs and clunks, his two-pound coin had been returned to him. The tepid coffee still tasted like it had been dredged straight from the Thames, but that wasn't enough to dampen his spirits. Yes, it was going to be a good day. No doubt about it.

His thoughts were interrupted by the arrival of Eleanor Campbell. Her expression was thunderous, signalling that she had either just ended or was about to start a conversation with her sort-of boyfriend Lloyd. He gave what he hoped was a sympathetic smile.

'There's a wee breakfast Mars Bar here for you Eleanor if you're feeling peckish.' He knew she wouldn't want it. She was vegan, and from the militant wing.

'They're completely disgusting,' she replied. 'And I've told you about rennet a million times.'

This time he was prepared. Extremely well prepared. 'Oh aye, rennet. It comes from the stomach of wee calves, doesn't it? So any product containing it is not suitable for vegans or vegetarians.'

'Very good Frank. Have you been swallowing Wikipedia or something?'

'No, no,' he lied. 'I've known from birth that rennet is a chemical sourced from calves' stomachs used in the production of whey. One of the first things I was taught on my mammy's knee.'

She laughed. 'So like, how long did it take you to memorise that?'

The laugh was a good sign. Because he had something he needed to quickly bring up with her before the phone call, and he sensed it might be difficult.

'Eleanor, I've got a wee thing I'd like you to take a look at. To do with this Operation Shark thing. You know, if you can fit it in to your busy schedule.'

'Case number?'

Eleanor would do anything you asked, within reason, as long as you had a bloody case number. He assumed that even Lloyd had to produce one when he wanted to make love to her.

'Absolutely,' Frank lied, but in an authoritative tone. 'I have one. All signed and sealed by DCI Smart.'

'I'll check.'

'I know you will. Quite right to. I'd do the same,' he lied again.

'Ok, what is it you want?'

'I remember you told me about some cool new software you'd got from GCHQ?'

She gave him a guarded look.

'We get lots of cool new software from them. Like everything they send us is way cool. But I assume you're talking about the verbal style recognition processor that Zak was working with.'

'Who's Zak?'

'Well, he's Zak,' she replied, as if it needed no further explanation. 'I don't know his job title or anything but he's got admin rights to all GCHQ's beta software.' Clearly, that was all that mattered.

'Aye, well I think that would be it. Is that the one that uses that A-I stuff?'

What A-I was, he could not say, but he wasn't going to admit that to Eleanor. But he should have known that she wasn't going to let a golden opportunity like this slip by without comment.

That A-I stuff? You've no idea what A-I is, do you Frank?'

'No,' he admitted, giving a wry grin, 'except that it's way cool.'

She gave him a derisive look. 'Well it's artificial intelligence, and trying to explain what *that* means would take like longer than we've got on this planet. Especially trying to explain it to *you*.'

He shrugged. 'You're not wrong there Eleanor. But Charles Grant, the boy's father, has been getting what you young people call trolled on his social media accounts. Obviously privacy laws mean the publishers don't reveal who is behind these postings, but I thought that maybe this...' He was about to say A-I stuff but checked himself. .'. this cool software might be able to reveal his or her identity.'

'And what's this got to do with Operation Shark?' she said suspiciously.

God, thought Frank, you'd think she was spending her own bloody money. Admirable in a public servant of course but a complete pain in the backside nonetheless. But this time he was able to tell the truth.

'His son you may remember was abducted two years ago. That *is* Operation Shark.'

Eleanor nodded, seemingly satisfied by the explanation. 'Well then I suppose I'll need to go over to Maida Vale and talk to Zak. I think it takes like ages to run these web-crawls but I'm not sure. As I said, I need to talk to Zak.'

He had no idea what a web-crawl was, and though vaguely interested, decided against asking her about it for now. Instead he said,

'Well that sounds great. So you'd better get over there after our call.'

She grimaced. 'But the traffic's a nightmare at this time in the morning.'

He shook his head in mock sympathy. 'I know, it's really awful. Look, I can get someone else to do it if you're too busy.' He expected that would do the trick, it always did. And he wasn't disappointed.

'No no,' she replied hastily. 'It's fine, I'll get over there as soon as we're done. Have you got any details you can give me?'

'Da Vinci.'

'What?'

'Da Vinci. That's the name of the troller or trollist. I don't know what you call them, but that's the name he uses.'

'His handle you mean. And that's all you've got?'

'More or less. But I thought this stuff used artificial intelligence? It should be able to work everything else out, shouldn't it?'

She shook her head in disgust. 'You owe me one mate. Big time.'

Frank smiled at her. 'I always do. Anyway, are we all set up for the conference call?'

He had asked her to join him for two reasons. Partly, it was because he was concerned that the Lyon guys might only speak French and he needed the polymath forensic officer to be his interpreter. But mainly it was because he didn't know how to operate the meeting room's speaker-phone.

'All set up?' she replied. 'You mean am I like all set up to press that big button labelled 'answer' when it rings? Yeah, I think I'm good for that. I've been on the training course.' She wasn't being sarcastic, she had been.

As he gave her a thumbs-up, the phone rang. Right on schedule. Eleanor lent over to answer. 'Good morning, this is the Metropolitan Police, Detective Inspector Frank Stewart and Forensic Officer Eleanor Campbell.'

'Bonjour. This is Inspector Marie Laurent from the Interpol international liaison section. I hope I find you both well this morning.'

She sounds lovely, thought Frank. It was the French accent of course, designed to seduce, a bit of a contrast with his rough Glaswegian. But you never know, maybe French women found Scottish accents equally enticing. He doubted it.

'We're both very well Inspector Laurent. All right if I call you Marie?' Quite a smooth chat-up line, considering that he didn't do chat-up lines, smooth or otherwise.

'Of course Frank. And hello Eleanor.'

'Sweet,' Eleanor replied.

'That's great,' Frank said, shooting an admonishing glance at his colleague. 'So, thank you for calling me back. I was wondering of course how you've got on with that enquiry I made? Is there any progress to report?' He was conscious that for some reason he had adopted his mother's telephone voice, speaking uncharacteristically slowly and taking extra care with the consonants. It was clearly unnecessary since Inspector Laurent spoke excellent English. With a beautiful accent too.

'Not a great deal at the moment Frank. You see, we don't really have a database that coordinates random individual crimes so I have had to send out special requests to my contacts across Europe. So far I have asked Holland, Belgium, Denmark, Germany and of course here in France. But I think it will take a few weeks to gather their responses. For most forces, it won't be a priority I'm afraid, but I have told everyone that it might be important, and I will call them weekly to remind them.' Her tone was apologetic, and he was grateful for that, for his previous dealings with the International Criminal Police Organisation had left him with a rather jaundiced view of its effectiveness. His optimism in this case was borne out of hope rather than experience.

'No, that's fine, I understand,' he said. 'I suppose I was unrealistic in expecting a breakthrough so soon. But no, I'm really chuffed that you've put so much effort into it already Marie. It's fantastic, it really is.'

'Chuffed did you say? I don't think that's a word I've heard before.'

Frank laughed. 'Yes sorry Marie, I'm not surprised. It means pleased or grateful. So when I say I'm really chuffed, I mean I'm really grateful.'

Out of the corner of his eye, he saw that Eleanor was taking the mickey out of him, her hand mimicking a phone handset with her little finger and thumb. He furrowed his brow and stared at her, which only succeeded in making her laugh out loud. With an expression that said I'm going to kill you later, he returned to his phone call, but this time, he dialled down the telephone voice.

'Yes, so Marie, maybe we can touch base every two weeks or so. I like to get a work in progress rather than wait until all the forces have made their reports, if that's all right. But as I said, I'm so grateful for your help.'

There was a pause before she replied.

'That's ok Frank. But I should tell you that I have the personal interest in this too, so I won't let it go, believe me.'

Her words made his pulse quicken. Quietly he said, 'What do you mean Marie?'

'It was about eighteen months ago, when I was a detective sergeant in the Gendarmerie. That's where I worked before I transferred to Interpol here in Lyon. At that time I was based in Bordeaux and we had a case that was very similar to the one that you described to me. I wasn't in charge of the case of course, I was just one of the team, but it was still very hard for me. For all of us.'

Frank indicated to Eleanor that she should take notes. She smiled and pointed to her phone, which was in *record* mode.

'I know how hard it can be, believe me. So what was the background on your case, if you don't mind me asking?' He was trying not to sound too excited.

'Well in our case, it was a little girl and she was just four years old. Her name was Kitty Lawrence, and of course it is easy for me to remember because her surname is very like mine. It was in May and she was at a kindergarten club where the boys and the girls too played outdoor games. Afterwards, her mother came to collect her at around four-thirty and then as they walked home, a car drew up and they were attacked by two men. The little girl was pushed into the car, leaving her mother very badly injured by the roadside.'

He could feel his heart beginning to pound. 'Marie, that is just *so* similar to our case here in London. But did you say her name was Kitty Lawrence? That sounds English.'

'New Zealand in fact. You see her father is a well known-figure. Harry Lawrence. He was a rugby player, but now he is a coach. You know the game is very popular in the South West region. He played for the local professional club and also for his country, before he took up his current position.'

'Marie, did you say he played for his country? So he was an All-Black?' He gave Eleanor a raised-eyebrows look, who returned it with a blank stare.

'Yes, I think that's what you call it. I don't know much about the game, but I know he was a very good player.'

'And did you think that was significant?' Frank asked. 'That he was in the public eye I mean.'

'Do you mean was he targeted? Yes we believe so. Because there was of course a ransom demand.'

'And don't tell me. It was paid, but the kid wasn't returned.'

There was silence on the line, before Marie finally answered.

'Yes. It was a mistake on our part. A big mistake.'

He nodded. 'Aye, we made the same mistake over here.' And the Met were still struggling to come to terms with the consequences. 'But do you have any leads as to who might have done this.'

'No, not really,' she said. 'We could find no witnesses other than the girl's mother and her recollection was of course not so good because of her trauma. Little Kitty just vanished without the trace, as you would say. Every lead we followed led to the dead end. The case was our priority for over a year, but there was nothing. So then our commanders were so embarrassed by it that they pushed it into the cold-cases locker and disbanded the team. It was not for all of us a great thing for our careers. For me perhaps not so bad because I was only a sergeant, but it was very bad news for my chief inspector.'

Frank thought again of what the Jamie Grant case had done to his colleagues.

'Yes, I know how terrible it can be when a case goes like that. It hurts, it really does.'

'But there was one thing Frank. We did not get much from Mrs Lawrence but she thought she remembered her attackers speaking to each other.'

By the way she said it, he knew what was coming next. Intuition or experience, call it what you will, but please, please let it be true.

'And the interesting thing was, she was sure they were speaking in English.'

Frank was silent for a moment as his brain furiously processed what she had just told him. It was the same MO, exactly the same, and the father, like Charles Grant, was someone in the public eye. And now he'd learned that maybe the abductors were Brits. Surely it was just too much of a coincidence?

'Tell me Marie, do you know if this Harry Lawrence guy was especially active on social media?'

'On social media? I'm not sure if that came up in our enquiry. But I guess you must have a reason for asking?'

'Aye, in the case we're looking at in the UK, we think it might be a factor. Maybe if you don't mind, you can take another look at yours and let me know?'

'Of course Frank, I will get the Bordeaux police to look at it. And I'll e-mail a photograph of Kitty over to you.'

'To Eleanor please,' he said hurriedly.

He heard her laugh. *'Very well Frank, and I will let you know if anything else comes up. Speak to you soon. Au Revoir.'*

Of course, it was only one incident. It might mean nothing, nothing at all. But Frank didn't believe that, not for a minute. As far as he was concerned, *Operation Shark* was now up and running, and he could allow himself a smile of satisfaction. Correction, a smile of *smug* satisfaction. Because when he thought about it, his two amateur pals just didn't have the advantages he had. They couldn't make phone calls to lovely French Interpol officers for a start, and they didn't have access to super-smart forensic scientists who would, more or less, do anything asked of them. Naturally it wasn't a competition, but if anyone was going to be first to find out what had happened to wee Jamie Grant, one thing was for sure.

It wasn't going to be them.

Chapter 13

Like Frank, Jimmy had been forced to make an unwelcome early start that morning. In the army, you were up at every ungodly hour under the sun or moon but it didn't matter how long you served, you never really got used to it. Especially since the things you had to get up for were usually unsavoury. He reckoned that's why so many squaddies found jobs in nightclub security after their demob. It wasn't because they were hard-men, it was because in that line of work they didn't have to get out of bed until noon.

As he left the tube station he glanced at his watch, squinting to focus through sleep-deprived eyes. Six-forty-five, the sun already beaming through wispy clouds on this early-summer morning. Luckily, the Met boys liked their lie-ins too and he didn't expect there to be anyone turning up for duty until eight at the earliest, even if it was the scene of a murder. As if he was ever going to forget that, having found the body. The mission briefing from Maggie was as detailed as many he had been given as a soldier. *'Pop round there and see if you can find out what Allegra was on about.'* Allegra David had been going to tell them something, but now of course she was dead. Pop round there, see what you can find out. *Brilliant.*

From the outside, it was impossible to tell that the house had been witness to such horrors only a few days earlier. The scene-of-crime mobile laboratories had gone from outside and even the 'do not cross' tapes had been taken down. Parsons Green was a genteel neighbourhood and he supposed that the residents had lobbied to ensure that disruption to their genteel lives, and to their rising house prices, had been kept to a minimum.

There were a lot of advantages to owning an end-of-terrace property, but enhanced security wasn't one of them. With a furtive glance behind him, Jimmy crept up the narrow gap formed between the end wall of the house and the sibling's Range Rover. It was still only half-light and in his black jeans, black puffer jacket and black beanie hat he knew he would be difficult to pick out. He paused at the end of the wall to survey the outlook from the rear of the property, specifically weighing up if the house was overlooked or not by neighbouring properties. The garden was of a good length, probably thirty metres or more, and was bordered at the rear by a row of leylandii which did an excellent job of screening the house from the rear of the properties on the parallel road. Cautiously, he peered round the edge of the wall. Good, next door's property had also been extended and in fact their kitchen protruded a couple of metres further into their garden than this one. So that was one potential sight-line he didn't have to be concerned about. He could still just about be seen from one of the neighbour's upstairs windows but as long as he kept tight against the bi-fold doors that stretched the entire width of the David property, the angle would make observation difficult.

The doors were secured by an elaborate triple-deadlock system which the manufacturers claimed had repelled every attempt to break in to in the ten years they had been on the market. But that didn't worry Jimmy, because he had the keys, having on his last visit found a spare set hanging on a hook just inside the entrance to the basement. Now *that* had been a smart idea, pocketing them. He had had a vague hunch they might come in handy, and now here was the proof. He checked the handle but as expected it was locked. In normal circumstances, a burgling villain would have to worry about the alarm, but he was fairly certain that today it wouldn't be set. The police wouldn't have bothered because of all the hassle it would cause going in and out of the place, and in any case, with the death of both residents, there was a pretty good chance that the four-digit code had died with them.

He took the bunch of keys from his jacket and examined them. Helpfully, the manufacturers had stamped their distinctive logo on their key which averted a lot of tedious trial and error, and a second later he was in the luxurious kitchen. A sensor detected his entrance, bathing the room in cool blue mood lighting. Tasteful, and enough for what he wanted to do. But what exactly was he looking for? He only had the vaguest of plans. All the electronic stuff like laptops, computers and phones would have been taken away for examination by the scene of crime guys, and probably anything else of obvious interest too. But this was a house where a high-profile pair of siblings had lived, a high-profile pair who spent their lives in the public eye and who had been brutally murdered within days of one another. There had to be a motive for their killings, and somewhere in this house, he might find something that would offer a clue.

He took out his phone and fired up the camera. It would take a lot longer, but it wouldn't be exactly smart to remove any items from what was still a crime scene, so they would have to make do with photographing anything of interest that turned up. Working methodically, he combed the room, opening every drawer to locate the one that every home had. The one where all the latest bills and correspondence were stuffed to keep the place tidy, and where bad news too could be buried out of sight and out of mind. It was the second-last one he tried. *Bingo*. He grabbed a handful of papers and spread them out across the worktop. The usual stuff, credit card and utility bills, old greeting cards shoved in and forgotten after the event they celebrated had passed, mail-shots for wine clubs and cruises and designer-label clothing, evidence of the high-end marketing demographic the Davids occupied. He dragged out a few bank statements and examined them more closely. Nothing to worry about here. Healthy five-figure balances despite the evidence of a high-spending lifestyle. So it didn't look as if either of the siblings had been in financial difficulties.

He finished taking photographs and stuffed the documents back in the drawer. Where to next? A quick survey of the front lounge and rear sitting room revealed nothing of obvious interest. He slipped back into the hall and bounded upstairs. The second floor contained two bedrooms and a large family bathroom. The first one he tried was evidently that of Allegra, furnished with a king-sized double, dressed with a vermillion duvet with colour-coordinated pillows and contrasting cushions. One wall was given over to fitted wardrobes, matching the bedside drawer units. Starting on the left, he pulled out each drawer in turn and rummaged through the contents. For some reason he felt a deep sense of embarrassment as he came across the one that contained her underwear. There was some very nice stuff in there, all satin and lace and expensive too. Suspender sets, seamed stockings, flimsy knickers, negligees. He didn't know who, but someone had been a very lucky boy indeed.

A cursory check of the other drawers turned up nothing of interest. That just left the wardrobes to deal with. Opening the first door, he saw that it was stuffed to bursting, Jimmy estimating that the actress owned about fifty dresses and not far off the same number of tops and trousers. Of more interest was the pile of handbags on the floor of the wardrobe. With no real idea what he was looking for, he began to rummage through each bag in turn. Ten minutes later, all he had harvested was a handful of coins, a few receipts, mainly from bars and restaurants, and a couple of cheap ballpoint pens. Mundane stuff in the main.

It was disappointing but it still left one obvious place to look. The pile of cash hidden under the mattress might be a hackneyed old cliché, but it had become a cliché precisely because sometimes it was true. He kneeled down beside the bed and started at the top, slipping his hands between the divan base and the mattress, stretching his arms out to halfway across, then gradually working his way down to the foot of the bed. *Nothing*. Moving round to the other side, he repeated the same routine except this time he started at the bottom and worked his way up. Then about three-quarters of the way along, he found it. As he felt his way around the object, there was no mistaking what it was. A book of some description, and from the texture, leather-bound. But having seen the contents of her underwear drawer, he was one hundred percent certain it wasn't a bible. *Allegra David kept a diary.*

Of course, it was the obvious place to keep it if you wanted to shield its contents from those around you. A leather strap was wrapped around the cover, attached to a brass clasp secured by a tiny lock. But that was purely symbolic, signifying that that the contents were for the eyes of the author only. Jimmy removed his penknife from the pocket of his jeans, inserted a slim blade in the keyhole, and a second later the clasp sprung open. And as he opened it, something fluttered to the ground.

The photograph had been taken in a garden somewhere, the backdrop an elaborate trellis clad in a beautiful yellow climbing rose. The archetypal father and child picture, beloved the world over, although it wasn't easy to tell if the kid was a boy or a girl since the face was hidden behind an outsize pair of comic sunglasses. Whatever the gender, the child looked about three or four years old. The only problem was that as far as Jimmy knew, Benjamin David wasn't a father. *So why the photograph?*

He checked his watch. Yes, pretty efficient. He had been in the property less than twenty-five minutes, and of course he still had the keys, so he could in theory come back any time he wanted. He would have liked to have had a quick read of the diary, but that would have to wait until later. So that was it. Not a bad morning's work, all in all. Jimmy thought he might find more if he had more time, and he hadn't even looked at the basement yet, but this was enough for now.

As he slipped back out on to the landing, he thought he heard the faint sound of a key being inserted in a lock. Shit, was someone trying to get in? That was a surprise, since it was still only quarter-past-seven and the day shift coppers weren't supposed to be here until eight. If whoever it was decided to venture upstairs, then they couldn't help but see him standing there on the landing, and yet he didn't dare try to get back into the bedroom. On his way in he had noticed the creaky floorboards, a certain giveaway. All he could do now was stick it out and hope that their business was on the ground floor and that it was short in duration.

But then, shit, shit and triple shit. As he recognised only too plainly that distinctive beep-beep-beep-beep sound, he realised with a sinking feeling what was coming next. Someone had nipped round to set the bloody burglar alarm.

***

It was easy to deduce from their home's luxurious appointments that the David siblings didn't do anything on the cheap, and so it was no surprise to Jimmy that the alarm system too was state-of-the art. A barrage of motion sensors covered every cubic centimetre of the property, and the siren was loud enough to pin you to the wall. He'd had torture training in the army, but this was on a whole different level. Unable to think above the bedlam, he tumbled down the flight of stairs until with just a couple of steps he was at the front door. He flicked back the latch and yanked the handle but it wouldn't open. Bugger, the deadlock was on. Then he remembered that he hadn't locked the bi-folds behind him. Thank god for that. Feverishly, he sprinted through to the kitchen and swung them open, leaping out into the garden and into the waiting handcuffs of PC Heather Green.

Chapter 14

Their regular Fleet Street Starbucks was as packed as ever, but they managed to find three adjacent stools along a sidewall shelf. She knew Frank would have preferred a pint but had been confident if she offered him a grande Americano with a gratis blueberry muffin on the side he would turn up, and he did. Service for once being swift, they were soon mainlining copious oral injections of caffeine and ready to discuss developments.

'Thanks a lot for coming Frank,' Maggie said. 'I know you must be really busy with *our* Shark case.' She noticed he ignored the deliberate provocation.

He nodded. 'Well, that's not a problem, but actually it's what my wee brother mentioned on the phone that's really brought me here.'

Jimmy took the diary from his pocket and carefully removed the photograph, laying it on the shelf. 'This is it. I guess it might be a nephew or a niece or maybe even some fan's kid I suppose. But I think it looks a bit creepy.'

'Nice garden though,' Frank observed.

'Yeah, but it *is* a bit creepy,' Maggie said. 'So this is what you concealed from pushy PC Green? Clever boy.'

'What's this about a PC?' Frank sounded suspicious, but then Maggie knew that came naturally to detective inspectors.

'Nothing for you to worry about,' Jimmy said. It didn't sound too convincing. 'Anyway, how are *you* getting on with the case.' Maggie couldn't help but notice the hint of a challenge in his voice. And the mild deflation when Frank told him about his conversation with Interpol and the Kitty Lawrence abduction.

'So do you think these cases might be linked?' Jimmy asked.

'I don't know,' Frank said, 'but there are a ton of similarities. I just haven't figured out what the connection could be, but that will come. Anyway, tell me, how did you get a hold of this diary and that photograph?'

Maggie smiled uncertainly. 'You'll need to tell him.'

'Tell me what?'

So Jimmy told him, and as she had predicted, it didn't go down well.

'Bloody hell! You broke into a *murder* crime scene? You used a set of keys that you had stolen on a previous visit. You traipsed all over the house no doubt leaving fingerprints and DNA behind which could screw up the evidence, and by the way, get you fitted up for the murder. You know, I really should arrest you myself.'

'I'm sorry Frank,' Maggie said, back-pedalling. 'It was my idea. Jimmy was just doing what I asked.'

'Well in that case I should bloody arrest you too. For god's sake Maggie, it was a really stupid thing to do. Damn stupid.'

'I was only in there for half an hour,' Jimmy said, evidently in an attempt at mitigation, 'and I don't think I disturbed anything. I don't know why you're getting so excited mate.'

The words 'red rag' and 'bull' sprang into Maggie's mind.

'You think this is funny, do you?' Frank spat out the words.

'But I thought that's what Department 12B did,' Jimmy said, not helping at all. 'The things that other cops can't touch?'

Frank grimaced. 'This case has got sod-all to do with me. As for the murders, if the team need more evidence they'll get it through the proper procedures, not through some bloody amateur subterfuge. And you Maggie are a bloody lawyer so you should know what *inadmissible as evidence* means.'

She had never seen him quite this angry before, and now began to wonder if they had overplayed their hand. 'Look, I'm sorry Frank, it's just my enthusiasm getting the better of me. You're right, I know you are.'

He seemed to soften a bit as Maggie gave him what she hoped was a little-girl-lost smile. 'Aye, well no harm done yet I suppose. But we're going to have to hand that diary and the photograph over to Barker, and god knows how we're going to explain how we came by it.'

And then he beamed a smile.

'But let's make sure we give that diary a thorough read-through first. And get a scan of that photo as well.'

Jimmy gave them a wry look. 'Well, actually folks, I've already had a good read. And it's *very* interesting to say the least.'

'We're all ears,' Frank said, through a mouthful of muffin. Jimmy undid the clasp of the diary, opened it and began to read.

'Aye, so here we are about six months ago, and Allegra's all loved up. *F asked me to dinner. Bit awkward with his wife on-set. But he's v. nice.* And then a couple of weeks later it's all getting a bit x-rated.'

She was amused to see the faint tint of crimson that now suffused his cheeks as he explained about her underwear drawer.

'So it sounds as if Allegra was having an affair with one of the actors on the soap,' Maggie said. 'Someone who was married to someone else on the show.'

Jimmy nodded. 'Seems like it. As I said, it all gets a bit steamy so I won't bother reading any of *those* ones out if you don't mind. But the thing is, interesting though it is, I doubt if it's got any relevance to our case.' He paused for a moment. 'But they next bit has. *Definitely*.'

Somehow Maggie could sense he was going to tell them something that would turn out to be of critical importance to the case.

'Ok, tell us,' she said quietly.

Jimmy nodded. 'Listen to this. *Wednesday May 21st. Benjy told me something awful tonight. Everything is ruined. Distraught and broken*.'

'Everything is ruined?' Maggie repeated, open-mouthed. 'What does that mean. Isn't there anything else?'

Jimmy shook his head. 'Not that I can see. There was just one thing. The next day. *Need to see Edwina*. That was all she wrote.'

'Edwina?' Frank said. 'Who's that?'

'A friend I suppose,' Maggie said. 'Or maybe a sister?'

'Not a sister,' Jimmy said, his voice betraying excitement, 'she's their agent I think. I found a few greeting cards stuffed in a drawer when I was in his house and there was an old birthday card for Benjamin. *To a wonderful client,* it said. *From Edwina*. That was her name.'

***

It had only taken a couple of clicks to locate the website of The Talent Partnership, the agency for whom Edwina Fox worked. Their office it turned out was located on Warwick Street in the heart of theatreland, barely a ten-minute walk from their Fleet Street Starbucks.

'I can't believe she agreed to see us right away,' Maggie said. They had been shown into a comfortable reception area, its walls plastered with portraits of famous clients old and new.

'My goodness, that's Lawrence Olivier, isn't it?' Jimmy said. 'With his wife Vivien Leigh. These guys must be really big-time to have had them as clients. And long-established.'

She hadn't heard of either but declined to admit it. 'Wonder if they represent Melody or Charles as well, what do you think?' she asked.

Edwina Fox was a woman of plain but intelligent appearance, Maggie imagining she would not be out of place as a blue-stockinged Oxbridge don or a chief librarian in some provincial town. According to her Wikipedia profile, she had started as an actress but then decided early on that her theatrical career was to be made out of the spotlight, and she had made rather a success of it. Beautifully dressed in a Prada pinafore subtly set off by an alarmingly expensive pearl necklace, she exuded the quiet confidence of someone at the top of her profession, but it wasn't hard to tell she had been through a lot in recent days. Her eyes were ringed with dark circles and her complexion had a dull pallor that a generous application of foundation had failed to disguise. 'Sit down please,' she said, as she ushered them into her tastefully-decorated office. More portraits lined the wall, Maggie assuming them to be some of Edwina's current roster. One face in particular she recognised.

'So you represent Sharon Trent do you?'

Edwina turned to look at the photograph. 'Her? I do, yes. Between you and me, she's not much of an actress, but as you probably know, sex sells in this profession. Always has and always will. Naturally it limits their shelf life, but she will find that out in due course.'

'And what about Melody Montague? Do you represent her too?' Maggie couldn't help reflecting that *she* was still selling sex, and she was approaching her fifties.

'Not personally.' Her tone was cold. 'She is represented by one of my colleagues.' She didn't sound as if she approved.

'You don't like her then?' Jimmy asked.

'I don't. But that does not matter because as I said, I don't represent her, and in any case, it is not necessary to like one's clients.' Maggie wondered if that was a reference to her relationship with Sharon Trent.

'Edwina,' she smiled, 'I know this must be difficult, but we wondered if either Allegra or Benjamin David had been speaking to you in the days before their terrible murders.'

Edwina gave her a sharp look. 'How did you know about that?'

'We came across her diary,' Maggie said. 'In it she mentioned wanting to talk with you.'

'She came here, very upset. About something Benjamin had told her. But she wouldn't tell me what it was, or she didn't know herself, I don't know which it was. It concerned his impending marriage to Melody, that's all she said.'

'So what did she want from you?' Maggie asked, puzzled.

'I'm not sure. I think she was trying to find out if I knew anything too, if perhaps Benjamin had talked to me. But he hadn't and I didn't know any more than she did. I think she went away disappointed, and very uncertain what she should do about what she had discovered. But of course, had she told me her concerns, perhaps I could have helped her.'

'I'm so sorry,' Maggie said. 'I really don't know what to say. It must have come as a terrible shock to you.' She knew there was nothing you could say that would be any good.

'Can we get someone to get you a cup of tea or something?' Jimmy said awkwardly. Maggie guessed he was wishing they hadn't come. But it seemed that Edwina was glad to have someone to talk to.

'You see, I've never really liked Melody Montague,' she began. 'So *common,* don't you think? But she and Benjamin seemed to be happy and there were great plans to start a family and build the perfect picture-book life that she so obviously craved. And she was so *old*,' Edwina continued, sounding bitter. 'Too old to be a mother really, although they can do so much with medical science these days. But she was completely obsessed with playing happy families. I'm pretty sure that's what caused the breakdown of her marriage to Patrick Hunt.'

Jimmy gave her a searching look. 'You don't represent him too?'

'I do as it happens,' Edwina said. 'A very reliable client, always in demand for telly work. Not a high flyer of course, but we can't all be one of them, can we?'

Maggie wondered if the agent was comparing her own stellar career with that of her *Accident & Emergency* client.

'We've met him,' she said. 'He seems rather bitter about the break-up.'

'Well perhaps,' Edwina said. 'But like many actors there is only one important person in his life and that's Patrick himself. I'm sorry to be cynical, but that's the truth about our profession.'

'You don't like him then?' Jimmy said.

'I don't need to,' she said matter-of-factly. 'He's a client, that's all. Whether I like him or not is neither here nor there.'

Maggie nodded, but made no comment. Instead she said, 'So Edwina, is there *anything* else you can think of that might give a clue to what Allegra was worried about?'

The agent frowned 'Well I suppose there are the Kemp brothers.'

'What do you mean?' Maggie asked, interested.

'Her brothers,' she repeated. 'I guess you know Melody Montague's a Kemp? Roxy Kemp, that's her real name, and she has two brothers, Terry and Harry I think that's their names. They're apparently well known in the East End as a pair of gangsters, if that's not an old-fashioned term, although I don't of course move in these circles myself. And they're a very unsavoury lot by all accounts, so it did occur to me that Benjamin might have got to know about some of their...well let's call it *activities*. And then perhaps he shared something he'd found out with Allegra. That's all I could think of.'

'But it must have been something incredibly serious,' Maggie said, furrowing her brow, 'because Allegra said that everything was ruined.

That was her exact words. Everything is ruined. Have you any idea what she could have meant by that?'

'I really can't help you. I wish I could. Perhaps it would help me make sense of their murders.'

Jimmy nodded. 'And do you have any idea who might have wanted to do your clients harm?'

She shook her head. 'No I don't, really I don't. They were of course involved with Charles Grant's little gang of revolutionaries, but I doubt if that had anything to do with it.'

'There was that attack in the period before the murders,' Maggie said. 'By Darren Venables I mean. At the Hyde Park rally.'

She gave a half-smile. 'Yes, but that was just a bunch of thugs lashing out because they hated their politics. I doubt if it was a reason for murder. Benjamin in particular wasn't a fanatic you see. He did care about injustice but he wasn't an obsessive like Charles. Allegra, well perhaps she was more in the Grant mould.'

'I take it you know Mr Grant then?' Maggie asked.

Edwina nodded. 'I've represented Charles for many years, and I would go as far as to say we are friends. He is the kind of client I like. Honest and hard-working, always turns up on time, and not too precious about the roles he takes on.'

'We know him too,' Maggie said. 'In fact we are helping him in the disappearance of his son.'

Edwina gave a weak smile. 'Really? Well I do hope you are successful because it was such a terrible business. That poor man needs closure so badly. He knows his son is dead of course, but without a body, well...' She tailed off, her eyes moistening.

'We will do everything we can,' Maggie said. 'And you've been a great help.' That wasn't exactly true, but it seemed the right thing to say. Getting up, she indicated to Jimmy that it was now time to leave.

***

She pushed open the door, the pair of them emerging into the busy hubbub of Warwick Street, already thronging with theatre-goers making their way to their pre-show suppers. As Maggie and Jimmy threaded their way through the crowd, they discussed how matters now stood. Had the meeting with Edwina Fox accelerated their understanding in any material way? It had been interesting enough, but as to the plaintive entry in Allegra David's diary, they were no further forward. *Everything is ruined*. What had she been told by her brother that had left her, in her own words, distraught and broken? Was it the same thing that left her dead at the bottom of her basement steps just two weeks later? Whatever the reason, it was clear that they were now running a murder enquiry. Although it was probably best not to mention that to Frank.

***

After Maggie and Jimmy had left the coffee shop, Frank had sat quietly for a few minutes chewing over what Jimmy had discovered. Angry though he had been about the method, there was no arguing the importance of what his brother had uncovered. He had looked again at the photograph with its beautiful garden backdrop and air of innocence. And it *might* be innocent of course, as Jimmy had suggested, maybe Benjamin David's nephew or a wee fan perhaps, or the offspring of friends. But after twenty years in the force, you learned to trust your gut, and his gut was saying something quite different. There was something odd going on here, and he meant to get to the bottom of it. The child wouldn't have a criminal record obviously, so Eleanor's jazzy new app wouldn't be much use in identifying him or her. But he remembered they had used some other fancy facial-recognition software in the Alzahrani case a couple of years ago and wondered if it might be time to dust that down again. Time for another call to the wee forensic genius.

Chapter 15

Maggie laughed to herself as she read the press release. Headed *exclusive* and rushed out by the actress's PR agency, it breathlessly announced that yes, the rumours were true. *Grieving Melody Montague signs Bow Road contract extension*. After days of press speculation, it could now be confirmed that she was staying in the show, something the actress had decided to celebrate by throwing a party. The do would also celebrate the completion of the extravagant renovations to her home, the works rumoured to have cost over a million pounds. The showpiece was what she called the west wing, a huge oak-framed entertainment space with floor-to-ceiling panoramic glazing looking westwards across the beautiful garden. Beneath the house, a high-spec basement had been carved out, said to feature a swimming pool, gym, cinema room and servants' quarters. For over a year, the building work had been highly disruptive to the day to day life of the neighbourhood, but no-one dared to complain. Not because of the celebrity of the owner but rather due to the notoriety of her brothers. Terry and Harry Kemp were not a pair to be messed with, so nobody did. Whether they event could be said to be in the best possible taste was in Maggie's opinion questionable, given the recent tragic events. But perhaps it was the start of the healing process, because as she knew only too well herself, life had to go on, no matter how rubbish the hand that fate had dealt you.

She guessed that Melody herself was not responsible for any of the planning, the organisation of the event being sub-contracted out to a professional party-planning outfit, the likes of which could only exist in London. It was scheduled to start at three in the afternoon and the good news for young Ollie Bainbridge was that children were most welcome. Welcome too were divorce lawyers and their private-investigator side-kicks, which accounted for the presence on the guest list of Jimmy and herself, and Asvina too, who was accompanied by her husband Dav and their two sons.

It was a perfect mid-summer afternoon, the sun splitting the sky and just a hint of a breeze cooling the air. They had arrived unfashionably early, the boys burning with excitement at the prospect of meeting Danny Walker. Not because of his upcoming new role in *Bow Road*, but because he had recently taken over as one of the hosts of *Overdrive*, the hugely popular Sunday night motoring show.

'Mummy, mummy, will I get to meet Danny, will I get to meet Danny?' Her little boy tugged at her sleeve with his free hand, the other holding on tightly to the large white chocolate lollipop that had been handed to him on arrival by one of the hired-in hostesses.

Maggie bent over to kiss him on the forehead.

'I don't know darling. He will probably be very busy with his grown-up guests but we'll see.'

She laughed. Ollie had heard 'we'll see' many times before and had worked out what it really meant was 'probably not.' Now, rather cleverly she thought, he was trying a change of tack.

'Uncle Jimmy, Uncle Jimmy, will you help me meet him please? Honestly I'll be good.'

Jimmy laughed. 'Ollie, you're always good, but of course I'll see what I can do. I love *Overdrive* too, you know, it's my favourite show.' Maggie guessed he wasn't lying either.

'And Danny's the best driver,' Ollie said in a serious tone. 'He always wins all the challenges.'

That's because it's written into his contract, Maggie thought with a hint of cynicism, but she wasn't going to burst her little son's bubble.

'Yeah, he is mate,' Jimmy said, 'isn't he? And some of the cars he gets to drive are just awesome. Did you see him doing doughnuts in that F40 last week?'

Ollie's eyes were sparkling with excitement. 'I'm going to drive a Ferrari too when I grow up.' Maggie didn't have the heart to tell him that by the time he grew up Ferraris would almost certainly be driving themselves.

If the motoring hero Danny Walker was the centre of attention for the kids, there was no doubt the topic that was way out in front with the adults, especially the women.

'Asvina, have you any idea how much this place must have cost?' Maggie whispered as she sipped on her champagne. 'I mean the garden must be about half an acre, in *Richmond*. And that house, Arts & Crafts, is that what they call it?'

'I don't know, but I remember Melody telling me what they were doing to it.'

'Worth a ton of money I'd guess,' Jimmy said.

'Eight million, minimum.' He'd forgotten Dav Rani was in property. 'We sold one just up the road for that three months ago. And it didn't have the basement or the sun room, and it had a much smaller garden too.'

'So this one might be more than that Dav?' Asvina said, smiling at her husband. She looked at Maggie and raised an eyebrow.

'Yeah, that's what I'm thinking too,' Maggie said. 'Where on earth does all this come from?'

They had been overheard by a pretty but stern-faced young woman who had been hovering nearby. They recognised her as the girl who had met them at the Bow Road set when they had first been introduced to Melody. But evidently she didn't remember them.

'I'm a production assistant on the show,' she said. 'Bow Road. I look after Miss Montague mainly.' In what way the actress required looking after was not specified.

'Aye, we've met,' Jimmy said, smiling. 'We were just admiring Miss Montague's house.'

'Ah yes, I remember now,' she said, giving a nod of recognition. 'Yes, the house is beautiful, isn't it? She bought it with her first husband Mr Hunt, but Miss Montague has been spending a fortune on it after they separated.'

'Really?' Maggie said, surprised. 'I didn't know they'd bought it together.'

Across the garden she noticed the actress Sharon Trent deep in conversation with two men. From a distance, it looked as if they were arguing.

'That's Jack Redmayne and our executive producer Robbie Wright,' Lucy said, answering the question that was on their lips. 'Jack's a writer on the show. And Robbie's my boss. Well, he's everybody's boss I suppose.'

'Do you know what they're arguing about?' Maggie asked Lucy.

She found her reply both surprising and deliciously indiscreet. 'Sharon's a right diva, she's always bitching about something, complaining about the lines she's given and moaning if she doesn't have enough scenes. She's a total nightmare to work with.'

Jimmy smiled. 'So do you know what this one's about?'

Lucy gave a conspiratorial look and dropped her voice to a whisper, evidently enjoying the actress's travails. 'Oh yes, I know all right.' Was she going to tell them more? It seemed like she was.

'You see, with the sad death of Mr David, they needed to do a big re-write. Sharon's character was meant to have a big steamy affair with Benjamin's but now that can't happen of course.'

'That would have meant less screen time for Melody, wouldn't it have?' Jimmy said. 'But now they've brought in Danny Walker. That's a big signing, isn't it?'

'That's right,' Lily said. 'The producers were devastated by Benjamin's murder and the effect it would have on poor Melody. So they had a re-think and her character Patty West is going to be centre-stage once more.'

'At the expense of Sharon's character?' Maggie asked.

'That's right. I don't think the writers have exactly worked out her character arc at the moment but I don't think she'll be featuring as much in the new season. The definite direction of travel over the next twelve months or so is towards Melody and Danny's characters. It depends what the scriptwriters come up with I suppose, but I wouldn't be surprised if they write in some sort of a breakdown for Sharon's character and she's out of the show for a while.' Lucy suddenly turned silent, perhaps worrying she had already said too much.

A marquee had been provided in the event of inclement conditions, and in their absence the sides had been rolled up, the shade providing welcome relief from the hot sun. Inside, a well-stocked bar in the charge of improbably good-looking staff of both sexes was doing brisk business, hardly surprising on account of it being free. Melody stood at the bar, in the process of ordering another glass of champagne. She was not alone. Her companion, a well-built man in his fifties stood alongside, puffing on a cigar, in defiance of the 'No Smoking' sign pinned to one of the supporting pillars. Anyone who thought for a moment of admonishing him would have soon thought again when they clocked his cropped hair, scarred cheek and general appearance of menace.

She saw them approach and smiled. 'I'll only be a second guys, just finishing up here.' On cue, her companion leaned over, kissed her lightly on the cheek, then moved as to leave. 'See you around doll.'

With the briefest nod of acknowledgment to Maggie and Jimmy he sauntered off, still smoking his cigar.

'That's Terry,' Melody said. 'He looks after some of my business interests.'

'Is he your agent then?' Jimmy asked.

She laughed. 'My agent? Good god, no, he's my big brother. I've got two but Harry couldn't be here today. Anyway, that's not why you're here is it?' she said, rising to greet them. They might have been long-lost friends such was the warmth of her embrace, Maggie feeling Jimmy's perhaps lasted rather longer than was strictly necessary.

She said, 'I hear congratulations are in order.'

Melody beamed. *'Thank* you, yes as you can imagine, I'm completely thrilled about it. Danny is a fantastic actor and I'm sure we'll make magic together. Now it's all going to be about the two of us, it's really going to be sensational viewing. They're even talking about having us adopt a child, a Syrian refugee or something, I don't think they've worked that out yet. I mean, how amazing will that be? Me, a mum at nearly fifty.' Maggie thought if that was the direction of travel, as Lucy had described it, she could see why Sharon Trent might be upset.

'Anyway darling, you must come for the grand tour. I assume you two would like to see round the house?'

Maggie and Asvina didn't need a second invitation, so keen were they to see the inside of this palace. Jimmy, it seemed, had other plans. She saw him looking over to Danny Walker who was standing in a quiet corner of the garden, surrounded by a scrum of excited boys, including her own Ollie and Harjinder and Hammi Rani.

'I'll leave that to you Maggie, if you don't mind,' he said, giving a mock grimace.

'Got your autograph book with you?'

'Naw, I'm hoping for a selfie,' he responded. She guessed he wasn't lying.

***

Jimmy made his way over to them, where Walker seemed to be in the process of organising some kids for a group photograph.

'Right, you, Ollie isn't it, could you stand up straight, I can't see your head. And Hammi, stand a bit closer to your brother, will you? And can we get this little girl over too please? What's your name darling?'

He looked like a harassed wedding photographer trying to round up the more inebriated guests for the final shot. He shouted across the garden.

'Eddie, where's Eddie?'

A man in his mid-forties appeared from behind a verdant azalea, adjusting his flies, holding a pint glass, a cigarette dangling from his mouth.

'Whoa, that's better,' he said to no-one in particular. 'Got it all sorted then boss?' His accent was more authentically East End than anyone in Bow Road could muster. 'Come on, hand over the phones and let's get on with it. Haven't got all day, have we?'

'Cheers mate,' Walker replied. 'Where's Melody? Melody doll, get your arse over here pronto.'

Hearing her name being called, she broke off her conversation with Maggie and Asvina and skipped over.

'This is nice,' she said smiling, then addressing the photographer, 'Get me and Danny on either end, then boy-girl-boy-girl. Here, can we have this nice little boy next to me.' She put her arm round Ollie and kissed him on the forehead. Jimmy could see his disappointment as his new friend Hammi got to stand beside Danny Walker.

'Right everybody say a big cheese,' she said. *'Cheeeeeeese!'*

This caused the children to collapse into a fit of giggles, requiring the scene to be re-composed and the shots to be re-taken. Next, Melody decided she wanted the same shot but with Jimmy in place of Danny, and so there was another five minutes of chaotic rearrangement until she was happy.

'Here, give us your phone mate,' Eddie the photographer said. 'I'll get you one for the family album.' Jimmy passed him his phone, setting off a third bout of messing about until finally Eddie deemed himself satisfied. Now there was only one picture to be taken to complete the shoot. Jimmy took Danny to one side.

'Any chance of a picture with the boy?' he asked, nodding towards Ollie. 'He's a huge fan.'

'Yeah sure mate, no problem. Make sure you get my good side Eddie my son.' He placed his arm around Ollie's shoulders and gave him a wink. 'And make sure you get a good one of this lad too. What's your favourite car mate?'

Ollie smiled an adoring smile, and replied with painstaking precision, 'A Ferrari S-F-ninety Stradale Hybrid. A red one. I saw you driving one last week.'

'The old Stradale? Yeah, that was a nice motor, and very good for the environment too. Hybrid you see, runs on its battery some of the time.' Yeah, for about two minutes Jimmy thought, wondering what the world's polar bears would think about it, but he said nothing. Danny Walker noticed him looking at him and a quizzical expression crossed his face.

'By the way, I don't think I know you mate. You one of the dads?'

Jimmy extended a hand. 'Not exactly. I'm Jimmy Stewart. I'm a sort of private investigator, helping Miss Montague with her divorce from Mr Hunt. Working for Asvina Rani.'

He shook Jimmy's hand, nodding. 'Ah yeah, Melody told me about you guys. You're making sure that that bastard Hunt doesn't get his hands on her money. Nice work.'

 Jimmy was quite sure how to react. Awkwardly, he said, 'I must say, it's very nice to meet you. *Overdrive* must be great to work on.'

Walker shrugged. 'Yeah, well it's harder than it looks, with all that first-class travel to exotic locations and having to swan around in all those fast motors. No, I'm taking the piss mate. You're right, it's a dream job. Better than all the shite I'll be doing on the *Road*, that's for sure. But the money's amazing and there's some pretty hot women on the show, know what I mean? Lots of opportunities in that department and that's what us blokes like, isn't it?'

Jimmy shrugged. 'I must admit I don't watch the show all that often, not like my partner Maggie. But what I've seen, I think you're really good, and I'm not just saying that.'

Danny gave a brief smile in response. 'Yeah, well cheers for that mate. Anyway, if you don't mind, I'll leave you to look after these lovely lads. I'd better circulate as I'm supposed to be the star attraction. Catch you later.'

***

Melody had kept up a running commentary as she led Maggie and Asvina through the house and up the stairs to her bedroom.

'The kitchen was a nightmare of course. We spent over a hundred grand and it took them three attempts to get the worktops to fit. Cost them a fortune of course and Benjamin was worried that they might go bust, but they got there in the end, and it is *lovely*, don't you think? And this staircase, pure marble and *so* heavy, it took three of their guys just to move each step. But well worth it I think.'

The bedroom was of impressive proportions and decorated in keeping with the opulence of the house, dominated by a super-king-sized bed with high-end fitted wardrobes around two sides.

As they entered, Melody was still in full flow. 'The decor in this room is *adorable*, don't you think? I found this simply excellent designer over in Twickenham who took care of everything. And it was her idea too that we should install a panic room. Apparently all of us celebs should have one, that's what she said. A wise precaution don't you think? The door leads off the en-suite and it's impregnable, I'm told. We've never had to use it of course, thankfully.'

A young woman in a pink apron holding a cleaning spray and cloth emerged from the en-suite. She smiled and greeted her employer in a thick East European accent.

'Good morning Miss Montague.'

'Good morning Bridget. This is Bridget, she's from Latvia or Lithuania, I always get them mixed up. She cooks and cleans for us. She lives in with her husband Gregor who looks after the house and the garden. I simply don't know *what* we would do without them.'

Jesus, thought Maggie, domestic staff? Who can afford them nowadays? And a panic room, for goodness sake. How the other half lives.

'I never had nothing like this, growing up of course,' Melody continued. 'My dad walked out when I was three years old and we never saw him again, me and my brothers. My mum took to the drink after that. Killed her in the end it did. And then we were taken into care.'

'I didn't know that,' Asvina said sympathetically. 'It must have been awful for you.'

'Yeah, it was. But I'm a survivor. We all were, me and my brothers.'

Maggie didn't know too much about Melody's tough upbringing, but she could see how it perhaps explained her desire to build a little family with Patrick Hunt. And when that fell apart, to try again with Benjamin David, hope triumphing once more over experience. As if she was anyone to talk, knowing that it was only the ticking of her own biological clock that had persuaded her that marrying Philip would be a good idea. But at least she had Ollie, and for that reason and that reason alone it had been worth it. Now she found herself hoping that Melody Montague too might find some consolation not too far in the future.

Chapter 16

In Frank's world, events were moving slowly, but he wasn't bothered about that, because in his head, the flaky hypothesis that he hoped might form the bedrock of Operation Shark was beginning to look a bit less flaky. Now there was news of an abduction of startling similarity to the Jamie Grant incident, and that was progress, no doubt about it. It had been a hunch and he had learned if not to trust his hunches completely, then at least to give them a decent shot.

It was a fair result, but he knew it was just one more piece in the jigsaw. Admittedly, it was shaping up to be a thousand-piece puzzle but figuratively he felt that he had now completed the border, and as all jigsawists knew, things always started to accelerate once you had the border in place. Now he judged it was time to have a wee word with his boss DCI Jill Smart. Jill was the gate-keeper between half-arsed conspiracy-theory bollocks and a live grown-up investigation, with an official case number and all that went with it. With a case number, you could pull together a team, you could bring suspects in for questioning, you had access to a full range of technical support services far beyond what Eleanor Campbell alone could provide. You could even call in a press officer to spout nonsense at the media if you wanted to. The only problem was, Jill Smart guarded case numbers with her life. Because once an investigation got a case number, it had broken cover from the murky secretive world of Department 12B and was out in the open for all to see. Specifically, it got onto the spreadsheets of Chief Superintendents and Assistant Commissioners, target-driven automatons obsessed with clear-up rates who asked awkward questions like why so much money was being spent on a case and why hadn't it been solved yet even when it had only been running for a week. A case number caused Jill a whole heap of hassle and so generally, she didn't give one up without a fight. Even to Frank Stewart, who was the only detective in the department she trusted.

And making the mission a whole order of magnitude more difficult was the fact that he had already suffered a bit of a set-back, when Eleanor's facial-recognition sweep of the world wide web had drawn a complete blank. The kid in David's photograph hadn't shown up, the problem being, as she had explained in her customary teacher-to-five-year-old manner that she always adopted when speaking to Frank, was that all the commercial recognition capability like Google and Facebook purposely did not work for children, for obvious reasons. On top of that, the GCHQ citizens' database, which by the way did not officially exist, did not hold details of citizens under the age of eleven.

Nonetheless he was determined to persevere, this time deciding to make his pitch in person rather than on the phone, reasoning he needed to see the whites of her eyes to judge how well he was doing. And they had much better coffee over at Paddington Green, properly expensive barista stuff with a rich nutty aroma that pervaded the whole building. As ever, the car park had been rammed, but as he never bothered to find a space on his visits anyway, it had been no effort to dump the battered Mondeo as close to the door as possible and block in the sleek Beemers and Audis which were the public-purse-provided rides of the most senior officers. He reasoned that since they were supposedly the smartest detectives on the force, it shouldn't tax them too much to find out whose motor it was if they wanted out.

DCI Smart occupied a cramped office on the third floor, overlooking the rear car park. Originally, she had been given a nice big one in the corner but DCS Colin Barker had objected, citing his longer service and seniority as a reason why it should be allocated to him. Cannily, Jill had acceded to the petty request. Everyone in the force thought Barker an arse, and this was just adding one more instance to the charge-sheet. God knows he'd been lucky to survive screwing up that Alzahrani terrorist case, and Frank figured he was now in the last-chance saloon. It was probably one more strike and he'd be out. And when that happened, Jill would move back into it before anyone else could grab it.

Today, however, nobody was in their offices, large or small. A desk in the middle of the vast open-plan space was piled with supermarket-bought cakes and savouries and all around the floor, officers were milling around, laughing and swigging bottled beer. Scanning the scene, Frank spotted his boss and made his way to her.

'Morning ma'am, so what's going on here? Somebody won the lottery?'

She laughed. 'Worse than that Frank. Barker's solved the David murders. They've been with the CPS team all morning and they've just given the go-ahead to prosecute.'

'What, he's solved the bloody thing in three weeks?' It was like hearing a supermodel saying she had brokered a Middle-East peace deal on a night out. 'No chance. Some poor innocent's been fitted up, more like.'

'Yes, well normally I would agree with you, but it seems on this occasion we may have to give him some credit. It does look like an open and shut case to me.'

Frank gave a bitter sigh. 'Come on ma'am, you and I both know there's no such thing as an open and shut case where Colin Barker's involved. It never is, and it never will be.'

'Jealousy and bitterness aren't a good look you know.'

'I'm not jealous or bitter,' he lied. 'So come on, what's the story? And is it all right if I grab a beer?'

Jill smiled. 'Yes, of course, and I'll have one too. To commiserate of course, not to celebrate.'

Frank sauntered over to the desk, picked up a couple of beers and scooped a large chocolate brownie onto a paper plate. His super-skinny boss basically didn't eat, so he knew she wouldn't think him selfish.

'So,' he said through a mouthful of dark crumbs, 'let's hear about how the genius detective did it. I'm all ears.'

She took a sip from her beer before continuing. 'It's that guy you had the run-in with at the Hyde Park demo.'

'What, Darren Venables? No way. Absolutely no way.'

'Way,' she said. 'Barker's team have worked out what Leonardo is all about, and that led them straight to him.'

'No way,' he repeated, conscious of the sinking feeling in his stomach. 'Come on ma'am, you know this can't be true.'

'I'm afraid it is,' she said. 'It looks that way to me.'

'Really ma'am? I know Venables is a piece of shit but I don't see him killing someone in the name of his poxy little party.'

But he knew in his heart that wasn't quite true. Venables and his White British League thugs were dangerous fanatics, and well capable of murder in pursuit of their deluded cause. It was just that he considered Venables, the history don turned champion of the neglected white working-class, to be too smart to do any of the dirty work himself.

'They had been looking at some of his published papers from his time in academia,' Jill said in way of explanation. 'You know he was a professor of history or something? At Oxford.'

'Well I'm not sure he was actually a professor. I think he was a reader, that's what they called it. That was until he got hounded out by the student body for not conforming to their narrow wee view of the world. Turned him a bit bitter after that.'

After arresting him, Frank had, out of interest, taken the trouble to read quite a few of the published papers of Mr Venables. The man's worldview was simple and unwavering. Socialist governments screw everything up and in particular, crush progress and innovation. Under socialism, according to D-V, there would have been no Einstein, no Henry Ford, no Crick and Watson. And, according to a particularly vituperative polemic he'd published a few years back, no Leonardo da Vinci either.

Jill laughed. 'Frank Stewart, I didn't see you as a foot soldier in the class war.'

'No no, don't get me wrong, he was an arse then, and he still is. But you've heard the old saying along the lines of I don't like what you're saying but I defend your right to say it? I kind of believe in it, that's all. But anyway, let's hear what you've got.'

'Well I know it's not your thing Frank, but it all hinges around Venables' social media and something he posted in response to a Charles Grant twitter message. Something that was mirrored in some of his academic work.'

Frank's eyes narrowed. 'Ok....'

'So obviously Barker's team have been interviewing friends and associates of the victim. And when they interviewed Charles Grant, he told them about a post Venables had made just after his son was abducted. *Commie bastards always get what they deserve.* He also told them he had been a victim of a long-running campaign of harassment by someone using the name da Vinci.'

'Aye, I've heard all about that.' Although he hadn't yet mentioned to Jill that he was intending to find out for himself who was behind it. Now he wished he'd made more effort to chivvy Eleanor Campbell along with her investigations.

'Really?' she said, surprised. 'Well anyway, Grant said he had his suspicions and was now pretty sure that it was Venables. You know, D-V is his nickname, and so there's the link to da Vinci. And that of course gave the connection to Leonardo.'

Frank was getting that sinking feeling he always got when a precious theory crumbled to dust before his eyes. The theory that Venables hadn't even been a suspect for the murder, let alone the killer.

'But come on ma'am, that's totally circumstantial, if it can even be described as that. Even by Barker standards, it's a massive pile of crap. I mean, who's going to write their bloody name on a victim, even if it is just a bloody nickname?'

She nodded. 'Well this *is* a Colin case, so the case is always going to be flimsy, but the CPS have passed it so I guess it must be half-credible.'

'Half-credible?' Frank said bitterly. 'That's all they need nowadays is it?'

'Don't be so cynical until you've heard everything,' she replied. 'So firstly, it turns out that Venables was seen at the awards ceremony where David died. You know what that means don't you? That they can place him at the scene of the crime. And they've checked his alibi and he hasn't got one.'

Frank was struggling to process what he'd just heard. 'So come on, how did Venables explain that away?'

Jill gave a half-smile. 'He said he'd gone with the intention of apologising to Benjamin and Allegra David for what had happened at the Hyde Park rally. Complete rubbish of course, especially in light of the other things Barker's team found.'

'What other things?' Frank said despondently. 'What other things?'

'They found his fingerprints on Allegra David's front door. And there was a note. A threatening note, pushed through her door.'

'No way.'

'I wish you would stop saying that Frank,' Jill said irritably. 'Yes, it is the case. A note, printed on A4 paper and bearing the symbol of the White British League. It was addressed specifically to Allegra and bore the message *commie bastards always get what they deserve*. And for the record, Venables has been unable to produce a verifiable alibi to cover the time window of the Parsons Green killing.'

'But if he *did* do it, and I'm not suggesting for a minute he did, I ask again. Why would he leave that Leonardo message on their hands? Or any message at all?'

But as he said it, he could hear himself answering that question. Because Venables was an arrogant self-regarding little shit and it would be entirely in keeping with his character to leave some sort of calling card. If he'd done it, that was. Which of course he hadn't. *No way*.

But now Frank could feel himself boiling up inside, and he recognised at least one of the reasons. He was angry at himself for his arrogance in assuming that only he could solve this case, and although he hated to admit *this*, there was anger and no little hint of envy that his nemesis had somehow outsmarted him.

The problem was, anger was never a good thing when he was within punching distance of DCS Barker. The last time he got so mad, bad things happened. But where was the fat arse? He must be here somewhere, it wasn't as if he was going to be absent for his big moment of glory. Yep, there he was, in the corner office, with a stupid grin on his face as he arse-licked a couple of the top brass. Two Assistant Commissioners, no less. No wonder he wasn't out on the floor sharing a spicy samosa with the *hoi polloi*. Glancing over, he caught sight of Frank and gave a barely-disguised look of disgust, before returning to his arse-licking.

'Don't do anything stupid Frank,' Jill said, clearly alarmed. She was smiling but the message was serious. 'It doesn't reflect well on the department, or me.'

'No, don't worry boss, I've learned my lesson,' he lied. 'Anyway, the real reason I came here was to talk to you about a case, you know, the one I mentioned on the phone. Operation Shark. The Jamie Grant abduction.'

But now his heart wasn't really in it.

***

So that was it then. No case number today, even though he'd told her about the Kitty Lawrence snatch and how it was almost identical to the Jamie Grant incident. *Ok, good work, but I need more than just some case that happens to have the same MO.* That's what Jill had said, and he couldn't really blame her.

And now against all the odds Barker appeared to have solved the David cases and the brass were going to make sure that it didn't get unsolved by some backwater has-been from Atlee House. The more he thought about it the more it became apparent that the evidence was rubbish, flimsier than a house of cards. *Leonardo leading to da Vinci, da Vinci leading to Darren Venables?* Even bloody Agatha Christie would have thought twice before coming up with that one. It was all wrong, Frank knew that, but there was zero chance of him influencing the course of events now.

So this morning had been a set-back, undoubtedly, but a few pints in the Kings Head and a good night's sleep would soon see off his temporary melancholy. Maybe Darren Venables was guilty, maybe he wasn't, but there was still plenty about the David murders that didn't add up. *Everything is ruined.* That's what Allegra had written in her diary, so it must have been something bloody serious, but what, he hadn't a clue. But at least when he got back to Atlee House he would have something to write on that wee blank label stuck to the front of that new folder. And this was a case name, which though obvious, he rather liked.

The Leonardo Murders.

Chapter 17

It was about a three and a half mile walk from their Fleet Street office up to HMP Pentonville on the Caledonian Road, but Jimmy was glad of the exercise. He'd let himself go a bit since he left the army, there was no doubt of that, but whereas when you were out in Iraq or Afghanistan maintaining peak fitness could be a matter of life or death, it wasn't such a big deal in London EC4. As an interim private investigator, which is how he would describe the current stage of his career, it didn't really matter if you had the odd beer or two or mainlined on stuffed pizza. And he felt he could carry a bit of excess baggage, an advantage of being broadly-built and six foot two into the bargain. Nonetheless he recognised a slippery slope when he was sliding down it, and accordingly put on a bit of pace as he headed northwards up Farringdon Street.

He reflected that today's mission was likely to prove difficult to execute, if not impossible, a pattern in his employment with Miss Maggie Bainbridge he was beginning to recognise. Generally, her mission statements were terse to the point of non-existent. *Break into a locked down crime-scene and see what you can find,* or this one, *ask the disgraced Blake McCartney to sign an affidavit saying he did actually draw up that bloody pre-nup in the way Melody said.* God, even in Helmand they sometimes gathered you in a room and gave you an hour's briefing in advance of sending you into action. Though to be fair, that would be the exception not the rule. But there was no arguing with the fact that Maggie Bainbridge would have made Major-General if she'd been in the army. Dish out the orders and let the poor bloody other ranks work out the details, that was her *modus operandi.* She was a natural.

Still, his mood remained upbeat as he approached the foreboding gates of the Victorian prison. Sure, the chances of success were two-thirds of not very much at all, but it would be fascinating in itself to see the inside of a jail, especially one that had opened as long ago as eighteen forty-eight, and McCartney sounded like an interesting character.

Signage directed visitors to a stark reception room where uniformed staff sat behind a glass panel, ignoring the assembling friends and family whilst they stared morosely at their computer screens. Every few minutes a name would be flashed up on a display screen and a guard would appear to lead the visitor into the search suite, where hi-tech scanning equipment was combined with a low-tech and highly invasive manual search by the assigned prison officer. It took nearly twenty minutes before the name 'Stewart, James' came up. A few seconds later, the automated door clicked and opened, and a hatchet-faced female officer emerged from the back office. At least, she was hatchet-faced until she caught sight of Jimmy.

'Nice day for a visit,' she said breezily, as she led him into a small windowless room, the walls painted a dull grey and harshly illuminated by a bank of fluorescent tubes. 'My name's Amanda Fletcher by the way. *Miss* Amanda Fletcher. I hope you don't mind being searched by a female officer today, but you see we're a bit short-staffed.' By her expression he gathered that whatever he thought about it, she herself was very much looking forward to it.

She handed him a large transparent plastic bag. 'Everything goes in there. Keys, coins, your wallet, your phone. Oh yes, and your trouser belt of course.' He was just waiting for her to offer to remove it for him.

He estimated her to be in her early forties, quite attractive but hard-looking, her hair bleach-blonde and eyes heavily-lined with black mascara. She looked as if she worked out too, her figure well-defined under the tight-fitting white shirt. A younger version of Melody Montague, that's who she reminded him of, and probably just as dangerous. Especially as it seemed they were to be on first-name terms.

And was it his imagination, but was the body search taking longer than strictly necessary? As she ran her hands methodically over his body - too methodically he thought, reaching places where he would have preferred her not to go - she kept up a running commentary describing conditions past and present in the prison. To Jimmy's amusement, it sounded rather like the chat you got from your tour rep on the airport coach on the way to your summer-sun hotel.

'Drones is the big thing at the moment,' she was saying. 'They can fly in all sorts with them. Drugs, mobiles, knives, razors, you name it. They even got a gun in once, can you believe? Can't seem to stop them, no matter what we does. And violence, there's a lot of trouble in this prison, I can tell you. We're in the top five in the country for that. Stabbings, slashings, we get it all here.' She made it sound like a badge of honour.

'That's why our searches have to be so thorough of course,' she said, in belated apology.

Jimmy nodded. 'That's ok Amanda, I understand.'

'Course you probably don't need to worry so much in B Block. That's where your McCartney is. Mainly white collar, pimps, fraudsters and con-men and the like.'

'And bent solicitors,' Jimmy said.

'Yeah, exactly. We don't get no trouble with them because we just threaten them with a move to A Block.'

'A Block?'

'Yeah, that's right. That's where all the hard men are kept. Murderers and gangsters, every one of them. Mental cases. I wouldn't like to work there, although of course they don't allow no female staff.'

But now it seemed that the search was completed to her satisfaction. She smiled at him and said,

'Well, you're clean. So this is your first time, right?'

Jimmy nodded again.

'So you keep your hands on the table where the officers can see them and no touching, ok?' She gave him a lascivious wink. 'Although I think Mr McCartney is going to have his work cut out to keep his hands off *you*. Yeah, I can see you being his night-time fantasy for the next twelve months at least.'

Brilliant, so that was another thing that Maggie had failed to mention in the mission briefing.

***

Fletcher had escorted him to a set of double doors with a sign above that read 'Gymnasium.' Observing his puzzled look, she said, 'Yeah, it ain't been a gym for more than twenty years. The prisoners have got a fancy place now over in the new East Wing. State of the art of course, whilst us guards get a load of old shit stuff over in our welfare building.' The bitterness sounded well-rehearsed, a grievance that he expected was shared with anyone who would listen. 'So anyways, I'll just drop you off with Andy at the door and then I'll be back to fetch you when you're done. You only get twenty minutes because you're not family.' She gave him a cheeky smile. 'And remember, no holding hands.'

The room looked just as he imagined, with wooden parquet flooring and narrow windows that were set just below the high ceiling. It reminded him exactly of his old school assembly hall back in Glasgow. Three prison officers were hanging around just inside the doorway, chatting and laughing.

'I'm looking for Blake McCartney please,' Jimmy asked the one Amanda had identified as Andy.

'Sure, no problem mate,' he answered pleasantly, and led him to a table in the middle of the room occupied by a slightly-built man who looked well into his sixties although Jimmy knew he had barely turned fifty.

'Well well McCartney, here's a turn up for the books. Someone actually wants to see you.'

'Thank you Mr Smith,' he replied, without apparent rancour, then nodded at Jimmy. 'Sit down please, make yourself comfortable. I'd shake your hand, but it's not allowed. He's a decent screw that Andy Smith actually. Slips me the odd fag and gets my mobile topped up although he charges the earth for it. We're not supposed to have them of course.' From his lack of discretion, Jimmy assumed that the authorities must turn a blind eye to these activities. Probably preserving the peace was given higher priority and he didn't blame them for that. But what he found amusing was how McCartney seemed to have adopted the *patois* of prison life. It wasn't as if he was a regular inmate, but maybe it was what you had to do to fit in.

Jimmy placed his hands in front of him as he had been instructed then said, 'I think you might have had a note from Melody, explaining what I wanted to talk to you about?'

'Oh it's Melody now is it?' he said bitterly. 'So now she's Miss La-De-Dah? But I suppose old Blake's not good enough for Roxy now. She was always Roxy to me, ever since we were kids. She's a Kemp you know. Roxy Kemp. Did you know that?'

'Yes I did,' Jimmy said, 'but I don't know much about the family.'

'Yeah well *I* do,' he said, reducing his voice to a whisper. 'If you knew what I done for them Kemps over the years. Got them out of all sorts of scrapes I did, and risking my reputation all the time.' Jimmy thought it unlikely that he had much of a reputation to risk, but he didn't say anything. In any case, McCartney was still in full flow.

'But do you think they supported me when I got into my little bit of difficulty? Did they hell. All I had was some cash flow problems which a few grand would have sorted out, but did they put their hands in their pockets, them Kemps? Did they hell. And so here I am, banged up for five years, and me an innocent man as well. It's a travesty of justice, that's all I can say. A pure travesty.'

Jimmy was conscious of the limited time he had to complete his mission and was already concerned that McCartney's venting of his grievances with the Kemps might easily take up the entire twenty minutes.

'Look Mr McCartney...'

'Blake, please.' He smiled what he no doubt imagined was a seductive smile, which caused Jimmy to mentally grimace, although he managed to hide it.

'Aye, so Blake, what I wanted to talk to you about is the pre-nuptial agreement you drew up for Melody - I mean Roxy - and her husband Patrick Hunt. About fifteen years ago it would have been. I wondered if you remember it.' It was all an act of course, Jimmy knew that, because McCartney remembered it perfectly well, having already shared with Asvina's team his version of events.

He screwed up his face, stroking his chin. 'Let me think. A pre-nuptial did you say? I used to do a lot of them, make no mistake. A lot of my clients were minted you see, and well, you need to protect yourself if you're in that income bracket, don't you? But Roxy and that Hunt guy? Yeah, course I remember that one. Sure I do. So what can I help you with in that regard?'

Jimmy gave him a sharp look. 'Well according to Roxy, it's gone missing. You told her you misplaced it during what you call your business difficulties. Is that right?'

He averted his eyes, staring down at the floor. 'Did I? Well you know, that time was all a bit of a blur I'm afraid. We had some stuff I thought we'd better get rid of quick, and, well to tell the truth I think it got mixed up with all that.'

'Brilliant,' Jimmy said wryly. 'So let me ask, do you remember the broad terms of that deal? I assume you do, given you had no trouble remembering drawing the thing up in the first place.'

He nodded. 'Yeah, I remember it no trouble. Fifty-fifty, straight down the middle. Everything. Pretty normal that is.'

'Are you sure?' Jimmy said, giving him a distrustful look. 'Because Roxy says there was a specific clause awarding her the primary residence. Do you remember that.'

McCartney shrugged. 'That's not my recollection.'

'But Melody's quite clear about it. It was signed on the set of Bow Road, in the presence of two witnesses, and Patrick himself of course.' He didn't tell him that Charles Grant had corroborated Hunt's version of the document, although they were still waiting to see the proof of that.

McCartney gave a short laugh. 'Yeah, but she would say that, wouldn't she?'

Jimmy gave a sigh. It was pretty clear that the conversation wasn't going anywhere, or at least not in a direction that would please their client Miss Montague. He smiled, adopting a conciliatory tone.

'Well I guess that's something we'll have to leave the courts to decide. I just came here to try and clear things up and you've helped me do that, so thanks.' Not that he had helped at all, but there was nothing to be gained by saying it.

McCartney relaxed back in his seat, evidently glad that the subject of the conversation was about to change.

'Well, that's ok then. So, if we're done... I'm a busy man you know.' He gave a low cackle at his own joke.

'Just one more thing before I go,' Jimmy said pleasantly. 'Did you know Sabrina Fellini?'

His eyes narrowed. 'Who?'

Sabrina Fellini. She was the young woman who was the other witness to the agreement.'

He gave Jimmy a wary look. 'She's dead, isn't she? An accident, just a few months ago. I think I read about it.'

'So you remember her then?' Jimmy said quietly.

'Not really. I think we only met that once, on the set.'

And then something came to Jimmy, something he and Maggie should have thought of before.

'Blake, has it ever occurred to you how convenient it was for Patrick Hunt that Sabrina's not around to give her version of events?'

'What're you suggesting?' he blustered, his voice rising to almost a shout. 'I don't know nothing about that, and that's the truth.'

Out of the corner of his eye, Jimmy could see Andy the prison officer approaching them, alerted by McCartney's eruption.

'Right sir,' he said politely but firmly. 'Time to wrap up. Come with me please.'

As Jimmy got up to leave, McCartney, evidently regretting his outburst, said.

'Look I'm sorry you didn't get what you came for. It isn't my fault if the agreement got misplaced. But it was nice Jimmy. I don't get many visitors. You're welcome to come back any time you want.' His eyes were pleading, like a dog begging for walkies.

'Sure, that would be great,' Jimmy lied. 'So take care, see you again mate.'

Prison Officer Amanda Fletcher was waiting for him in the hallway as scheduled.

'This way,' she said, pointing to the large sign marked *exit*. 'Sad bastard isn't he? All we ever hear from him is how he's innocent and how the Kemps done him down. I expect you got some of that, did you?'

Jimmy laughed. 'Aye, big time. He would have gone on all day if I'd let him I think.'

'Yeah, he would have. But I bet that was a treat for him. The poor guy doesn't get many visitors. His old mum came down from Liverpool a few weeks ago, but that's about it. Although strange to say he did get a visit from one of them soap stars a couple of months back. Said they were old mates. It was quite a talking point around here as you can imagine.'

Jimmy raised an eyebrow. 'What, Melody Montague was here? She never told me that.'

She gave him a puzzled look. 'Nah, it wasn't her. It was that guy, the one whose son's missing. You know, from Accident & Emergency. Charles Grant.'

Charles Grant. What the hell had he been doing here? What with his social media spats and now this, Mr Grant had a few questions to answer, make no mistake. And then there was McCartney's surprising reaction when the death of Sabrina Fellini was brought up. Did he know something, something he wasn't telling? Perhaps if they figured out what that was, they might start to make some progress at last.

Still distracted by his musings, he became vaguely aware that Amanda was still speaking.

'Look, if you want to visit again, there's no need to go through the official channels,' she was saying. 'Just give me a call, I'll give you my mobile. Here, I'll write it on your hand.'

Chapter 18

It was only a few weeks since they had taken on the Charles Grant case, advisedly or otherwise, but regular progress meetings had been part of the arrangement and another of them had now fallen due. And what a momentous period it had been with the brutal murders of Benjamin and Allegra David still hogging the front page of every newspaper. Maggie and Jimmy had learnt from Frank that Darren Venables of the White British League had been arrested for the crime, but all the media had been told at this stage was that a forty-six-year-old man was helping them with their enquiries. Reflecting the priorities of their readership, the entertainment correspondents seemed more concerned with the impact of the killings on Bow Road, speculating how the writers would deal with the loss of two of its leading characters.

Now of course the whole thing had become rather awkward, because Frank had made it crystal-clear he didn't want a bunch of bloody amateurs, as he rather unkindly described her and Jimmy, trampling all over his enquiry. Still though, she felt an obligation to help the wretched actor in any way she could, even if she now recognised that the heavy lifting of the investigation would have to be left to the Metropolitan police. They had offered to meet Grant for lunch, forgetting that eating in public could often be more pain than pleasure for those in the public eye, so instead agreed that he would come into their office at around eleven. 'And no selfies,' Jimmy had said to Elsa as he arrived earlier that morning, but he needn't have worried since she claimed never to have heard of Grant.

The actor arrived promptly, the young receptionist ushering him through to one of the office suite's shared meeting rooms.

'I've booked it for an hour,' Maggie said, smiling. 'Should be enough I would think.'

He nodded. 'I guess that means there's not been much progress?'

'To be fair, it's only been a few weeks,' Jimmy said, 'but actually we have got some ideas. Although it's early days it's not looking unpromising.'

Early days. Maggie smiled to herself as she recognised one of his brother's favourite sayings, although Frank seemed to describe every case as being in its early days until five minutes before he solved it.

'Yes,' she said, 'so I think I'm right in saying that from the start, the police always assumed it was about the ransom. You were targeted because you are a famous actor and they assumed therefore that you would be able to raise the kind of sum they were looking for '

Grant shrugged. 'Yes, well that's what the police thought. What else could it be?'

'And you definitely had no reason to think otherwise?' Jimmy asked.

He shook his head. 'No, why should I have?'

Maggie gave him an uncertain look.

'It's just that looking at your social media postings and your Guardian pieces, you're an advocate of what I think is described as progressive politics, is that right?'

The question did not seem to perturb Grant.

'Yes, that's correct. I've always been a strong supporter of the fight against inequality. It's in my DNA I think.' To Maggie, there was more than a hint of superiority in the way he said it and she wasn't sure if she liked it.

'But we can't help but notice that you seem to attract some pretty vitriolic trolling online,' Jimmy said. 'Doesn't it bother you?'

'On the contrary,' he replied, 'the far-right idiots hate to see their world view being challenged. I see it as my duty to do so. But I have to ask, why are you so interested in my political views?'

'I'm not sure how to put this diplomatically Charles,' Maggie said, 'but you do seem to have made some quite vicious enemies.'

Grant sighed. 'Ah, I assume you must be talking about the cowardly da Vinci. Yes, he does seem to get particularly angry, which makes me assume he is some pathetic inadequate holed up in a ghastly bed-sit in Streatham or somewhere equally horrid.'

'And you're sure it's a he?' Jimmy asked.

'Oh yes, I'm quite sure it's a he. Women tend to be much more polite and usually choose an identifiable user name like JaneX or suchlike. But, tell me, where are we going with this?'

Maggie frowned. 'We're not sure. But it presents a possible motive that wasn't considered in the original case, so we think it's worth looking into.'

'What, some sort of far-right plot directed at little old me?' He sounded sceptical.

'Why not?' she said. 'There are people out there with extreme views and violence is in *their* DNA. So yes, it is something we at least want to explore.'

Including finding out who the hell da Vinci was, although that wasn't something she was going to promise her client right now. That would depend on Frank and his tame forensic officer. But of course, it wasn't difficult to have an intelligent guess at who it *might* be.

'You don't think it could be the work of Darren Venables, do you? He's known as D-V, isn't he? And we know that he made a particularly nasty comment on your social media just after Jamie was taken.'

Grant shook his head. 'Well, it did cross my mind, and in fact I did tell the police of my suspicions when they interviewed me in connection with Benjamin's killing. But afterwards I was not so sure. You see, I think Mr Venables is too full of himself to hide behind a *nom de plume.*'

But Venables won't be so full of himself now that he's about to be charged with two murders, Maggie thought. That was a development they were not yet able to share with Grant and she'd need to be careful it didn't slip out by accident.

'I tend to agree with you,' she said, 'but da Vinci is very persistent isn't he? Because his activities have been going on for several years as I understand it.'

His tone was dismissive. 'Well, as I said, I'm sure he's just some inadequate holed up in a garret somewhere. I don't allow his activities as you call them to distract me from my very important work in the fight for equality.'

She shot Jimmy a raised eyebrow but made no comment. Instead she asked,

'And can I ask you about your relationship with Benjamin David? Were you friends, away from show-business I mean?'

'Not really,' Grant said matter-of-factly. 'I presume you are asking because you have found out about our little quarrel last year. I admit I may have been rather sharp with him, but surely you can see how it might hurt our cause when we have rather minor celebrities jumping on the bandwagon simply for the publicity?'

'And how did Mr David feel about that?' Jimmy asked. 'I mean having his sincerity questioned? Not too pleased I would imagine. And yet it didn't stop him turning up to speak at the Hyde Park rally, did it?'

'I don't wish to speak ill of the dead,' Grant said coldly, 'but, really, I rest my case. Benjamin and Allegra were hardly likely to turn down such a prestigious opportunity to display their virtue in public, now were they?'

Maggie gave him a look that betrayed her surprise. 'They were *murdered* Mr Grant, and yet that doesn't seem to be causing you the least concern.' He was a client and she knew she ought not to speak to him in that manner, but it was hard not to, given the breathtaking narcissism of the man.

'It is a terrible tragedy of course. I'm sorry if I don't sound more regretful, but I didn't like either of them. They were very average actors in my opinion.'

She looked at him sharply but didn't say anything for a moment. Then she said,

'So to change the subject, can we talk now about Melody Montague and Patrick Hunt's pre-nuptial agreement.'

He shrugged. 'That was a long time ago. But as you requested I've brought along my copy of the document.' He removed a slim booklet from the folder he was carrying and passed it across to them. 'You are welcome to keep it. It's of no use to me.'

Maggie picked up the document, and rifled through it until she came to the page that laid out the terms of the agreement. There was no doubt about it, none whatsoever. Hunt was due fifty percent of the total marital assets, including the primary residence, and in the absence of Melody Montague's copy, there was nothing to say otherwise.

'Well, it does seem to support what Benjamin told us,' Maggie said. 'Now there's just one more thing maybe you can help us with. Blake McCartney. Why did you visit him in prison?'

Grant peered at her over his glasses. 'Who says I did?'

'I visited him myself,' Jimmy said. 'To see what he knew about the pre-nup. And when I was leaving, a prison officer told me you'd been to see him.'

'Ah well, I've been found out then,' he answered, quite calmly. 'Before his imprisonment, he had been helping me with a contractual matter with regard to some corporate work I was doing. But I fell out with the client and was anxious to understand if I had any redress under the contract. You see, in this case I had lodged the only copy of the agreement with him. That was a mistake which I will not repeat.'

It sounded half-plausible to Maggie, especially the bit about him falling out with his client.

'And was he able to help you?'

'No. He couldn't recall any of the detailed terms and conditions I'm afraid.'

'And yet, you visited him twice.'

Grant gave a rueful look. 'Yes, and what a waste of time that was. You see, on my first visit he promised he would have something for me next time, but he hadn't. I think he just said it so that I would come back. So that he could get out of his cell for an hour. He doesn't get many visitors you see.'

Jimmy gave a wry smile. 'Aye, he does seem to be Billy no-mates. But actually, there was one thing that struck me as odd. I asked him about Sabrina Fellini. He behaved very oddly when I mentioned her name. Why do you think that was?'

'I really can't help you with that,' Grant said impassively. 'As I said, I only met McCartney three times including when I witnessed the agreement, and her just once. But he is an untrustworthy little man in all respects so nothing would surprise me about him.'

Evidently he was now anxious to draw the meeting to a close. 'Look, I'd like to help you but really there's nothing I can add. Now, if there's nothing else, I've got a lunch appointment.'

'Yes, I think we're probably done for today,' Maggie said, reflecting that their client seemed to have quickly overcome his aversion for dining in public, 'and obviously if anything turns up before our next meeting I will let you know. So enjoy your lunch. Going anywhere special?'

Grant laughed. 'Oh goodness no, I'm not going to a *restaurant*. Sharon is cooking for me. At her flat. She's a very good cook, and I expect we will have a lovely lunch and then, well, what could be a better than a little spot of afternoon delight?' He dropped his voice to a conspiratorial whisper. 'We're in love you know, head over heels. In fact I've already bought the ring and I have high hopes she will accept me. You see, Sharon Trent is the best thing that's ever happened to me. I would do anything for her, she really is the most wonderful woman.'

That would be the same Sharon Trent who a week or two ago had written her number on the back of Jimmy Stewart's hand.

Chapter 19

The call had come in at four twenty-two pm on that damp July afternoon. The fourteenth of the month to be precise and by coincidence, the national day of France. *La Fête nationale*, that was what they called it, but Frank Stewart knew nothing of French history. Bastille day? Up until that point in his life he'd never heard of it, but it was to be a day he was destined to remember for a very long time. In every investigation, there was a turning point, the sweetest of moments when all the hopeless hunches and futile going-nowhere speculations suddenly turned to gold, when the fog dispersed in front of your eyes and everything became crystal clear. That's how he felt after the phone call from Inspector Marie Laurent, still hard at work on her country's most important anniversary when most of her countrymen had buggered off to the beach.

He recognised immediately the three-three international dialling code, causing his heart to skip a beat. They had agreed to touch base once a month, but this call was barely a week since they had last spoken. Something must have turned up. Something big.

'Bonjour Marie, it's great to hear from you so soon.'

'Bonjour Frank, your French accent is improving, I must say.' And yours is lovelier than ever, he thought.

'I'm trying Marie, I'm trying, but us Glaswegians can't even speak English properly, never mind French.'

She laughed. *'Well I think it is very nice, and we French and Scots are great friends in history I think.'*

'That's right,' Frank said. 'We call it the Auld Alliance. Auld means old in proper old Scots.'

'Ah yes, I have heard of it. I think we had the common enemy in England, is that not true?'

'Aye, I think you're right Marie, but we're all big pals now. Us and the English I mean.'

'Well, I'm not so sure France and England will ever be lovers, but yes, I think we are quite good friends now.'

'Yes, I agree, I think. But I guess you're not calling me to give me a history lesson, are you?' Even though he clearly needed one.

'No, I'm not.' She hesitated before continuing. '*Frank, something has arisen that may be relevant to your enquiry. To our enquiry I should say.*'

He tried in vain to suppress his excitement. 'Goodness, that's fast work Marie. Tell me more, please.'

'*It's really just a very lucky break, but of course we are grateful for it. The big congratulations must go to our Dutch colleagues in the city of Leiden. To them it is very important to have the international cooperation especially within Europe and so they always consider Interpol in their investigations and communications. Frank, you remember I told you about the Kitty Lawrence case in Bordeaux?*'

How could he forget? That was the case that had transformed his crazy hunch into a reasonable each-way bet. Now he was longing for more, something that would turn it into an odds-on favourite.

'Sure Marie, I remember. Go on.'

'*Well I have been told of a new case in Leiden in Holland which is very interesting. It is a big university town, in fact it has the oldest university in the Netherlands and one of the biggest too, with over one thousand teaching and research staff. Which brings me to the name of Professor Henk van Duren.*'

'Should I have heard of him?'

'*If you are Scottish like you or French like me, no, you will probably not have heard of him. But if you are Dutch, yes. He is very famous in Holland, a popular historian who is always on television. And not just here in the Netherlands. He worked for many years in America at the famous Princeton University and is very well-known on the history channels over there too. You may have seen him too in England.*'

Frank laughed. 'I'm afraid history's not my specialist subject. Now if he was a rock guitarist, that would be a different thing all together. But I'm getting off the point, sorry. Tell me what's happened.'

'*There has been another kidnapping. Exactly like our other two. Exactly like them.*'

'Goodness Marie, this is good news.' He knew the words were a clumsy choice but he was sure she would know what he meant. Another case with the same MO meant more information to get your teeth into and more chance that the perpetrators would make the stupid little mistake that gave them away. And they always did, no matter how clever they thought they were. So from the selfish point of view of the investigation, it *was* good news.

'*This time it was a little boy, his name is Brandon and he is just six years old.*'

'Hang on Marie. Brandon did you say? Is that name popular in Holland?'

'*I don't know, but it seems Mrs Van Duren is American and Brandon was born there when his father was at Princeton so I think that is the reason. But Frank, I have to tell to you there is something terrible about this case which has caused a great public outcry in the Netherlands.*'

'What was that?'

'*Brandon had been left in the car outside a convenience store whilst his mother ran in to buy some milk.*'

'Bloody hell, don't tell me,' Frank said, feeling his heart sink. 'With the keys in the ignition and the engine running.'

'*Yes, I am afraid that is the truth. The shop-owner told the police that this was the habit of Mrs van Duren almost every day.*'

'And someone only had to jump in to the driver's seat and speed off with the boy in the back.'

'*That is what happened, yes. That was three days ago. And now of course if the cases are connected, we must wait for the ransom call.*'

***

This time the dialling code said three-one. Eight in the morning and barely ten hours since he had got the news from Interpol in Lyon, it seemed the Dutch *politie* already had something to share with him. This was all turning out too good to be true but he would take it any day of the week. The voice at the other end of the line was loud, authoritative and over-familiar. That didn't bother Frank. He'd met a few Dutch cops in his time and recognised this as perfectly normal.

'*Hi Frank,*' boomed the voice, '*this is Marco from the Leiden police. Inspector Marco Boegenkamp. A good day to you.*'

Instantly, Frank could tell he was going to like this guy. He didn't know why, it was just a gut feeling, and over the years, he had learned to trust his gut. He decided to reply with matching familiarity. 'Hi Marco, good to speak to you mate.'

'*Ah, I hear from your voice Frank that you are Scottish. Kenny Dalgleish, Alan Hansen, Graeme Souness, I loved them all when I was a boy. They were great footballers and we Dutch know something about great footballers don't you think?*'

Frank laughed. 'Aye, you're not wrong there, you've had a few in your time. Van Basten, Van Nistelroy, Bergkamp, and not forgetting Johann Cruyff the master. But I take it you're a Liverpool fan then Marco? You must be happy with how it's going at the moment.'

'*Yes Frank, we're not normally great fans of Germans here in Holland but it is my opinion that Herr Klopp is a genius.*'

'Yes, I think the fans would agree with you there Marco. Not the Manchester United ones though.'

A loud cackle blasted down the line. '*Ha ha, that's true. Anyway, I have an update for you on our van Duren investigation. It is a very big deal over here as you can imagine because the professor is quite famous here in the Netherlands.*'

'Aye, so I've heard.'

'*Yes, but now it is his wife who is the subject of all the attention. I think it is true to say that she is now the most famous woman in Holland. And not in a good way also.*'

Frank knew someone else who had suffered that fate and he didn't envy Mrs van Duren one bit.

'So Marco, I guess you're expecting the ransom demand any time soon, am I right?'

'*We have it already. That is just one reason why I'm calling you. And not only because the demand is in English. Because you see, we think the kidnappers might be from the United Kingdom also.*'

'Why do you think that Marco?'

'There was CCTV footage from outside the convenience store. And we saw the driver at first went to the wrong side of the car.'

'Ah,' Frank nodded knowingly, 'we Brits do that automatically. But I guess you will have found the car by now?'

'Yes and as you would expect it has been burnt out to destroy any evidence. About twenty kilometres from where the boy was taken.'

Frank let out an audible sigh of disappointment. 'That's a shame Marco, but I can't say I'm surprised. We didn't find anything in our Jamie Grant case either. The hoods running this thing are obviously very careful. But you say you've had a ransom demand?'

'Yes that's right Frank. It was sent to the family by post and arrived this morning. We have checked the note of course for DNA and fingerprints but we have nothing. They received also a text and of course we have been unable to trace the owner of that number.'

'And the note. Where was it posted?'

'Here in Holland, in Leiden.'

That wasn't a surprise to Frank. The kidnappers would have been holed up in the city for quite a few days, allowing them to observe Mrs van Duren's routine. A routine that included leaving her son in an unlocked car with the engine running.

'And how much are they looking for?'

'A million Euros Frank. A lot of money.'

Frank gave a sharp intake of breath. 'Aye, that is a lot. You know there were ransom demands in the Jamie Grant and the Kitty Lawrence cases?'

'Yes, I know that Frank. And I know the kidnappers did not return the children. It is a very worrying situation. Here the van Duren family is very anxious for the ransom to be paid but we are advising them that they must not.'

Worrying situation? Marco was right, although Frank wasn't sure if his choice of words spoke for the difficulty the police faced. An impossible situation might describe it better, because no matter how you looked at it, there was no win-win scenario. If you didn't pay the ransom, you'd never see the kid again. If you did pay the ransom, you'd never see the kid again. Same difference. They only way there was going to be a happy outcome was if they caught the bastards who were doing this. And that wasn't going to be easy.

'Marco mate,' Frank said, more in hope than expectation, 'have you got *anything*? Anything at all?'

'Almost nothing Frank.'

Almost. So perhaps there was a sliver of hope after all.

'It is a very long shot I'm afraid, but we have a detective sergeant on our team who was born in the UK. And she said that the wording of the ransom note was slightly unusual. Of course we Dutch would not have noticed this because we are not native speakers of the language.'

Which made Frank laugh to himself because he'd yet to meet a Dutch person who didn't speak perfect English. Apart of course from that random *also* thing they peppered throughout their sentences. He'd need to watch he didn't start doing it himself. *Also.*

'What does it say?'

'I have it here Frank. It says "Make no mistake about it, I'm not joking you when I says it. A million Euros or the kid dies". Our sergeant says that is quite an unusual construction.'

'Is that all?' Frank said, failing to hide his disappointment. 'I assume you're talking about *I'm not joking you when I says it*? It is a *bit* unusual but I have heard it before. Plenty of times.'

Boegenkamp seemed unfazed. 'Well perhaps Frank, but you see here in the University of Leiden we have some of the greatest cyber-crime experts in Europe, maybe even the world. That's what they tell me and I have no reason to doubt them.'

'That sounds great mate. But how does that help us?' He didn't mean it to sound as churlish as it came out, but if Boegenkamp was offended, he didn't reveal it. The more he got to know this guy, the more he was getting to like him.

'One of our team has worked in the past with a very clever young lady called Hanneke Jansen. I am told that Doctor Jansen has developed a web-crawler technology that can search the entire world-wide-web with next-generation phrase matching algorithmic processing.'

Frank could hear him convulse into laughter at the other end of the phone.

'I'm sorry Frank but I'm sure you can tell that I don't really know what I'm talking about.'

Frank didn't understand much of it either but he did catch on to one phrase. A phrase that he remembered from his chat with Eleanor Campbell just a few days earlier.

'Web-crawler did you say?

'Yes. You know of this technology?'

'Not got the faintest clue mate. But I know a woman who does.'

'Ah that is interesting,' Boegenkamp said. *'So maybe you have an expert in this technology also?'*

'Aye we do.' He didn't like to mention that Eleanor and her pal Zak-with-no-surname had been working on their wee da Vinci problem for nearly a fortnight, apparently without success.

'So perhaps we could get our two experts together to work on this case. I'm certain she would get on really well with our Doctor Jansen and we have a saying which I think you have also that two heads are better than one.'

There was no chance that Eleanor would get on with any woman she perceived as a rival, and in Eleanor's eyes, all women were rivals. But he tried not to sound too doubting.

'Well the thing is, our Eleanor isn't exactly a team player.'

Boegenkamp laughed. *'Well maybe Frank we will get some big fireworks when we put these two together, but I think it will be worth a try. When do you think your colleague can be here in Leiden?'*

That left a slight problem to overcome. True, he had failed with DCI Smart the last time he'd tried for the case number, but surely now with this new development, she couldn't refuse. A couple of hundred quid on a cheap flight and two or three nights in a budget hotel, that wasn't going to break the bank. Hell, if it came to it, he would pay for it himself.

'Marco, I think we can get her out to you in the next couple of days, depending on what she's working on at the moment.' *Fingers crossed.*

'Tomorrow would be better Frank. You know we do not have much time. I will of course arrange for one of my team to pick her up at Schipol and take her to her accommodation. Let's hope these two clever women can work their magic, eh?'

Frank grinned. 'Aye, if they don't kill each other first. I'll get it arranged as fast as I can and let you know. Anyway, it was nice to make your acquaintance Marco and maybe we can meet up in person sometime.'

'You too Frank. And now I have to go and see the parents, to tell them that they should not pay the ransom.'

Not that it would make any difference to the outcome.

***

As Frank had predicted, this time he had little trouble convincing Jill Smart to release a case number into his care. Although to be fair, she had raised an eyebrow when he told her the first task would involve the expense of sending Eleanor Campbell to the Netherlands for a few days and that he himself would need to fly over, with only one overnight stay involved, for a review with Inspector Boegenkamp. Sensibly, he had waited until the case number was in his possession before revealing this latter information.

Speaking of Miss Campbell, he had been unsure of the reaction he would get when he told her of her urgent overseas mission, but in the event, he needn't have worried. By good fortune she was in the midst of one of her semi-permanent relationship dramas with her sort-of boyfriend Lloyd, and so jumped at the chance of an enforced separation.

'It'll like show the pig what he would be missing if we ever broke up,' she had said, with, in Frank's opinion, greatly misplaced optimism. He liked Eleanor but he was under no illusions that she would be anything other than a nightmare to live with. There was every chance that Lloyd would indeed see what he was missing and, concluding that it wasn't very much at all, resolve to make the separation permanent. Nonetheless, he knew that blind encouragement was the way to secure the result he was looking for.

'That'll show him all right,' he had said, with fake but convincing sincerity. 'He'll be grovelling at your feet when you get back, mark my words.'

'Yes, I like that,' she had said. 'Pig.'

Having secured her assent to the mission, the problem still remained as to how to ensure the visit was productive. There was a lot in Eleanor that Frank recognised in himself, both of them sharing a preference to work alone, and both having a barely-suppressed inability to suffer fools gladly. The last thing he needed was for her to have a punch-up with the Hanneke woman over at Leiden Uni. So there would need to be a briefing. A brief one.

'I've heard that this Dr Jansen is pretty good,' he started. 'She's a cyber-crime specialist at the university so she should know her onions. Maybe not with your depth of hands-on experience of course, but she should be able to help you with some of the easier stuff.' He was pleased with how that sounded overall. Except for his stupid schoolboy error, which Eleanor immediately picked up on.

'*Dr* Jansen? So she's like a PhD or something?'

Frank shrugged. 'I think they dish them out like Smarties over there. Honestly, it's nothing to worry about, you'll get on great I'm sure. Anyway, are you clear on what we are trying to do out there?'

'Yeah, like it's a no-brainer. We're to phrase-match across cyberspace for that weird *joking you* phrase.'

'And does that involve web-crawlers?'

She gave him an amused look. 'Is that your new word of the day?'

'Two words actually. But I don't know what it means. Can you tell me?' And then wished he hadn't bothered.

'Like sure. So the tech giants have like catalogued the web into a giant cross-referenced multi-zillion terabyte database to support their search technologies but because of privacy *they say*, but really to protect their commercial interests, they won't share it with law-enforcement agencies. So governments have built this huge capability to roam all over the net and build their own ad-hoc search indexes using mega supercomputers that run at like mental speed.'

'Good to know,' Frank said. Normally he would have added a sarcastic quip, but he was painfully aware of the need to tread carefully given that she had already spent a frustrating fortnight trying to crack Charles Grant's da Vinci thing, without success.

'Aye, and it sounds as if they have some fancy tools over in Leiden that even your mate Zak hasn't got.'

Her eyes lit up with anticipation. 'Yeah, I've been on their website and they've got like two mega supercomputers. It's two Cray XC45s working in a cluster and they're like the size of a tennis court. And the cluster can generate twenty million database hits a second, which is beyond awesome.'

Beyond awesome? At last, Frank could relax, because if there was one thing he knew about Eleanor Campbell, it was that she was a sucker for big expensive kit, and these Cray thingies sounded as if they were both big and expensive. Brilliant, the trip was going to be a success.

Then not more than five minutes after he had got back to his desk, Marco rang him again. And before they reached the end of their short conversation, it was arranged. Frank was going to be out there himself, sooner that he expected. Because the van Durens could not be persuaded that the ransom should be paid, and now Boegenkamp wanted him in Leiden to see if he could do any better.

All things considered, that had every prospect of being a red-letter day. Or *een bijzondere dag*, as his new best pal Marco would say.

Chapter 20

At about the same time as Eleanor Campbell was meant to be flying out to Schipol, the highly-paid lawyers of the Crown Prosecution Service were filing the paperwork that would charge Darren Venables with the murders of Allegra and Benjamin David, the task already having consumed an estimated thirteen hundred and thirty man hours at a cost to the public purse of one hundred and ninety thousand pounds. It was therefore inconvenient to say the least when on that very day another body turned up with the identical MO as the earlier victims.

It was an early-morning jogger who found it, slumped against the wall of a dark tunnel at the point where the north-bound lines out of St Pancras Station crossed the Regents Canal. At first she thought someone must have dropped a glove, pausing to pick it up with the intention of placing it for safe-keeping on the thin ledge that ran along the brick-lined wall of the tunnel. A second later, she was screaming uncontrollably as she realised with horror what she held. In her panic and shock, and quite understandably, she tossed the severed hand into the middle of the dirty canal, which was to cause the police diving team no little difficulty in the hours following the discovery of the dead man. But eventually it was recovered, and despite it having been submerged for some time, it was still just about possible to make out the message scrawled on the back. *Leonardo.*

Two hours later, in a darkened room somewhere on the top floor of Paddington Green police station, DCI Colin Barker was fighting a desperate rearguard action, pleading with anyone who would listen that nothing had changed, that Darren Venables was *clearly* responsible for the first two murders and so this one *must* have been the work of a copy-cat killer. The brass were in full damage-limitation mode, and had issued strict orders that under no circumstances should the MO of this new killing be released to the media, which resulted of course in it being leaked little more than five minutes later. Over at the *Chronicle*, the young award-winner Yash Patel was already salivating over the award-winning possibilities of a juicy miscarriage of justice story. One that would keep him on the front page for a week at least, with another month's worth of human-interest spin-offs. And that jogger who had found the severed hand, she looked so hot in her little running shorts and tight vest. Her picture alone was guaranteed box-office.

And for the second time in two years, DCI Jill Smart was being called in to clear up an almighty Barker-generated mess, and where Jill went, DI Frank Stewart went too. In charge of proceedings that morning once again was Assistant Commissioner Brian Wilkes, a competent detective of the old school just weeks from retirement. You could tell he was old-school among other things by the way he addressed his charges as ladies and gentlemen and not guys.

'So ladies and gentlemen,' he began, 'who's going to give me the whole gory details of this monumental screw-up?'

No-one seemed keen to take the stage except Frank.

'Sir, I will do my best, although we're new to this case of course.' By we, he meant Department 12B, the rag-tag bunch of misfits headed up by Jill Smart of which he was part.

Wilkes smiled. 'Getting your excuses in early are you Stewart? Proceed, if you please.'

'The victim is one Daniel George Walker. Forty-seven-year-old male of mixed race, well-known TV presenter and more recently, an actor in that soap Bow Road. Don't know if you watch it at all sir?'

'I am aware of its existence Stewart. Carry on.'

'Very good sir. Well Mr Walker was seemingly on his normal jogging route, which according to a neighbour we spoke to, he does pretty much every day, leaving around seven-thirty in the morning and returning around one hour later. We can only speculate at this stage, but it appears that his assailant was waiting for him under the railway bridge. He was killed by two severe blows to the back of the head, we assume on the towpath, and then the body was dragged to the piece of waste ground where it was found. Probably that's where the hand was severed and the message written on the back. *Leonardo*.'

Wilkes nodded. 'So exactly the same MO as the David killings?'

Frank shot a cruel smile in the direction of Colin Barker.

'Exactly sir. The same MO. No difference.'

The AC shook his head in disgust. 'This is going to be totally embarrassing if it gets out. Just to reiterate, let's make sure we keep schtum on this, understood?' Everybody nodded, although everyone knew it was already too late for that. 'What a bloody foul-up. So where are we with this now? Any leads, suspects, witnesses?'

'Aye sir, well we can assume it wasn't Darren Venables, unless DCS Barker let him out on compassionate leave.'

Jill Smart shot him an admonishing look.

'My little joke sir, sorry. No, we don't have any serious leads or suspects at the moment, and as far as we can see there's only one obvious connection.'

'Ok, so spit it out then.'

Frank smiled. 'It's that actress Melody Montague, she's also from Bow Road as you probably know. You see, our victim was drafted into the show specifically to get her to sign an extended contract. And she was due to be married to Benjamin David, victim number one.'

Wilkes was now pacing the room, evidently in an effort to focus his thoughts. 'So this Montague woman, did her name come up in the earlier enquiry? It must have, I assume. We always suspect partners and former partners. Ninety percent of the time it's one of them who has done it, isn't that the case?'

Jill Smart intervened. 'We weren't involved at that stage sir, but I'm sure Colin will be able to help you with that question.'

DCS Colin Barker's expression suggested that was the last question he would want to help anyone with.

'Eh...I don't think it *exactly* came up sir,' he squirmed. 'We did not think she had a motive or the opportunity, and she was able to produce convincing alibis for her fiancé's murder. And also the team felt the case was so strong against Venables, we concentrated all our resources into that line of enquiry.'

Concentrated all your resources into fitting up the WBL's leader thought Frank, not that he felt sorry for *that* guy, not after that wee run-in they'd had at Hyde Park. Wilkes contented himself with a shake of the head. There was a long and awkward silence, which no-one felt like breaking. Until finally the AC said quietly,

'So, anything else anyone wants to tell me?'

'Well DCI Barker dismissed it at the time,' Frank said guilelessly, 'but shortly before the first death, a private investigations firm was engaged by Miss Montague to sort out a dispute with a pre-nuptial agreement. Concerning her first husband.'

Barker was staring at the floor, no doubt dreading what was coming next. He wasn't to be disappointed.

'Bainbridge Associates is the firm in question,' Frank continued. 'As it happens, my brother Jimmy works for them too. I think you met Maggie and Jimmy in connection with the Alzahrani enquiry.'

Wilkes nodded. 'Ah yes, I remember them. Sound bunch, as I recall. Should work with them more often.'

'Yes, well I'm sure they would like that,' Frank said, storing it away for future use. 'So as I said, there's a major dispute between Miss Montague and her former husband, concerning the contents of a pre-nuptial agreement they signed fifteen years ago. The dispute of course is about money, and we're talking millions here sir, not just five bob. The sort of dosh that can make people do bad things.'

'So what's your line of thinking?' Wilkes asked.

Frank shrugged. 'It's only a sketch of a theory sir, but the former husband - he's another actor called Patrick Hunt, pretty well-known - well he's pretty bitter about the break-up and specifically about the money situation. I doubt whether he would have been wishing Benjamin David a long and happy marriage, that's all I'm saying.'

'And was he ever questioned?'

'I believe not sir. At least not as a potential suspect.'

Frank heard him swear under his breath.

'And what about the other two killings? Do we have any theories about them?' Now he was ignoring Barker, directing his questions at Frank and Jill alone.

'Early days sir. In the case of Miss David, it's reasonable to suspect that she was killed for the same reason as her brother. As to Danny Walker, I've no idea about that at the moment. But there must be a connection sir, mustn't there? Because it must be the same killer. And so probably the same motive.'

'And you've no idea what that motive may be?' Wilkes said.

'No idea at all sir. It needs work.'

Wilkes shook his head in disgust. 'Well, you and DCI Smart better get onto it right away then, hadn't you? And as for you, DCS Barker, I think you need to come with me.'

***

Of course, it needed work, a lot of work. There was something missing, something big, something that would tie the whole ragged mess together, but he just couldn't put his finger on it. At least now he could bring Hunt and Montague in for questioning and make up his own mind if any of them were capable of murder.

But the truth was, knowing what he knew about them, he didn't much fancy any of them in the role of a serial killer. Because he was sure that was what this case had now become. It was a serial murder case, there was no doubt about it. Luckily Wilkes hadn't focussed too much on the *Leonardo* thing, because he didn't have a bloody clue what that was all about. Of course in Barker's simple view of the world, it led right back to Darren Venables and the White British League. But unless one of D-V's acolytes had picked up the baton whilst their leader had been in police custody, that theory was now dead in the water.

However, that didn't mean that the scrawled message wasn't important to the investigation. The exact opposite in fact, and he had a feeling that until he'd figured out where it fitted, the investigation would go nowhere. And so that was it then. Three identical murders, same MO, no credible suspects, no ideas. For the first time, he began to wonder what had possessed him to open that bloody file in the first place.

Chapter 21

'Bow Road Filming Suspended after Sharon Stroke' read the headline, the quality *Chronicle* for once following the tabloids by putting the story on its front page. The photograph that accompanied the article did not feature the actress's lover Charles Grant, instead picking and image of Melody Montague with the stricken woman captured together on-set.

Frank tossed the paper across the desk and gave a wry smile. 'It's hard not to laugh, isn't it? It's like a scene from some terrible old Carry-On film.'

'You're bloody awful,' Maggie said. 'Just because they were in bed together at the time it happened. It must have been a great shock for Grant.'

'I know,' Frank said. 'I was only joking. But apparently he was asking her to marry him at the time, although they're saying the drugs might have been partially to blame.'

Maggie nodded. 'Yes, apparently she has a cocaine habit. They're thinking it was a combination of that and shock that seems to have caused it. Poor woman, she's been completely wiped out and they can't say whether she'll make any kind of recovery.'

He shook his head. 'Aye, strokes are awful. And she's only forty-two, same age as me. Mind you, I think I might have a stroke if anyone proposed to me.'

'Yes, very tasteful Frank,' she said, frowning. 'But you're right, she obviously wasn't expecting him to propose to her.'

'But for it to cause a stroke?' Jimmy said doubtfully. 'Seems pretty unlikely to me.'

They were holed up in Atlee House, Frank having persuaded Jill Smart that he found it easier to think when he was away from the stifling bureaucracy of Paddington Green. It wasn't a lie either, but it was also a lot easier to sneak Jimmy and Maggie into that decrepit cesspit, with its almost complete absence of any security measures. Irregular yes, but it wasn't as if what he was doing was without precedent. The Met often availed itself of the services of private eyes, and where would it be without its network of paid snouts, many of whom moonlighted in the murky waters of the investigation trade. And hadn't Assistant Commissioner Wilkes himself opined that they should use them more often? So that was it then, it was all good. He was doing no more than following orders, although he had taken the precaution of making sure the two of them were tucked away out of sight in an obscure corner of the building. That wasn't difficult, Atlee House consisting of little more than obscure corners.

Jimmy was already at his adopted desk, pouring over an inch-thick document, addressed to his brother, that had landed earlier that day. Literally so, because although he could have had it delivered electronically, Frank liked to work with a hard copy, the ones that were professionally printed and bound at the government print works over in Elephant& Castle.

'Oh, hi guys,' Jimmy said brightly. 'Hope you don't mind Frank, it's the interim forensic report on the Danny Walker case. I've just given it a quick skim. It makes interesting reading, that's for sure.'

'No problem bruv, you just keep on reading.' He looked at the document with satisfaction. Yes, it had been the right decision ordering that hard copy. With a hard copy you could scribble notes, draw a ring round passages that interested you, turn down the corner of the pages you wanted to go back to again and again. And you could take it with you when you went to the bog, something you really didn't want to do with your police-issue laptop. He wouldn't have minded getting stuck into it himself, but in less than ninety minutes he was due to be sitting opposite Jill Smart over at Paddington Green for his monthly meeting. He was expected to have produced an advance briefing paper, centre stage of which would be the report on the proposed visit to Leiden, but with one thing or another, somehow he hadn't quite got round to it.

'Look, I've got to sort a few things out before I nip over to see Jill. Why don't you two do some work on the report, see if you find anything? And obviously, let me know if anything turns up. And then I'll see you back here at three-ish.'

Maggie winked at Jimmy. 'Don't worry Frank, we're not going to hide anything from you. So just leave us in peace and we'll get onto it. And yep, we'll see you at three or thereabouts.' Frank gave a distracted thumbs-up and scuttled towards the door.

***

'Ok then boss, where do we start?' Jimmy asked.

Maggie shrugged. 'From the beginning, I suppose.'

Scanning the frontispiece, they saw it was a Doctor Ashley Stone who had put this report together. Obviously neither of them had ever met this Dr Stone, didn't even know if it was a woman or a man, but a few pages in, it wasn't hard to recognise it as a great piece of work. Meticulous but concise, with summary tables laying out the facts of Walker's murder and comparing them with those of the earlier killings. Clear photographs of the scene and of the body as it lay in the morgue, the impact point of the head trauma which had killed him clearly labelled, but without aimless speculation about the murder weapon, which had not yet been found. As they thumbed through it page-by-page, enthralled, their attention was drawn to a sidebar captioned *Issues and Concerns*. Half a dozen bullet points, some pretty trivial. But not the one at the top of the list, helpfully underlined and picked out in bold type.

Jimmy looked at Maggie with an amazed expression. 'Are you reading what I'm reading?'

She nodded. 'I think so. The top line of that table...'

'... where it says the method used to sever the hand in the Walker case...'

'...in the balance of probability, was not the same as that of the earlier murders. Frank is going to have a complete heart attack when he hears this.'

'So if I understand this right,' Jimmy said, 'in the first two murders, the cut which removed the hand was neat and precise...'

'... probably done by a meat cleaver, I think I saw that earlier in the report,' Maggie agreed.

'Aye, that's right. Whereas in Walker's case, it was much less precise. Dr Stone thinks it was probably done by hand using a large hacksaw, and would have taken at least ten minutes...'

'...as opposed to just one expert chop with the cleaver. This is dynamite, isn't it?' Looking up, she was surprised to see Jimmy trying hard to suppress a laugh. And failing.

'What? What's so funny?'

'I know, it's no laughing matter, but you know what this means, don't you? It means that Frank's best pal Colin Barker was right all along. It looks very much like this one *was* a copy-cat killing. You can't believe how much I'd love to be there when Frank has to tell him. He might even have to say sorry. I mean, can you imagine how hard that's going to be?'

Maggie giggled. 'Whatever happened to brotherly love, Mr Stewart?'

'No, you know I'm only kidding. But it is a bit of a bitch for him. Seriously, we'll need to break it to him gently. And soon. Maybe you should call him, do you think?'

They caught him just as he was pulling into the car park, Maggie leading the call and her colleague listening in on the speaker-phone. Frank's reaction, as had been predicted, was not positive.

'Aw for god's sake, that's all we need. Shit shit shit.' Maggie imagined him banging the steering wheel in frustration before reaching for the figurative hip-flask. *'Everyone in the force has been pissing themselves laughing at Barker's copy-cat thing, but unknown even to the idiot himself, it turns out he's been right all along. Shit and double shit.'*

***

The annoying news from Maggie and Jimmy had kicked Frank's brain into overdrive and now he struggled to process this fresh and vital information. So whoever had killed Danny Walker, it probably wasn't the same person who had killed Allegra and Benjamin David. And more than that, there was something else that differentiated the killings, something obvious. The first and second ones spoke of preparation and knowledge, specifically a knowledge of how difficult it was to sever a limb and therefore how important it was to have the right tools for the job. A professional killing, carried out by someone with prior experience. The third one seemed quite the opposite, an amateur job, almost certainly. But amateur or not, it didn't make the case any easier. Having one killer on the loose was bad enough, but now that there were two, the complexity of the case had risen exponentially. *Bugger.*

He was still trying to figure it all out as he walked through the front door of Atlee House. And then another thought struck him. Apart from the media who had been at that shit-show of a press conference with Barker, nobody outside the immediate investigation team knew the detailed MO of the earlier killings, and certainly not the *Leonardo* bit which was the signature-mark of the earlier crimes.

Yeah, apart from the media. There had been nearly fifty journos at that Paddington Green do, and what was the chances that each of them had kept schtum as instructed? Precisely no chance at all, that was the answer to that question. Keeping their mouths shut just wasn't in their DNA and they only needed to tell a couple of mates, and then they in turn told a couple of theirs, and well, the maths was beyond him, but it was a lot. As the depression enveloped him like a Victorian pea-souper, there remained only one possible course of action. Once again, and breaking every rule in the book, he found himself fumbling in his jacket pocket for the hip-flask. And then one restorative swig later, it came to him. For there was *one* other individual who most assuredly knew the MO of the murders.

The individual who had formally confirmed the identity of Benjamin David as he lay in the morgue.

Chapter 22

It had been quite a relaxing flight, all in all. The Met's travel team had done him a huge favour by booking him on British Airways from Heathrow rather than shunting him out to Luton or Stanstead on one of those ghastly low-cost jobs. The departure time was a civilised six-thirty in the evening and by good fortune he had been allocated an extra leg-room seat, and on the aisle too so he didn't have to clamber over a stranger to get to the loo. The food wasn't much to write home about, the main course being some sort of warmed up cheese and tomato croissant, but it filled a hole and importantly, there was a complimentary bar service, unusual in this day and age. The only thing that stopped the journey being perfect was that the traveller next to him was one of these guys who liked to talk, and the talk had continued without a break from the moment Frank had sat down beside him until the flight attendant was welcoming them to the Netherlands and reminding them to set their watches forward an hour. Not that he was by nature antisocial, far from it, but there was only so much interest you could squeeze from the subject of interlocking flooring systems, apparently the specialisation of his companion. Still, he had managed to anesthetise himself from the worst of it with a couple of double gin and tonics, and his spirits were undampened as he now scanned the small group of people milling around the arrivals area. At last he saw him, a tall figure of around forty years of age, crop-haired and wearing a vivid orange sports jacket, green open-necked shirt and blue chinos. Inspector Marco Boegenkamp was holding up a small whiteboard on which had been scribbled 'Mr Stewart,' sensible insurance in case they didn't recognise each other from their pictures.

Frank walked over to him and gave a broad smile. 'I'm guessing you must be Marco,' he said, extending his hand. 'I'm Frank. It's good to meet you at last.'

The greeting was returned with obvious warmth. 'Yes, and I'm Marco of course. Welcome to the Netherlands. Good flight?'

Frank laughed. 'Yep, on time and smooth, what more can you ask for?' Well, not to be seated next to a crashing bore would have been nice, but he didn't share that thought with his new friend. Twenty minutes later they were threading their way south in Boegenkamp's Audi, the busy motorway still thick with rush-hour congestion.

'It's always like this I'm afraid. I could put on the blue lights of course,' he laughed, 'but we are a very orderly society here in Holland and it wouldn't be right since we are only going to a little meeting in Leiden. But don't worry, the traffic usually thins out in a few kilometres and then we should be there in about an hour.'

Given the primary reason for his visit, Frank wasn't really in any hurry.

'What state are they in, the van Durens?' he asked. 'Pretty bad I'd imagine.'

'Yes very bad,' Boegenkamp agreed. 'Professor van Duren of course blames his wife for everything and he is finding it difficult to deal with his anger.'

'Not surprising. But they're still adamant they want to pay the ransom?'

'Yes, I'm afraid so. That's one of the main reasons I wanted them to meet you. So they can hear directly from you what happened in the other two cases.'

Leiden police headquarters was located in a nondescript low-rise office block located on a nondescript business park about three kilometres outside the old town. Boegenkamp led Frank through a warren of corridors to a small stuffy meeting room, windowless but ventilated by a noisy air conditioning unit. The room was sparsely furnished with a table and a half-a-dozen plastic chairs and seemed to have been purposely designed for maximum discomfort. The van Durens were already there, accompanied by a detective sergeant introduced as Johann.

'This is Inspector Frank Stewart from London,' Boegenkamp said, his tone serious. 'He is here to help us with our case.'

Professor van Duren was of medium height and slim with a shock of thick greying hair swept back from his forehead. His wife was small and petite and strikingly attractive, although the effect was diminished somewhat by the dark rings that circled her eyes, no surprise given what she had been through. From his opening remarks, it was evident the Professor was a man very much used to being in control.

'We've had the advice from the police here in Leiden,' he said briskly, 'but of course we do not intend to follow it. We must have our child back and therefore we have no option but to trust the abductors will return him as they have said they would. We wish to pay the ransom.'

'Well that would be a mistake sir,' Frank said, making no attempt to sugar-coat the message he was about to deliver. 'Look, I don't want to trash your faith in human nature, but criminals aren't wired the same as you and me. I don't know if you have the saying over here about no honour amongst thieves, well it's true. Professional criminals like these guys are driven by greed, pure and simple. They'll take your money all right, but they won't give you back your child.'

Mrs van Duren began to sob, drawing a look of cold disdain from her husband. The poor woman had been destroyed by one stupid mistake and it was clear he wasn't going to let her forget it. *Ever.*

'Shut up Rachel. This isn't doing anyone any good. So Inspector Stewart, what do you suggest we do?'

Frank knew the question was coming and he hadn't been looking forward to it one bit. Boegenkamp would have already told them about what had happened in the Grant and Lawrence cases, but it seemed they were in denial, so they would have to hear the unpalatable truth again from him. But luckily he had an idea, a stupid, crazy idea. An idea that might give them hope where there ought to be none.

'If you simply hand over the ransom money, then it's odds-on they won't return your child. I'm sorry to be blunt, but that's the fact of the matter. You see, from their point of view, doing a handover just introduces unnecessary risk and complication into the whole thing. So why bother if we still get the money, that's the way they look at it.'

'I'm sorry,' van Duren spat at Boegenkamp, 'but I don't see how *he's* helping the situation.'

And the guy was right of course, he wasn't helping much. Because nothing would help until they tracked down the scum responsible for this, and any prospect of that was a long way off right now. Which left only his crazy idea.

'Look, I said it was greed that drives these people. So there is *one* thing we could try.'

'What?' Rachel van Duren cried desperately, 'please tell us.'

'It's a risky play,' Frank said, catching Boegenkamp's eye, 'but if we make the reward worth their risk, there might just be a chance they'll go for it.'

And then he explained his crazy idea, and in the light of day it sounded even more stupid than when he had dreamt it up on the journey down from Schipol. But there was no denying Professor van Duren had an aura about him, an aura that radiated dignity and importance. *A man of honour.* On that, everything depended. Well, not quite everything.

'It depends on whether you can raise another half-million Euros,' Frank said.

'We can raise that on the Connecticut beach house?' his wife said, pleading to her husband. 'Can't we?'

And so it was arranged. Three-quarters of a million Euros would be paid in advance, with a further three-quarters of a million to be paid if the child was handed over unharmed. A deal that put the ball back in the court of the abductors. All they had to do was trust that Professor van Duren was a man of his word, a man who would keep his part of the bargain. In Frank's mind, the enticement of that three-quarters of a million gave it at least a fifty-fifty chance of success. And anyway, this was the only game in town.

The proposal was pinged off to the mobile number they had been given, obscured behind a wall of encryption somewhere on the dark web. Six minutes later they received the terse reply.

Deal.

***

It had always amused Frank that in the movies, ransom handovers were conducted in dark and dank abandoned warehouses in some moody and windswept riverside location. Of course it was great for creating the atmosphere of dangerous foreboding sought by the director, but it was hopelessly stupid in real life. No way of arriving un-observed for a start, and generally just one way out too. *Dumb.* Which is why he'd agreed with Boegenkamp the perfect location for this most high-risk of operations. Centraal Station Amsterdam, used by over a quarter of a million passengers every day, constantly teeming with arrivals and departures from all parts of the Netherlands and beyond.

Half an hour earlier, the money had been electronically transferred as instructed, to be laundered through a network of shadow servers hosted in a quiet Moscow suburb, the mafia-funded provider charging a flat ten percent fee for their expertise and discretion. And now all they had to do was wait for the appointed time. Eight minutes past eight o'clock, bang in the middle of the morning rush hour. *Send just the mother and no police.* That was a joke and both parties knew it. The place was already swarming with dozens of Boegenkamp's plain-clothes team, melting with ease into the background amongst the throng of commuters. Hard to spot, but then that worked both ways. Frank stood with his Dutch counterpart about fifty metres from where Rachel van Duren was waiting, her face etched with worry, at the entrance barrier to platform twelve. *Wait there, we'll bring him to you.* Neither spoke, but each knew what the other was thinking. *Fifty-fifty at best, but please for once let the odds fall in our favour.*

Out of the corner of his eye, he saw a man in a conspicuously-branded puffer jacket kneeling down, talking to a child, pointing in the direction of the barrier. Was it his imagination, or did the child look scared? Frank touched Boegenkamp on the elbow, catching his attention and together they peered at his phone, studying Brandon van Duren's photograph. Was there a likeness? It was hard to tell from this distance. But then they saw Mrs van Duren had seen the pair too, and immediately they knew from her body language. *False alarm.*

They watched as the huge digital clock, mounted high above the travellers on a steel column, ticked over to the handover time. *Eight minutes past eight.* Earlier, they'd speculating on how the handover might be effected. Would the boy have been pushed onto a train in some outlying suburb, eliminating the possibility of his abductors being caught in the act? Or would he be dropped off in person, his chaperone melting seamlessly into the crowd? Less likely, given that they would know the police would be observing the scene. But right now, that was all academic, because nothing was happening. Above them, the clock clicked over once more. Then another minute. And another. *Nothing.*

This was exactly what he feared the most, the raising of false hope only for it to be cruelly dashed. Never mind her marriage, he doubted if Rachel van Duren's sanity would survive this. But then a thought suddenly came to him. *God, I've been so dumb.* For the abductors, it was all about eliminating the risk of being caught, was it not? So why would they drop the kid exactly at the spot where every bloody cop in Amsterdam would be watching?

'Rachel,' he yelled, sprinting towards her, his tone urgent, 'Rachel, you need to come with me. Now.'

She spun round, her expression a mask of confusion. Without waiting for an answer, he grabbed her hand and began to run across the concourse, dragging her behind him, Boegenkamp following several steps behind.

'Where are we going Frank?' she shrieked, but not resisting. 'I need to stay at the barrier. Brandon will be here soon.'

'Trust me, he won't. But it will be ok. Come on.'

God, how he prayed his hunch was right. They were heading to the Western tunnel, which if he'd read the map correctly, burrowed below several of the platforms before emerging on the waterside. And according to the map, that was the side where the taxi rank stood. They barged their way down the escalator, Frank not bothering to apologise as they pushed aside an army of indignant commuters. Reaching the bottom, it seemed that the flow in the tunnel was in the opposite direction to theirs, and every second person had their head buried in their smartphone, making no attempt to get out of their way and thus slowing their progress. But at last they reached the up escalator, taking the steps two at a time, ignoring once again the protests of those who they had bundled past, until they reached street level once more. To his left, he saw the giant illuminated sign above a pair of automated sliding doors. *Taxi*.

'Come on, this way,' he shouted, dragging her in the direction of the doors. Boegenkamp had now caught them up and was on his radio, bringing his team up to speed on the change of plan. Not that they would be needed, the kidnappers being already over the Belgian border on their way to Calais. It had been, as far as could be arranged, a risk-free operation. Shove the kid in the back of the cab, slip the Leiden-based driver a hundred-Euro note and remind him it would be good for his health to forget who gave it to him. Now they just had to sit back and wait to see if the van Durens honoured their side of the bargain. If they did, then *result*. Three-quarters of a million in the bank, a tidy little job and no mistake, and plenty of other kids to go for to fill the vacancy. If they didn't, then they'd better not let the kid out of their sight ever again.

The boy was standing there, alone and bewildered, as the doors slid open. Boegenkamp was there first, bounding through the gap and gathering him up in his arms. Frank smiled at Rachel van Duren and gave her a thumbs-up, then watched as she ran towards her son. You didn't get many happy endings in this job, so you needed to savour them when they turned up. He might stay on another night, see if Marco fancied a wee pub-crawl around the city, maybe even check out the famous red-light district, although strictly as a social observer. They'd been bloody lucky, he knew that, because he was certain that the villains' original scheme hadn't included handing back the kid. But at least now he had a blueprint that he could use next time it happened, assuming of course the next victim's family had a cool million and a half going spare.

Because there would be a next time, he was sure of that.

Chapter 23

'Hi Amanda, nice to hear from you!'

Jimmy hadn't exactly been surprised when he glanced down and saw who was calling him. Whilst it was true that for most of his life he had been pretty hopeless at reading signs of attraction even when to an outside observer they were bloody obvious - at least that's what Maggie kept telling him - with Miss Amanda Fletcher of Her Majesty's Prison Service even he could tell there was an interest. An interest that was *definitely* not going to be reciprocated. For a moment Jimmy had debated whether he should take it or not, but eventually admitted to himself that he would like to know the reason for her call, and the easiest way to find that out was to answer it. She had seemed momentarily taken aback by the fact that he had actually picked up and by the effusiveness of his greeting.

'Yes, well thank you!' There was a pause during which he assumed she was catching her breath. *'It's lovely to talk to you too. I was beginning to think you'd lost my number.'*

'No no,' he said, quite truthfully, 'just been a bit busy, that's all.' He had been busy but that wasn't the reason he hadn't called her.

'All work and no play makes Jimmy a dull boy. You should come and play with me, we could have a lot of fun.' That wasn't the first time he'd heard someone say that, and he didn't doubt that it might be true, but it was how to escape afterwards that would be the problem. Especially given her profession.

'That would be nice,' he lied, 'but well, it would be a bit difficult, let's put it that way.'

'Don't tell me, you're with someone,' she sighed. *'All the nicest ones always are.'* By her tone he guessed that the revelation, untrue though it was, had neither surprised nor particularly upset her.

'Nicest ones? I don't know about that,' he laughed, 'but I guess you didn't call me just to tell me how amazing I am.'

'I did actually, but there was something else too,' she answered. *'It's your friend Mr McCartney. He's in hospital.'*

Jimmy couldn't hide his surprise. 'What? What happened?'

'He fell over. In his cell. Smashed his face against the wall five or six times and broke his nose. He was unconscious when they got him to the Royal Free.'

'Fell over? Really?'

'That's what it will say in the official report. But no, of course not really.'

'So what did happen then?'

'Well the first thing is when I hears that our boy is getting moved to A Block.'

'What, where all the nutters are kept?'

'That's right, well remembered.' From her tone he could tell that she was enjoying the story, and that she was in no hurry to get to the end of it. 'I mean, that's highly unusual. Normally the only reason you get moved from our wing over to A is if you have done something really bad or upset someone very important, so I thinks, oh-oh, this doesn't look good for our Blake.'

'So what did he do?' Jimmy asked. 'A bust up with one of the officers or something?'

'Well, not exactly,' she said, sounding evasive. 'It was because he got on the wrong side of one of the organised crime crews. Not that I'm surprised because he's a right twat, isn't he?'

'So, these guys can arrange for someone to be transferred to another part of the jail. As if they run the place?' Jimmy said incredulously.

She laughed. 'Well more or less. It's all about the give and take of prison life, ain't it? You do this little thing for us and we'll do something for you. Bob's your uncle then a couple of weeks later the governor is boasting to the Home Affairs Committee about a nice little drugs bust or about finding a stash of mobiles in the shower block.'

'So who do you think beat him up then? Because I'm assuming he didn't actually fall over six times.'

She laughed again. 'Oh, I know who did it all right. Everybody around here knows that. It was Johnny Watson and Pete Smart. A right couple of hard bastards they are. You wouldn't want to get on the wrong side of them, believe you me.'

He was struggling to get his head around the fact that someone could order a beating inside a jail as easily as ringing for a takeaway. And that the authorities apparently knew who were responsible yet did nothing about it.

'This is an eye-opener for me Amanda, it really is. So what are these two guys in for? Murder or something I assume.'

She grinned. *'What are they in for? Watson and Smart aren't inmates, they're screws. Do you think we allow our guests to just wander into anyone's cell and do this sort of thing? What sort of establishment do you think we're running here?'*

'Jesus Amanda, there's a lot about the prison system I'm obviously ignorant of. But I'm guessing you must have some idea what it was all about?'

'Yeah, well sort of. My mate Andy Smith, remember the officer you met on your last visit, well he's kind of mates with the two of them and apparently it was all to do with some legal document or other.'

'You're kidding,' Jimmy said, unable to hide his surprise. 'It wasn't about a pre-nuptial agreement, was it?'

'I don't know the details, might have been mate. 'Course, that's why you came to see him, I remember now.'

'Aye, that's right.' Now his mind was racing as he skimmed through all the possible reasons he could think of why someone might want to beat up McCartney. With his history, there probably was no shortage of folks who might bear him a grudge, but surely the timing of this was too much of a coincidence just a few days after his own visit. And it was not as if that would have been kept a secret in that place. Someone had been doing some digging into McCartney's visitor log.

'So Amanda,' he asked her, 'do you or your mate Andy have any idea who ordered this?'

'And do you think if I knew I would tell you?' she said disbelievingly. *'No way mate, I value my health too much for that. Some people are saying it was one of the Irish firms, but I don't think Andy knows and he doesn't want to know either. But you know Jimmy, you could always visit McCartney in hospital and ask him yourself, I'm sure he'd be very pleased to see you. We've got a rota for guard duties and as it*

happens it's my turn tomorrow afternoon. And then maybe we could go for a drink afterwards.'

Jimmy couldn't help but chuckle. 'Nice try Amanda, but some other time eh? But listen, thanks for letting me know all this.' And he *was* grateful to her, although at that moment he had no idea what it meant for the case, but he could figure that out a bit later. Satisfied he had all he needed, he was just about to bring the call to a close when she said,

'*Now you just wait a minute Jimmy Stewart, because I've kept the best for last.*'

'You're a right tease Miss Fletcher,' he said, grinning to himself. Aye, a tease in more ways than one. 'Come on, tell me.'

'*So Andy says that the story going round is that McCartney was paid twenty grand by someone to make a document disappear and this seems to have displeased someone important. That's all Andy has heard.*'

'Amanda, you're a wee darling!' And he meant that too. This was dynamite. Someone had been prepared to pay good money to make the Hunt-Montague pre-nup evaporate, and there was only one person who stood to gain from that happening.

Time they paid another call on Mr Patrick Hunt. That was, if the Kemp brothers didn't get to him first.

***

It was seven thirty in the evening, and for Maggie this was her sacred no-work time, the blissful hour she got to spend with her son before bedtime, just the two of them, united in love as step by step they erased the trauma that had upended their lives almost two years earlier. But the implications of Jimmy's earlier call with Amanda Fletcher were so startling that for once she had to make an exception. Which was why he was now sitting opposite her in her tiny kitchen hugging a mug of coffee and munching on a chocolate digestive. Ollie was naturally delighted about his visit, racing around in his P-Js and excitedly urging him to examine his latest Lego creation.

'It's a Buzz Lightyear, Uncle Jimmy. To infinity and beyond!' He picked up the spaceman and holding it aloft, circled the room at speed, accompanied by a loud *whoosh*.

'Aye, I can see that mate. It's really good. I love Toy Story, it's one of my favourites.'

Maggie laughed. 'Now then Ollie, leave Uncle Jimmy alone, will you? I tell you what, if you're a good boy, you can watch it for ten minutes. Go through to the sitting room and I'll set it up for you.'

Ollie adopted a serious tone. 'But not the *original* film mummy, I like Toy Story Three best.'

'Already a wee film critic eh?' Jimmy said, smiling. 'You know, I think that's my favourite too.'

'And then can we play football Uncle Jimmy? *Please*.'

'Of course mate. I'll go in goal and you can take penalties at me, how about that?'

Satisfied, Ollie followed his mum out of the room, leaving Buzz in the care of Jimmy. A few seconds later Maggie returned, grinning from ear to ear.

'I doubt whether he'll sit there for five minutes, but you never know, now that he's got a promise of a game a football with you.'

'He's a great kid Maggie, a real credit to you. After everything you've been through, I mean, it's just amazing.'

She nodded. 'Well maybe, but we just get through it day by day. And it's getting better, much better.' She wondered if she should tell him how much of that was down to him. Jimmy Stewart had saved her life, in more ways than one, and she knew she would be grateful to him forever.

'Well, as I said, he's a fine boy. But anyway, I suppose we'd better get down to work, don't you think? I don't want to waste your whole evening.' As if she could think of a better way to spend it.

'Yeah, so what about our Mr McCartney then?' Maggie said, shaking her head. 'Not the smartest sandwich in the picnic, is he?'

'Aye, you could say that. I bet he wished he hadn't taken that twenty grand now.'

'He's a troubled soul, let's put it that way.'

'And Charles? How did he get roped into it?'

Maggie shrugged. 'We can only assume Patrick Hunt paid him to do it. That's all I can think of.'

'Aye, or maybe Patrick had something on him,' Jimmy said uncertainly, 'because we know that our Charles is a very complicated man. So you never know what might be hidden away in his back-story.'

'The thing is,' Maggie said, thinking out loud, 'the poor man is completely broken, isn't he, so he wouldn't have been thinking straight whatever the reason. And then he decides to invest his whole future in Sharon Trent, and well, I think we knew that those feelings were all one way. And now of course the poor woman has suffered that terrible stroke.'

'Aye, poor woman and poor guy too, because I've been there, done that.'

She gave him a surprised look. Surely it was impossible that there was a single woman on this earth who wouldn't fall for Jimmy Stewart? But then she remembered. Astrid Sorenson, beautiful, desirable and dangerous. The woman for whom he had left his adored Flora, only to find out when it was too late the terrible mistake he had made.

'Top-up?' she asked, indicating with the cafetiere.

A mumbled sound which might have been 'Aye' emerged through a mouthful of digestive crumbs. He gave her a thumbs-up, evidently to ensure she understood his intention. Carefully, she filled his mug to the brim. 'But you know the thing with the pre-nup, that's really serious,' she said. 'Twenty grand to make Melody's copy disappear, I mean that's naughty.'

'And pretty stupid too as it turns out. Messing with the Kemps I mean.'

Maggie smiled. 'So you think that's what happened? That they found out?'

He nodded. 'I would have thought so. And I guess they would have plenty of - well let's call them associates - inside who could take care of stuff like that. And I'll tell you what, Patrick Hunt better look out too. Because it wouldn't surprise me now if he becomes the next murder victim.'

She laughed. 'No, somehow I don't think that will happen. The link back to Melody would be a bit too obvious, wouldn't it?'

'Aye, I suppose you're right,' he said, giving a shrug. 'So what's going to happen now do you think?'

'Well assuming McCartney makes a full confession, Asvina will put the matter in front of the family court and argue that Melody's recollection of the terms of the agreement, though not backed up by actual evidence, can be taken to be true.'

'But do you think it *is* true?' Jimmy said doubtfully. 'Because McCartney's story has really only come out under duress, hasn't it? What if these bent wardens threatened to kill him if he didn't say what they wanted him to say? What if Grant was actually telling the truth about the reason for his visit to see McCartney and it had nothing to do with the pre-nup, just like he said.?'

There was a moment of silence as she thought about what he had said. And then she realised that of course there was another way of looking at the whole thing. What if the seemingly disorganised McCartney really *had* lost Melody's copy of the agreement and couldn't even remember what was in it in the first place? What if Melody had realised that gave her an opportunity to challenge the true contents of the agreement? *What if it was Melody Montague who was lying, not her ex-husband Patrick Hunt?*

'The whole thing's a bloody mess,' she said finally. 'We're bloody useless aren't we? We've got nowhere with the abduction of Charles' little boy and nowhere with this pre-nup business.'

And it was true. As far as the Jamie Grant affair was concerned, they were way out of their depth, but at least with that one, Frank and his Department 12B were all over it. But had they fallen hook, line and sinker for Melody's version of the pre-nup story when, like *proper* investigators, they should have treated it with more scepticism?

Whatever the case, she knew now there was no option. They had to confront Melody and get her to tell them the truth. Or at least, when she said *they*......

***

'Well just hang on a minute,' he protested. 'What, you want me to go *now*?'

'Why not?' she said, trying and failing to suppress her laugh. 'It's a lovely evening and it'll only take you twenty minutes to get there. I'll send her a text, tell her it's urgent and you'll be there by half-past eight. You only need to stay five or ten minutes. In fact you don't even have to go in if you're a real scaredy-cat.'

'I'm not scared,' he said, furrowing his brow. 'But why can't we both go and see her? We could go back to the set of Bow Road tomorrow maybe. That was good fun and she'll be more relaxed there, surely?'

Maggie chuckled. 'Oh my goodness, what's the world coming to? Captain James Stewart of Her Majesty's Royal Ordinance Regiment refusing an order. I'll have to have you court-martialled or executed at dawn.'

'I'm not in the blooming army any more, thank god,' he railed, 'but I'd take the firing squad anytime over an evening with Melody Montague.'

'Don't be such a drama queen Jimmy, it needn't take more than a few minutes. Not unless she entices you in to her boudoir, that is.'

'I'm sorry, I'm not doing it. No way.' She could see he was doing his best to sound angry, but not really succeeding. A moment later, his face cracked into a smile.

'You're a bloody awful woman and a bloody awful boss, Maggie Bainbridge. But go on then, I'll do it.'

She tried not to sound triumphant. 'I knew you would. But thank you. I've already texted her to say you're on your way.'

***

The traffic had been quiet on the early August evening, the sun still warm but slowly sinking in a lovely pink-tinted sky and the journey had taken barely twenty minutes. Now steeling himself for what lay ahead, he jabbed the button on the intercom that was mounted on one of the sturdy stone brick pillars of the entrance gates. The voice that answered was accented and unfamiliar. Of course, she had a maid. Bridget, that was her name, Latvian or Lithuanian. Maggie had told him that even Melody did not know which.

'Miss Montague is in the garden. She is expecting you sir.'

There was a click and then one of the automated gates began to swing inwards. He slipped through the narrow gap then looked around. She was seated in a shady corner, the table set for two and a bottle of something already on ice, the elegant silver wine-cooler alongside the table glistening in the fading sunshine. Champagne, if he knew anything about their client. The furniture was, as he expected, high-end, of a design that could be found in expensive Mediterranean hotels and on board private yachts, not that he had much experience of either. The garden was in full bloom, expertly-designed formal borders surrounding the luxuriant shaped lawn, clematis, honeysuckle and climbing roses clinging to ornamental trelliswork, the garden a secluded oasis walled on three sides by weathered dusky brickwork. A paradise, but a paradise that needed money to sustain. A ton of money.

He'd seldom seen Melody in anything but a dress but this evening she was informally attired in light blue jeans and a black loose-fitting T-shirt. She still looked nice, pretty alluring in fact although he hated to admit it.

'I expect you're more of a beer man Jimmy,' she was saying, 'but I hope you can make an exception this evening. I must say though, this is an unexpected pleasure. And *so* intriguing.'

He smiled uncertainly. 'Well, we're a wee bit worried about the pre-nup business. We hoped you could help us straighten things up.'

Unnoticed, the maid had appeared beside them, filling both their glasses then slipping silently back through the patio doors and in to the kitchen.

'Straighten things up?' she said, a slight steeliness in her tone. 'I thought I was paying you guys to do that.'

'Well aye, but there's one or two kind of, well *issues*, as I said.' Bloody hell, he thought, this is going to be difficult. *Curse you Maggie Bainbridge, we're going to have to have words about this in the morning.* But for the moment, he decided that perhaps he'd been a bit too direct and searched for a change of subject.

'How are you coping Melody?' he said, feeling slightly awkward. 'With Benjamin's tragic death I mean. It must still be very difficult. Particularly since they still don't know who actually did it after that Darren Venables cock-up.'

She gave him a baleful look. 'I'm still in shock. I can't believe it has actually happened. But life must go on, what else can you do?'

He wasn't quite sure how to react to this, because no matter what you said, they were just hopeless platitudes, of bugger-all use to anyone. *It'll get better in time, believe me. I'm so sorry for your loss. If there's anything I can do just ask.* So he didn't say anything, instead hoping his look was warm and sympathetic. It was a look that must have been open to misinterpretation, because out of the blue, she leant across the table, straining to kiss him. *Shit.*

'I shouldn't really be doing this, should I?' she said. 'But life is short as they say, and well, you know I've never been one for resisting temptation.' She extended a finger and ran it down his cheek. 'And you are *so* beautiful.' That explained it then. She just didn't do faithfulness. Even to the dead.

'Beautiful?' he replied, tensing up. 'I don't know about that. Melody, I can't believe I'm saying this but perhaps this isn't such a good idea. Look, you're incredibly attractive, but maybe you're aren't thinking so clearly at the moment...'

She drew away and gave him a surprised look. 'Well Jimmy boy, it will be your loss. Because no man ever leaves my bed disappointed.' He didn't doubt that was true, but that didn't mean it wasn't an extraordinary thing to say. And now all he could think of was how to get out of there. *And fast.*

'I'm sorry Melody,' he said. 'It's not you, it's just that I'm looking for something more at the moment.'

She shrugged, evidently accepting his explanation. 'Yes, I'm sorry but my head is all over the place at the moment. It would have been nice, that's all. You see the loneliness and emptiness, it's quite unbearable. But whatever, I'll always be here when you change your mind.' There was an awkward silence and then she said,

'So, if it's just to be business, well, to the pre-nup. That's why you're here, isn't it?'

'Aye it is,' he said, relieved. 'It's just....well, we were wondering about whether you were being entirely straight with us. Sorry, but that's the fact of the matter.'

He'd wondered how she might take that, expecting an outburst of anger or at least some kind of frosty response. But her answer took him completely by surprise. Because she smiled and said,

'Well now I *can* put you straight on that.' Reaching down below her chair, she picked up a blue transparent folder and placed it on the table.

'I have it here. That's what you came for, isn't it?' She handed him a blue transparent plastic folder.

'What's this?' But he thought he might have already guessed what it was.

'You know what it is,' she said, smiling. 'My copy. We've found it. Isn't that lucky?'

He gave it a brief glance. 'So how did you come by it? Because when I spoke to McCartney he was adamant he had lost it.' He had tried not to sound suspicious but it didn't come out that way.

'Yeah, that's what he said, but it was his paralegal girl, Paula Rogers who managed to find it. Blake said she was having a sort-out and came across it, that was all. Hidden away in the bottom of my file, where it seemed to have been all along.'

Yes, he thought, Miss Rogers just *happened* to come across it after her erstwhile boss had been beaten to within an inch of his life. What a coincidence that was. But coincidence or not, he was done here. He said,

'Melody, I think it's time I was off. It's been lovely, really it has. And very useful. Thanks.'

 He got up, walked round the table and placed his hand on her shoulder. It was meant as an expression of sympathy, but she clasped it tightly and stood up to face him, her lips almost touching his, her gaze steady as she looked into his eyes. Almost imperceptibly their lips came together and he felt the tip of her tongue in his mouth, gently probing, the physical reaction as inevitable as it was irresistible. *Bloody hell*. Time to make his excuses before it all got out of hand.

***

Back in his flat, he picked up the plastic folder and carefully removed the agreement. Idly he flicked through the pages, vainly trying to make sense of the dense legalise, but after a few minutes, gave up the struggle. Sod it, it didn't actually matter what it said, the important thing was they had it back in their possession and so they could, however improbably, complete the mission they had undertaken for Asvina.

But then his attention was caught by the faint dark stain that had, unnoticed, spread across his fingers. Which struck him as odd, because you would think the ink would be dry by now on a fifteen-year-old document.

Chapter 24

They had been forced into a bloody huge change of plan and all because of an unexpected obstacle that had arisen in relation to that bane of his life, the case number. This particular one being the case number which had, belatedly, been allocated to his *Shark* investigation. The blame fell to some administrative assistant's assistant buried down in the basement of Paddington Green police station, or more accurately, to the stupid bureaucracy the Met had put in place to make everything three times more difficult than it needed to be. For it seemed an extra signature, rank of Chief Superintendent or above, was needed on the travel requisition form before a relatively junior employee like Eleanor Campbell could make an overseas trip, and since no officer of that rank could be arsed to sign it, there it sat in the stern and matronly clerk's virtual pending tray, ignored. From whence no amount of persuasion by Frank, subtle or otherwise, could release it. He'd even tried mild bribery, being rewarded with a stony stare and a threat to report him to his superior officer. As if Jill Smart would give a monkey's about that. *His* travel requisition had got signed without any such obstacle, and so at about the same time he'd been heading to the Netherlands to meet the van Durens, Dr Hanneke Jansen was heading the other way.

Now, back in London and four days after Jansen's arrival at Maida Vale labs, he was due to meet them for a progress report. But that was a couple of hours in the future, giving him time to catch up with his amateur colleagues in the Fleet Street Starbucks they seemed to call home. To tell the truth, he was in desperate need of a caffeine infusion on account of a crashing headache, induced by the extended drinking session he'd enjoyed with Marco last night. He had only been returning the favour extended by Boegenkamp when he'd stayed over in Amsterdam a couple of days earlier, but now he was paying the price. Still, there was no denying it was good for international relations and he was looking forward to seeing what state his Dutch mate was in when they met up later that day.

Maggie and Jimmy were already there, sharing some private joke at the cramped little table they'd managed to secure. He was pleased to see they had already ordered for him, a steaming black Americano which he hoped benefitted from a double shot of Espresso. She smiled up at him, causing him to reflect again how simply lovely she looked. Not that he had yet plucked up the courage to do anything about it, and probably never would. But he didn't have time to think about all of that now.

'Hey guys, how's tricks? Solved the Jamie Grant case yet?'

'Sod off,' Jimmy replied, grinning, 'but we're following a number of promising lines of enquiry, that's all I can tell you.'

'Oh aye, is that right? Because I told you not to follow any lines of enquiry, promising or otherwise.'

'We didn't, honest,' Maggie said, 'but there have been developments.'

'Developments?' He was willing to bet they wouldn't be as interesting as what he'd recently found out from his useless mate DC Ronnie French.

'That's right,' she nodded. 'Jimmy will tell you all about them. But I heard about your big success with the rescue of the van Duren boy. You must be incredibly relieved how it turned out.'

'Aye, I am,' Frank said, trying not to sound too pleased with himself. 'Gives us some hope if it happens again. But come on, let's hear these *developments*. What have you got?'

He listened intently whilst Jimmy told him about McCartney being beaten up in prison, and about the alleged twenty-grand payoff, and the unexpected re-emergence of Melody Montague's copy of the pre-nuptial agreement. And about the traces of ink on his hand. It was interesting enough, but how any of it had anything to do with either the Jamie Grant case or the Leonardo murders was beyond him.

'You see Frank, this all seemed like some sort of scam engineered by Patrick Hunt to cheat his ex-wife out of a couple of million quid. But now it seems the scammers have been scammed.'

He shrugged. 'Aye well, we know that money corrupts, don't we?. But I'll leave you two to sort that one out.'

The fact was, he'd already dismissed any connection between the Montague-Hunt pre-nuptial agreement and the murders or the abductions. It was just a wee spat over money, and nothing else, of that he was convinced. The only problem was, right now he didn't have a better theory about any of it, especially the Danny Walker murder. And then he remembered Jimmy and Maggie saying they had met Walker at that house-warming do over at Richmond.

'What was he like, this Danny Walker?'

'Nice enough,' Jimmy said. 'A bit of a lad perhaps, but nothing wrong with that I suppose. But here, I've got a couple of photos from the do. Take a look.'

He took Jimmy's phone and peered at it.

'Good-looking guy. Him I mean, not you. A nice wee snap with the kids and Melody too. They must have been pleased, meeting their hero.'

'They were. And if you swipe through, you'll see wee Ollie got one with Danny too.'

Frank nodded. 'Nice picture. The wee lad would be thrilled I guess?'

'He was,' Maggie said, smiling. 'We've printed it out and he's got it stuck on his wall alongside the Ferraris.'

'But *somebody* must have wanted Walker dead,' Frank said. He knew it was stating the bleeding obvious and he wasn't really looking for a response, but he got one anyway.

'Well, what if it was something to do with *Bow Road*? Because there's a connection there to Benjamin and Allegra David, isn't there?' Maggie said. 'Maybe that's something for us to look at.'

He laughed. 'What, you think it's the cast of a rival soap bumping them all off? That would be quite a plot-line.'

But there was no denying it *was* a connection. Tenuous perhaps, but not as tenuous as the link to Charles Grant and the abduction of his toddler. Sure, Grant had been in Bow Road too, but that had been years ago. Which brought him back round to Frenchie and the meeting he'd had yesterday with Mrs Vivien Grant.

'My esteemed colleague Ronnie French finally got off his fat backside and went to interview Charles' wife. He said she was in a bit of a state and already hitting the vodka and oranges at ten in the morning. But the interesting thing was, she seems to blame wee Jamie's abduction on some photo-shoot the family had done for one of these glossy lifestyle magazines. It hit the newsagents just a month or so before the incident and she says it put her boy in the shop window. A funny way to describe it I know, but that's what she says.'

'Gosh, that's interesting,' Maggie said. 'Did that come up in the original enquiry?'

'*Nothing* came up in the original enquiry. But it makes you think doesn't it? Some villain sees the article and thinks, yep, that boy will do nicely. Not that it takes us any further forward in terms of who did it.'

'Not really,' Maggie agreed. 'But you know, it might be interesting to know if the other two kids were involved in one of these photo-shoots too. Their parents were in the public eye after all.'

'Maybe that's one for you and Jimmy to look into,' he said, draining the dregs of his coffee, 'but I need to head off. Got some hot-shot boffin over from Holland who might be able to nail this da Vinci bloke for us. I'll keep you informed.'

***

On the way over to Maida Vale, Frank reflected that he had to do some serious thinking about what the press was now calling the Bow Road murders. Danny Walker's killing was definitely a copy-cat job, he now accepted that. And now Colin Barker was back in charge of the case, more smug and more stupid than ever, and with renewed determination to stitch up Darren Venables for the two David killings. The far-right thug had barely been free for twenty-four hours when he was re-arrested, and all that da Vinci social media stuff was going to do for him. Frank would bet his pension that he was innocent, but he realised with some reluctance he would have to leave that for the jury to sort out. As for the Danny Walker murder, where did you start? The only half-lead he had so far came from Jimmy, from that meeting at Melody Montague's place. A bit of a lad, that's how his brother had described him, the sort of guy who regarded infidelity as a wee hobby like fishing or golf. So was this the revenge of a wronged husband, a husband who somehow had got to learn the MO of the earlier killings and staged a neat if flawed re-make? He shook his head, swearing to himself under his breath. Of course it sounded ridiculous, because it *was* ridiculous. There had to be more to it than that.

***

Boegenkamp was waiting in reception when Frank arrived and, annoyingly, looked none the worse for his session the previous evening, where he had out-drunk Frank in a ratio approaching two to one.

'Good afternoon Frank. A little bird is telling me we have some good news to look forward to.'

Frank forced a smile despite his pounding head. 'A little bird called Hanneke is that?'

He nodded. 'Yes, she called me on my way over from my hotel.'

Frank collected their passes then led Boegenkamp up the stairs to the corner conference room where Eleanor and Dr Jansen had been installed for the duration. Eleanor smiled warmly in Frank's direction, a smile which he recognised as her pleased-with-herself one. Which was a surprise to him since she had been far from pleased when he told her she wasn't going to Leiden after all. However, the source of her good cheer was soon revealed by her first words to him.

'Hanneke got me access to her Cray. It's like beyond awesome.'

She looked as if she hadn't slept for a week, dark rings surrounding her eyes and her hair dull and matted, her favourite lavender t-shirt crushed to within an inch of its life, but then again, that wasn't much different from her normal look. Dr Hanneke Jansen by contrast was fresh-faced and smartly dressed in new-looking jeans and a crisp white tailored shirt. She was tall and slim, almost as tall as Boegenkamp in fact, and her general academic appearance was accentuated by a pair of circular wire-framed spectacles perched on the end of her nose. Despite the outward differences, it was clear that a bond had developed between the two women over the few days they had spent together, as they now shared a quiet joke which Frank suspected, correctly as it happened, featured himself in some way.

'Eleanor has told me so much about you,' Hanneke said in way of introduction. 'I have been very much looking forward to meeting you in person also.'

He gave her a suspicious look. 'Is that right? I can't imagine what she's said about me.'

Eleanor grinned. 'We were just trying to work out how to explain what we've found out, you know, in a simple way, as if you were like a five-year old.' The words may have been unkind, but the tone was affectionate.

He shrugged. 'Aye, well I'm sure you'll keep it dead easy, that's what I need.'

'And me also,' laughed Boegenkamp.

'So anyway,' Frank said, 'enough of this hilarity Campbell. Just tell us what you've found.'

'Can we wait for Zak?' she asked. 'He's just gone to the loo.'

He remembered her mentioning him before.

'Oh aye, he's the web-crawler guy.'

Dr Jansen let out an involuntary giggle.

'I'm sorry Frank,' she said, 'it sounded so funny.'

'I gather that,' he replied, without malice.

A few seconds later, they were joined by a smooth-skinned youth who looked as if he should still be at school. *Primary school.* He wore old-fashioned horn-rimmed spectacles with a mass of thick brown locks tidied into a ponytail. Frank knew the dress code in this building was shirt and smart trousers, and whilst Zak's attire just about obeyed the letter of that law, his light blue shirt though clean, was clearly antique and had not been ironed that morning or any other. The trousers were of a brown corduroy, and they too were un-pressed. The general effect was of a second-world war code-breaker, brilliant but so scruffy that he had to be hidden out of sight in some top-secret country manor house.

He raised a hand in greeting. 'I'm Zak. Zak Newton. Welcome to Maida Vale Forensic Labs. Eleanor probably told you, I've been trying to help with your da Vinci guy thing?'

Zak seemed already to be ending his sentences with that rising inflection thing that had become the norm for anyone under thirty-five, so Frank wasn't sure if he was expected to answer. But he did anyway.

'She told me.'

'Sweet. So I've been running the sweeps through GCHQ's Hitachi for the last couple of days. It's awesome capability but the beta version that we've got is fairly slow and a bit unstable.'

'Beta version?' Frank had heard Eleanor use the phrase earlier in the case but couldn't remember what it meant.

'It's like untested software,' Zak explained. 'It's got lots of bugs and it falls over and some things don't work at all, but the developer guys get feedback from us so that they can fix it and make improvements and stuff. Once they've done that it goes alpha.'

Frank smiled. 'Sounds a bit like what my bank does to me every time they have an upgrade to their app.'

'Yeah, just like that,' Zak said, smiling. 'So this software is all about replacing manual analysis. It's state of the art and a lot more accurate. It can identify thousands of phrases and scan two hundred thousand documents an hour. Pretty awesome.'

Out the corner of his eye, Frank saw Boegenkamp giving a subtle tip of the head. Cottoning on, he looked over at Dr Jansen, who was wearing a face like thunder.

'Aye, nice one Zak,' hoping to steer proceedings in Jansen's direction. But he didn't need to intervene any further because Zak had picked up the atmosphere in the room. Not that you could miss it.

'But of course, it's nowhere compared with Hanneke's kit and well, her software is just off the scale, capability-wise. So I decided to hand over the problem to her and Eleanor. Always best to use the right tools and the right people for the job, don't you think?'

Frank chuckled to himself. This lad should dump his career in tech and join the diplomatic corps.

'Awesome,' he said, shooting a smile in Boegenkamp's direction. 'So Dr Jansen, perhaps you could take up the story from here?'

Returned to centre stage, her frown melted away. This was a woman who obviously craved the limelight. Something to remember for the future, although he wondered why Marco hadn't mentioned it to him. Maybe he hadn't noticed. Or maybe it was just her Dutchness.

'Of course Frank. So perhaps I can start with some history?'

'Please do.'

She smiled. 'We are the cyber security research group at the University of Leiden, and I of course am the leader of that group. For this project, we worked with the admissions administrators to recruit a control group of a thousand student volunteers. Each of them were asked to write one hundred posts on various social media platforms, under their usual handles. And then my A-I software, running on some high-powered computer hardware set up specifically for the purpose...'

'That's the Crays,' Frank said.

'...right. So the Crays analysed all the posts, looking for commonalities in the phraseology, comparing them with a control document prepared by each participant also.'

'Cool'.

'When they compared the identification data with the control document,' Jansen continued, 'there was about an eighty percent match. And the cool thing is, my A-I software learns from experience, so it gets better the more data it gets.'

'I get it so far,' Frank said, lying. 'What about you Marco?'

'Crystal clear also.'

Frank shot him a smile.

'So once we were happy with our matching technology, then I needed to develop a method to search across the internet.'

'Isn't that simply google?' Boegenkamp asked. Riskily, in Frank's opinion, and being rewarded with a withering look from Dr Jansen.

'Many people would think that,' she said in a smug tone, 'but of course we cannot use that facility because that is owned by the American corporation Alphabet Incorporated and they do not grant access to their databases or algorithms.'

'Aye, so *that's* why your team had to develop the web-crawler thingy.' Frank remembered Eleanor explaining this to him earlier and he was feeling pleased with himself for recalling the conversation.

'My team was involved, yes, but it was mainly me,' she replied, a hint of frostiness creeping into her voice. 'It is something I specialise in also.'

'Well that's all great Hanneke,' Frank said, trying to hide his impatience. 'So the big question is, how have you got on?'

It all went a bit quiet at that point. Meaning it didn't take long for him to realise that Dr Jansen might have oversold the good news bit when she'd spoken to Boegenkamp earlier.

'Frank, do you know the song, two out of three ain't bad?'

He nodded vaguely. 'Aye, Meatloaf, isn't it? But a bit before my time.' Jesus, did he look *that* old?

'Yes perhaps it was. But it is a very good old rock song in my opinion, one of my dad's favourites. Well this week, we change the song to be one out of two ain't bad. That's what we have achieved this week, so maybe we can call it a little success.'

And then came the excuses, which, showing great leadership, she left Eleanor to deliver.

'It's like a problem,' Eleanor said, frowning, 'if the person we are trying to detect doesn't have a big web presence. If they like don't have a Twitter or an Instagram for instance.'

'So, like if they're like over forty?' He hadn't meant to mock her way of speaking but it had just come out that way. 'It like, won't work? *Not* awesome.'

'It's not our fault,' she said defensively. 'If the data isn't there in the first place, we can't make a match, can we?'

There was no denying it, even he could see that. But then, totally out of the blue, an idea popped into his head. And if he made a fool of himself in front of these techie geeks, then so what?

'Listen, I get what you're saying. The guys we're looking for are villains, not bloody social-media stars. But I know one place where their words of wisdom are faithfully recorded for all time. You see the chances are we would have had them in for questioning at some stage in their pathetic little careers. And when we have them in for questioning, they have to make a statement, don't they?'

'And we record these statements in our computer systems,' Boegenkamp said, catching on.

'Exactly Marco. So why can't we connect Dr Jansen's magic phrase-matching technology up to the Met's criminal records system?'

'It would be very difficult,' Jansen said, frowning. 'Several months work I would think.' He detected the sour tone, the tone that said it won't work because I didn't think of it.

'Our criminal records system has an API,' Zak said suddenly. 'An application program interface. You don't need to know what that means, but it lets us connect to external systems very easily. I know some of the network services guys and I'm sure they could help set it up if it's too technically difficult for Eleanor or Dr Jansen. A day or two's work at the most.'

God, thought Frank, *I love this guy*. And evidently he wasn't yet finished.

'And of course Hanneke, I assume your software has an API too? It's pretty much mandatory these days, isn't it? You wouldn't write an app like yours without it.'

Ambushed. But to her credit, she seemed to get over it quickly, and five minutes later she and Eleanor were buzzing with excitement as they savoured the interesting technical challenge that lay ahead. One day, two days at the most, and they'd be able to do a sweep against the Met database, when maybe the abductor would be nailed on account of not paying attention in his English class.

That left just one question to be answered.

'One out of two ain't bad, that's what you said. So does that mean you've found out who da Vinci is?'

They had. And when they told him who it was, he couldn't help but laugh out loud. Now he couldn't wait to tell Maggie and Jimmy the news.

Because when it came down to it, professionals were going to beat amateurs every time.

Chapter 25

It was a rare treat indeed for Maggie to get the opportunity to collect her son from school. Theoretically since she worked for herself she could have arranged her workload around the school schedule, but in practice it seemed there was always things to do and people to see which inevitably got in the way. Today however it had been forced on her because her nanny Marta had to fly to Poland at short notice to tend to her sick mother. Inconvenient, but in truth it wasn't much of a problem. In the last day or two they had received a few enquiries for new work, and so Jimmy had been sent off to Kent to interview a local councillor who had contacted them directly about some irregularity or other in the accounts of the local leisure centre. It wasn't their normal line of work, but bills had to be paid whilst they were waiting for the next big assignment from Asvina. To his credit, Jimmy had assented to the mission without protest, citing the opportunity to look up an old army chum whilst he was down there. It seemed to Maggie that he had an old army chum in all four corners of the country and probably beyond too, and for a brief moment she mourned the loss of camaraderie she had suffered after her semi-successful barrister career had crashed and burned. But then when she thought about it again, they were all shits, so really, it was no loss.

They'd had a laugh on the phone after Frank had told them the crazy truth about da Vinci. That their client Charles Grant, right-on warrior for social justice, had, unbelievably, been trolling himself. She could just imagine the headlines in the *Mail* and the *Telegraph* if it ever got out. *Leftie actor invents fascist foe to reinforce victimhood narrative.* It hadn't been his smartest choice, that was for sure, but that seemed to be the pattern of his life, evidenced by his bonkers decision to invest his whole future in Sharon Trent, when the feelings were all too clearly one way. And now she lay in a nursing home, her brain ravished by that terrible stroke.

But then Maggie thought about it again. If this ever got out, the poor guy would be totally humiliated, and knowing his strong self-regard, it would surely break him. What if Benjamin or Allegra David had found out about it, and threatened to reveal his embarrassing secret? With Grant's fragile state of mind, she could quite imagine him seeing murder as the only way out. This was something she would need to bring up with Frank as a matter of urgency. But that would have to wait until after she'd fetched Ollie.

The school stood at the head of a leafy cul-de-sac on the northern edges of Hampstead village. After the terrible events of the Alzahrani affair she had moved Ollie from his old private school to this state primary. It wasn't in any way a political statement on her part, the school having been chosen mainly for its convenient location to their home, and she knew it wasn't exactly an inner-city catchment area. The parents were no less middle-class than those of his old school, but tended to be of that group who liked to signal their virtue in all things, including and especially, the choice of education they had made for their kids.

The environment being the great concern of the age, the school encouraged parents if at all possible to leave outsized SUVs parked on driveways and to walk their children there instead. Encouragement was backed up by enforcement, the entire cul-de-sac a no-parking zone patrolled by a suitably officious female traffic warden in a conspicuous hi-viz jacket.

Maggie made sure she arrived outside the gates in good time, being unfamiliar with how long the walk would take. Group of mothers and childminders had already gathered, laughing and smiling as they enjoyed their familiar daily routine. She didn't know any of them, although she recognised a woman of about her own age who she recalled had recently moved in a few doors down the street from her and to whom she had spoken once or twice. Olivia, that was her name, easy to remember for someone with a son called Ollie. She stood a little detached from the others, her arms clasped protectively across her chest. From her City uniform of grey business suit, white silk blouse and heels, Maggie guessed an accountant or a banker, or heaven forbid, a lawyer like herself.

She smiled at her. 'Hi Olivia, I guess this isn't your normal afternoon. Me neither. But it's nice isn't it, to be able to fit it in occasionally?'

The other woman nodded. 'It's Maggie, isn't it, from number twenty-two? Yes, you're right, it is very nice. I don't generally get the chance. We've got a young French au pair who normally does it but we've only had her a couple of weeks and she's turned out to be hopelessly unreliable. Not because she's French or anything,' she added hastily.

Maggie gave a sympathetic laugh. 'No, I think it just comes as standard with these young girls, no matter where they are from.' Except for good old Marta, as solid and reliable as the day was long, and she was only twenty-four. 'It's Josh isn't it, your little boy? We must arrange to get together some time soon, I'm sure my Ollie would love to have a friend so close by. I bet they would get on very well.'

'Oh yes, that would be wonderful. Perhaps you could pop in for a coffee when we get back today and we can arrange something? Maybe this Saturday afternoon if you're both free.'

But now children were beginning to appear through the double doors of the school entrance, at first a trickle and then a steady stream, the noise level increasing exponentially as more and more emerged. Through the crowd she spotted her son, engaged in a mock-wrestle with another boy whom, as they got closer, she recognised as Olivia's Josh. She caught his mother's eye and smiled.

'Looks like our boys are ahead of us Olivia.'

'Mummy, what are you doing here?' Ollie shouted as he caught sight of her, immediately running over and throwing his arms around her waist, so forcibly that she was almost knocked off her feet.

'Wow, have you been doing rugby practice today darling? That was a great tackle.' She squeezed him tightly to her and kissed him gently on the forehead. 'Marta had to go and visit her own mummy in Poland so you've got me instead today.'

Momentarily he looked anxious. 'Can we still go to the shop for sweets on the way home mummy? Marta always lets me.' It was news to Maggie, and strictly against instructions too, but that was her good-hearted nanny all over.

'Well if you can show me the way, maybe we can do it as a special treat just for today. And perhaps Josh would like to come too if his mummy is ok with that?'

Olivia laughed. 'I don't think I could stop him even if I wanted to. Of course it's fine.'

They set off along the cul-de-sac, the boys hyper with excitement and the mums relaxed, chatting easily about work and houses and schools and husbands - dead husbands in Maggie's case. Time seemed to fly by as they trooped the half-mile along the busy main road to where they would turn off, disappearing into the warren of leafy suburban backwaters. Looking up, she saw that the two boys had sprinted ahead and then stopped at a junction which was unfamiliar to both the mothers.

'Do you know where you're going?' she shouted, struggling to make herself heard above the roar of the traffic.

'Of course mummy,' he shouted back. 'It's just along here a bit. Mr Aziz's shop is on the next corner.'

'Well don't go too far then,' she said, knowing they would ignore her. 'Wait for us!'

Across the street the occupants of a black BMW SUV sat quietly observing proceedings, as they had done for the last three days. If you were a politician or a celebrity or a prominent business person, you were likely to have had personal security training, which would have taught you the importance of avoiding regular routines in your day to day life. Change your times, change your route, change your mode of transport, that would make it more difficult for those that meant to do you harm. But kids going home from school, why would they know anything about that? Inside, the men had to make a decision. Same time, same place and there was the kid they were after, but today he wasn't with the fat girl, and today they weren't alone. It wasn't what they were expecting but a fraught phone call with the boss had left them in no doubt. It was to be done today, and so what if it was a bit more complicated, that was their job in the organisation. *Just get it sorted, understood?*

They left the engine running and clicked open the powered tailgate with the key-fob. It was quiet in this street, that's why they'd picked it, but it didn't pay to hang around any longer than was necessary. Just grab the kid, stick the bag over his head and cable-tie his hands, bundle him in the back, beat it. Didn't need to be more complicated than that.

To the mothers, now some eighty metres distant, the horror seemed to be unfolding in slow motion. There was two of them, a thick-set man in a leather bomber jacket, black jeans and trainers and a wiry youth in double denim. They looked around, hoping that they would be unobserved but not caring that much. In a second, they were on the other side of the street, the larger man grabbing Ollie by the hair and dragging him screaming over to the BMW. The boy, initially taken by surprise, now seem to realise what was happening and began to struggle, kicking his legs furiously and trying in vain to push himself away from his abductor. The second man, seeing what was happening, gave him a brutal slap across the cheek to subdue him, causing the other man to react furiously.

'Fuck's sake Vince, careful, we don't want no damaged goods.' He realised his mistake as soon as he said it, but Maggie and Olivia, who had now began running towards them, were still too far away to hear. With an expert motion he put two pre-prepared cable-ties around Ollie's wrist and jerked them tight, causing him to wince with pain. He yanked even more tightly on his hair, guiding him towards the open tailgate, and roughly pushed him into the luggage area. 'You fucking sit there and don't move, understand?' And then he remembered his slip of the tongue. 'Shit, we'd better take the other kid too, we don't want no witnesses. Come on, get him in the back of the motor.'

Throughout, Josh had stood stock-still on the pavement, open-mouthed with shock and fear, and it was a simple task for Vince to push him across the street and into the back of the SUV. At least it would have been, if at that moment Maggie and Olivia had not arrived on the scene.

Olivia flew at the youth, her arms flaying as she rained a barrage of weak punches in his direction. 'Leave him alone, leave him alone!' she screamed through her tears. 'Run, Josh, run. Get away!' but the boy was paralysed with fright, unable to comprehend what was happening to him and his mummy.

Simultaneously Maggie had rushed over to the BMW, where the older man stood guard, waiting to bundle Josh in the back. She tried to push past him to get to Ollie, but he grabbed her roughly by the shoulders and pushed her to the ground. As she fell, her forehead slammed against the pavement edge, driving a deep gash and drawing blood. Weakly, she got to her knees, her mind clear despite the pain. She had to free Ollie, she just had to, pleading with the gods to give her the strength, but as she tried to get to her feet, the hood smashed his fist into her face, shattering her nose and causing her to collapse into the road, ending up face down in a pool of her own blood.

Momentarily unconscious, she opened her eyes to see that across the street Olivia was still gripping desperately onto the younger man, who despite all his efforts, was unable to shake himself free. She could just about make out the words. *Fuck's sake dad, get the cow off me*. Then through her blurred vision, she caught the glint of steel in the sunshine as he ran across to his son and with a sickening movement, plunged the knife into Olivia's chest.

Chapter 26

Serious but not immediately life-threatening was how the young doctor had described Maggie's condition. Not *immediately* life-threatening, what the hell did that mean? That's what Jimmy was asking his brother, again and again, as they sat alongside her bed in a high dependency suite of the Royal Free Hospital. *How the hell would I know*, Frank thought, *you've seen more of this stuff that I have.* All he could say was that she looked as if she had come off second-best in a particularly one-sided boxing match. Her left eye was surrounded by a dark purple ring of puffy skin, causing it to be squeezed tightly and painfully shut. Her nose had fared even worse, the bone broken and the flesh swollen to twice its normal size, its colour a matching shade for her eye. Fortunately, the blow on her forehead, though causing a nasty bruise, had not broken the skin so no disfiguring stitches would be required. But along the corridor, Frank knew that Olivia Walton was fighting for her life, her distraught husband beside her, struggling to take in the shattering tsunami that had today, without warning, enveloped his family. He had been told not to hold out much hope, but he had not been listening. Olivia was just thirty-six years old and only yesterday they had received the news that she was pregnant with their second child. Thirty-six-year-old women didn't just *die,* of course they didn't, that was stupid, and seven-year old boys weren't abducted in broad daylight.

Jimmy and Frank had been joined by Asvina and DI Pete Burnside, who had been swiftly assigned to the case by DCI Smart. The stern male nurse had balked at having four visitors in the room, but Burnside had convinced him of the need for the police to be present when she awoke from her sedation, in case she had seen anything that would help them in the desperate search for the abductors of two young boys and the perpetrators of the vicious attacks on their mothers.

'What are we going to tell her about Ollie?' Jimmy whispered, his tone betraying his anxiety. 'I mean, it could send her over the edge, it really could.'

'What can we tell her? We know absolutely bugger-all at the moment,' Frank replied irritably. 'Look, I'm sorry mate, we just have to tell her the truth, she would want that.'

'Maybe it's best if I speak to her,' Asvina said softly. 'I don't really know what to say, but well, as a mother, maybe it would be better...honestly, I don't know.'

Burnside was trying hard to be positive, without much conviction. 'This whole abduction thing didn't turn out at all as they planned it, I'm absolutely sure of that. The crime scene will be awash with evidence, believe you me. We'll get the bastards this time, we will. There's no doubt about it.'

Frank nodded, wishing he shared his colleague's confidence. Six hours on and no witnesses had come forward and there was nothing on the CCTV around the scene, not that they had a bloody clue what they were looking for. Burnside had a squad of uniforms conducting door-to-doors within a five-hundred metre radius, but so far they too had drawn a blank. A near-fatal stabbing and the snatching of two children had taken place on a sunny school-day afternoon and no-one had seen a thing. With Olivia Walton at death's door, the fact was that now they were totally dependent on Maggie to make any progress, and goodness knows what state she would be in when she came round. Outside the door, another doctor had appeared and was immediately in deep conversation with the nurse. A moment later, she entered the room.

'Good evening, I'm Susan Sleaford, Miss Bainbridge's consultant. Nurse Hamlyn has just been sharing the background of the case with me. It's a terrible thing altogether.'

'Is she going to be all right?' Jimmy asked.

'I think so. She's suffered quite a severe trauma to her forehead and that would have led to rather bad concussion, but luckily we don't think she has suffered an injury to the brain. These can take some time to develop of course so she will have to be kept here under observation for a few days, but the signs are good. And she has a broken nose too, which is going to be very painful.'

Frank nodded. 'Aye, she's been in the wars right enough.'

'Indeed,' Sleaford replied, 'but my immediate concern is the effect any further emotional stress will have on her recovery. I've heard about what's happened to her son, and in my opinion, it may be sensible to keep her under light sedation when the news is broken to her. I'm genuinely worried about the effect any shock may have on her.'

'I understand that doctor,' Frank said, nodding in sympathy but anxious to make his point, 'but you know we really need to speak to her as soon as you think it's safe. She's probably our only witness at the moment and so you see, everything depends on what she can tell us. To help us find the boys.'

The consultant shook her head. 'Yes, well I can see it's important, but I have to balance that with the needs of my patient. Look, I'm happy with one of you staying with her but not all of you. And please, when she wakes up, no questions until the nursing team and myself are here, is that clear?'

'That's absolutely fine,' Asvina said. 'Her mum is on the way from Yorkshire and should be here in a couple of hours. Who's going to stay with her until then?'

They looked at each other, uncertain. Finally Jimmy said, 'I will.'

Frank knew his brother had plenty of experience dealing with trauma, probably too much if truth be told, but he guessed he'd never expected to have to face it in this job. Out in Helmand, telling an injured squaddie that some of their mates were dead was the worst thing he'd had to do, and now back here in London, Jimmy would somehow have to break it to Maggie about Ollie, and about Olivia and Josh too. He'd have no idea how much she would have remembered about the attack but whatever the case, she would be in deep shock. Of course, she'd been through a lot, about ten times more stuff in the last two years than most people saw in a lifetime, and seemed outwardly to have built up a resilience. But sometimes there was a tipping point, just one little thing, the straw that broke the camel's back. Frank prayed that this wouldn't be it.

He got up and patted his brother on the shoulder. 'Ok, we'll leave you to it mate. We'll be outside if you need a break, just give us a shout.'

***

Jimmy gave a thumbs-up as they left the room. For the moment there was nothing else to do but sit and wait, watching as she lay still and silent, her shallow breathing the faintest murmur above the background hum and rhythmic beep of the heart monitor. Hard to believe it was barely eighteen months since they had first met, both of them in different ways damaged goods, but to use the over-used phrase so beloved of celebs, they had since been on a journey together, and it was now quite impossible to imagine life without her. Yet it was difficult to put a finger on what exactly made the relationship so special. It wasn't romance, attractive though she was, but it wasn't like brother and sister either. Actually, when he thought about it, they were like comrades in the army, brought together by life experiences that few had shared. Yes, the more he considered it, the more he saw it to be true. Captain James Stewart and Maggie Bainbridge, the not-quite-QC, were comrades-in-arms, and always would be, if he had anything to do with it.

It was nearly ten minutes before she stirred, first her head slowly tilting towards him and then with an obvious effort she opened her eyes. Her face wore a quizzical expression as she struggled to take in her surroundings, and then the faintest of smiles as she recognised Jimmy. For a few moments she lay silent, and then with no warning she sat bolt upright, wincing as a wave of pain shot through her.

'Ollie, Ollie! My Ollie!' Now her breathing was laboured, her face turning a deathly shade of white.

Jimmy leaped to the door and yanked it open. 'Get someone in here quick!' It was a few seconds before Dr Sleaford arrived at her bedside, trailed by a young nurse. Gently, she placed her hands on Maggie's shoulders and guided her down so that again she lay on her back.

'You're ok Maggie, you'll be fine. Just lie down and we'll get you comfortable. That's a good girl.' She glanced at the nurse. '1ml of

Midazolam please,' and then to Jimmy, 'It's just a mild sedative, it's standard procedure.' The nurse bared Maggie's arm and then expertly administered the injection. 'It'll take a few minutes,' she said in way of explanation.

Now Maggie started to cry. 'Jimmy, Ollie, they took him, they took him... and Olivia...' She sobbed violently as the image evidently came back to her. 'God, it was so awful. That man... I can't believe it, what he did.'

Jimmy was struggling to find the right words. 'Maggie... I know, it's just... so terrible. But listen, Pete Burnside's got more than a hundred officers out on the streets looking for him right now, and it's all over the news and in all the papers. They'll find him soon, I'm sure they will.'

But the sickening feeling in his gut said otherwise. Of course he wasn't sure, he wasn't sure at all. After all, it was more than two years since Jamie Grant had disappeared, and they still hadn't found him, not the slightest trace. Praying was useless, he'd found that out only too starkly in Afghanistan, but he still did it because it was human nature to cling to any comfort blanket, no matter how illogical. So he closed his eyes and made a silent plea. *Please God, if you're there, for once just show your hand. Prove me wrong*, please please prove me wrong.

The sedative was evidently beginning to take effect and now she spoke more calmly. 'Jimmy, I need to get out of here. I need to go and look for him. I need to do *something* or I'll go mad. Please, where are my clothes, I need to go back there, I need to.'

'I know, I know,' he said soothingly, 'but Maggie, you have to get well first. And you should take a look in the mirror. You'll scare the horses if you go out in that state.'

She forced a weak smile. 'Yeah, very funny. But I can't just lie here doing nothing. I just can't. Tell the doctor I want to go home, at least tomorrow.'

He stared at her, alarmed. 'Are you mad Maggie? Hell, you're in no fit state to go anywhere.' Turning to the doctor he said, 'Can you tell her please, she won't listen to me.'

Sleaford nodded. 'Maggie, as your doctor, I have to say it wouldn't be advisable...'

'Advisable? Look, I'm really ok and I'm not lying here whilst Ollie is...is.' She tailed off, unable to bring herself to say the words.

Jimmy took her hand and squeezed it gently. 'Maggie, we'll find him, we will.' It wasn't much use, but what else could he say? 'But look, maybe you'll be ok to answer a few questions. Are you up for that... I mean, will you be ok?'

She spat out her response. 'Ok? Of course I'll be bloody ok, what sort of a mother do you think I am?'

The doctor smiled. 'There's your answer I think. But please, not too long. I'll ask the policeman to come in, shall I? But I'm staying, just in case.'

***

Maggie just about managed to pull herself up into a sitting position as DI Burnside entered her room. She saw him gave Sleaford a searching, as he sought permission for the interview.

'Just five minutes though, that'll be enough,' the doctor said. 'And then she needs to get some more sleep.'

Jimmy stood up to vacate the bedside chair and gave a thumbs-up.

'Cheers mate,' Burnside said, taking his place. 'Now Maggie, I know this will be difficult, but can you tell me everything you remember. Even the tiniest detail can help us to find your boy.'

'I understand,' Maggie said, and then she went on to tell him everything she could remember. Of the utter horror when she realised what was happening, the pathetic sense of helplessness when she could not free Ollie from the car, and of course, the stabbing. It was all a terrible blur, the order of events all jumbled around, like waking up in the middle of a nightmare and not knowing what was real and what wasn't. But there was something else, something she sensed was important, but it just wouldn't come to her. What was it? *Come on.*

Sleaford sensed her agitation and said quietly, 'Ok, I think that's enough for today Inspector.'

Burnside nodded. 'Yes, thank you Maggie, you've been absolutely amazing. It's been really, really helpful.'

But it hadn't been, not really, she knew that. She hadn't got the make or number of the SUV, and that was likely to be fake in any case. She had got a look at both men, but she wasn't sure if she could identify them if she saw them again, certainly not the younger of the two. She guessed it wasn't much more than the police had already worked out for themselves, and that was probably two thirds of bugger-all.

But then quite suddenly she remembered what it was. *Dad*. The man who had taken Ollie and who had stabbed Olivia. The younger man had called him dad, she was quite sure of that. How that would help, she had no idea, but it was something. But then another thing came to her. That man he had called dad. She couldn't think where, but she was certain that she had seen him before.

***

Outside in the corridor, Frank felt his phone vibrate. Glancing down, he saw it was Jill Smart.

'Jill, hi. What's up?'

'Frank, I'm in the ops room over at Paddington Green. We've just had something come in, and it's really bad news I'm afraid. They found a body, on some waste ground near Putney Bridge. It's a real mess. SOCOs and the pathologist are there right now, I don't envy them. But it looks like shot wounds to the head.'

'Don't tell me Jill, please don't tell me that.' With every fibre of his being, he hoped that it wouldn't be true, but already he knew from Jill's tone that it was.

'It's a boy. A little boy, about six or seven.'

Of course, he had feared this might happen, although he hadn't dared to admit it to himself. Because he knew they didn't need little Josh Walton. He had just been an unexpected complication in an operation that had very nearly gone tits up. A complication that had to be tidied away.

Chapter 27

As soon as she awoke it started to come back to her through the fog of pain and confusion. Something had happened, something so dreadful that her body and her brain and her entire nervous system had shut down, like a computer placed in that semi-vegetative state known as sleep mode. She remembered someone saying that they would give her something, a nurse probably, and then there was only blackness. Glancing at the bedside clock, she struggled with the calculation. Five-sixteen and the light was beginning to creep through the ward blinds, so that meant it was morning. What was it, fourteen, fifteen hours that she had been asleep? And then as her operating system kicked back into life, she remembered what it was and instantly she was wide awake.

'Nurse! Nurse!' Now she was sitting up, struggling to throw off the bed-clothes as she swung her legs round, her feet recoiling as they brushed against the cold floor. Shakily, she pushed herself up, becoming conscious for the first time of the crashing pain in her head. Ignoring it, she flung open the door of the bedside cabinet and pulled everything out.

'My clothes! Where are my bloody clothes!'

Two nurses had heard her cries and rushed from their station. The first put her arm around her shoulder and gently tried to guide Maggie back to bed.

'Now then my love,' she said in a kindly tone. 'We're not in any fit state to be up and about, are we? Let's get you back to bed, there's a love.'

Maggie struggled to free herself, but the nurse's hold on her was firm.

'My clothes. I need them. Please. It's my son you see, he's been taken and I have to look for him.' She could feel herself starting to shake as the emotion threatened to overwhelm her. The other nurse had turned down the sheets and now took Maggie's arm and helped her sit down on the edge of the bed.

'I know love, I know, it's a terrible thing. Look, there's a policewoman waiting outside. Let's get you back into bed and I'll send her in so that she can give you an update. And your partner Mr Stewart is snoring away in our dayroom.' She grinned. 'He actually fell asleep at your bedside and nurse Short and I had a right job to wake him. Now we'll get you a nice cup of tea and send them through.'

It was Jimmy who was first to arrive, unshaven and dishevelled after a night of fitful sleep, but it didn't prevent a gaggle of nurses turning to stare as he strode down the ward. He bent over and kissed her on the cheek.

'How are you feeling?' he asked quietly.

She smiled weakly. 'Rather shit, if you must know. But you've got to get me out of here Jimmy. We've got to look for Ollie.'

'Aye, you said that last night. Over and over again, as I recall.'

The young uniformed PC had been hovering discreetly in the background. Now she pulled out the chair next to Jimmy's and sat down.

'Miss Bainbridge, DI Peter Burnside has taken personal charge of the investigation. I think you know him. He's a very experienced detective and he will be pulling out all the stops to find your son. You're in good hands.' It sounded exactly like what it was. Classic platitudes from the victim support handbook.

'Is there any actual news?' Jimmy asked, looking at her.

She shook her head. 'They'll be doing more door to doors this morning and there's an update meeting at noon over at Paddington Green.' In other words, no.

Maggie tried to push herself up against her pillows, without success. 'Find me my clothes Jimmy, please I need to get out of here.'

He gave her a sceptical look. 'I don't think so Maggie. You're in no fit state...'

'They can't keep me here. I'll go crazy with worry. I've got to do something.'

***

He knew she was right, she would go crazy, but really, what could he do? Maybe they would give her something to help with the stress and anxiety, something to help her rest until she got strong again. That's what they had done with the worst cases out in Helmand. Pump them full of morphine so that they even forgot their own name. For their own good, that's what the medics said, and they had meant it too. And at that moment, that's what he wished for Maggie, more than anything in the world. He would squeeze her hand tightly as she drifted into a deep sleep, and only waken her when they had found Ollie safe and well. However long that took. But that was fantasy, not reality and he had to deal with the real world.

'Look Maggie, I need to talk to Dr Sleaford. She'll know what's best for you.' But he already knew what she would tell him. There was no way she was going to agree to her discharge, you only had to look at her battered face to tell how stupid that would be. And he already knew what Maggie would say when he reported Sleaford's advice back to her. Short of tying her to the bed, he wasn't going to be able to stop her. Which left him with one last option.

'Ok, promise me this. If the doctor says you will definitely die if you discharge yourself, you will agree to stay right here. If she says it would be incredibly dumb, foolish and stupid, and that you will need to sign fifty forms indemnifying the hospital from all responsibility in the matter, but you probably will not die, at least not right away, then you can leave with me.'

She did not reply but he took her silence as a yes.

***

Barely one hour later, they were outside in the cool air, a welcome relief after the stuffy hospital room. Jimmy was pushing the wheelchair which the discharge team insisted must be used for the journey to the car-park, Maggie wrapped in a blanket and clutching an outsized paper bag containing her medication. She had protested, but Jimmy had told her it was at least a mile to where he'd left his old Vectra and he wasn't carrying her, no way. Especially since the car was up on the seventh floor of the multi-storey and he'd noticed when he arrived that to save electricity they didn't switched the lift on until eight o'clock. He cursed inwardly as he propelled her up the steep accessibility ramp that wound its way up around the edge of the building. On another day he would have joked that she was putting on a bit of timber, but today wasn't that day. A few minutes later, and breathless, they were pushing open the double doors signed with a seven. The floor was almost deserted of vehicles and so he had no trouble locating his own car. He blipped the remote and wheeled her up to the door.

'Right then, let's get you in,' he said, grimacing as he once again caught a glimpse of her bruised features, 'and if I were you, I wouldn't bother with the vanity mirror. I just need to go and pay for this ticket.'

She smiled weakly. 'I won't. Are we going straight to the scene? I hope that's the plan.'

'Straight there,' he shouted back to her, though what the hell they were going to do when they got there, he hadn't the faintest clue.

They slipped through the barrier out onto Pond Street and a minute later they were on Haverstock Hill, the road quiet as they headed northwards against the flow of the early-morning commuters.

'Heath Crescent, wasn't it?' Jimmy asked. 'I think I spotted that on the map. Shouldn't be more than ten minutes.'

Heath Crescent had a distinctly genteel appearance, leafy and lined with twenties semis like so many more in the capital, although the average house price here was close to double the city's average. Maggie screwed up her eyes and scanned left and right as Jimmy slowed the car to a crawl.

'I think it was on the left, just along here a bit. Yeah, right here. This is it.' Following her instruction, he pulled up and jerked on the handbrake.

'Ok then,' he said slowly, 'right. I guess we should get out and take a look, what do you think?'

Yes, but look at what? Twenty-four hours ago, the place would have been swarming with SOCOs, working round the clock under the harsh glare of their portable floodlights. The fact that they had been and gone meant that their work here was done, the scene presumably having yielded all the evidence it was likely to yield. What were they going to find that the team of highly-trained and professionally-equipped experts had missed? But they had to do something, he knew that, for Maggie's sake. They couldn't just sit around and wait. That would be a killer.

He helped her out, taking her arm to steady her, the hospital blanket still wrapped around her shoulders. Softly he said, 'Do you remember anything?'

She shook her head. 'No more than I told Burnside.'

They stood on the pavement for several minutes, brows furrowed in concentration, hoping for inspiration, but none came. How could it? It wasn't as if they were suddenly going to magic up the solution out of thin air.

'Look, maybe we could try going door to door, if you're up to it,' he said. 'There's always a chance that someone will give up some information to you as the mum that they wouldn't give to the police.'

She gave the slightest nod of assent, but already he could see the hope was being drained from her. And of course it was hopeless. He knew he had to keep going for her sake, but after two hours, all they heard was the same story. *It was so awful what happened, but I'm really sorry, I didn't see or hear anything*. He glanced at his watch.

'Maggie, it's nearly twelve o'clock and you need to take your medication. I think we'd better get you home, get you a coffee and a bite to eat.'

'Yes Jimmy, I'd like that,' she said, her reply barely audible. Her house was only a half a mile away, and a couple of minutes later he was pulling up the Vectra outside her front door.

He'd forgotten that Marta would be there. As soon as she heard the key in the door, the young nanny rushed to comfort Maggie.

'I'm so so sorry, I don't know what to say. Ollie will be ok, I know he will. I have prayed to God and I know it will be ok.' He could see Maggie's eyes moisten as the young woman locked her in an embrace, desperate for anything that would provide a momentary relief from their agony.

'Marta, could you make us some coffee please?' Jimmy asked. 'And maybe a sandwich.' He took Maggie by the hand and led her through to the sitting room, settling her comfortably into the plump settee, tucking the blanket around her. Now all they could do was sit and wait. Wait for the phone call that said he'd been found, that he was perfectly safe and well and none the worse for his ordeal. Or wait for the phone call from the police liaison officer, the call that told her that her life would never be the same again. And he feared for her, if that was the outcome, after all she had been through. If anything happened to Ollie, he just couldn't see how she could carry on. He looked over at her, and to his relief, saw she was drifting off to sleep.

He slipped out of the room as quietly as he could and re-joined Marta in the kitchen. She had prepared a pile of cheese sandwiches that would have fed them for a week, but like her, his appetite had gone. She had been crying, her eyes black-ringed through lack of sleep and the tracks of her tears visible against her pale skin. 'Oh Jimmy, please tell me it will be all right,' she pleaded, but he couldn't comfort her, any more than he could Maggie.

'I hope so Marta. And I hope your prayer is answered, I really do.' He half-smiled and returned to the sitting-room, flopping down in the floral-patterned armchair that occupied the bay window recess. And soon he too was asleep.

He was awakened by a loud blast of *Feels Like Teen Spirit*, the strident opening of the Nirvana classic perfect as a ring tone but less than ideal as a wake-up call. It was Frank.

'Hey mate, how is she? Sorry I didn't call earlier but there's been some developments in the Danny Walker case and that tied me up all day.'

'She's not good Frank. What time is it?'

'Nearly eleven o clock. At night.'

'Is it? We must have been out for hours.' He looked over to her, checking she was still asleep. Lowering his voice to a whisper he asked, 'Has Burnside and his team made any progress?'

Frank sighed audibly. *'No, and there's bugger-all to work on. We know it's ninety-nine percent certain that it's the same gang that took those other kids but that's it. We've got Eleanor and her Dutch mate trying to do that phrase-matching thing and we've got old Mrs what's-her-name with her Henry, and Maggie with her dad guy and thinking* she might have seen him somewhere before. That's the sum total of concrete facts and it's two thirds of bugger-all.'

'That's not what I wanted to hear bruv,' Jimmy said.

'Aye, you're right but at least it's something. Oh by the way, Jill Smart's given me the ok to work on Ollie's case, not that I wouldn't have irrespective of what she said. I'm just going over to Paddington Green now to do some digging on father and son operations.'

'What, at this time of night?'

'Aye, I know. It's a long shot, but the fact is, I need to do something to take my mind off it. Anyway, must push on, just wanted to know how she was. Over and out.'

Maggie was now beginning to wake, yawning as she stretched an arm in the air. She saw Jimmy and smiled. 'What time is it?'

'Eleven. You've had a great sleep, you must have needed it. Fancy a cup of tea?'

'I'd rather have a whisky if it's that time. A large one please. There's a bottle of Glenfiddich in the cupboard over there. And some glasses.'

He fetched the bottle and glasses and placed them on the coffee table.

'Two inches?'

'Yes please,' Maggie said. 'Has there been any news?'

'Frank's moved himself onto the case,' Jimmy said. 'He's over at the station right now following up some leads on your dad thing. Looking at father and son teams as he called them. It sounds quite hopeful.' It hadn't sounded the least bit hopeful, more like clutching at straws, but he had to say something.

She picked up her glass and gulped a large measure and then another. The combination of sleep and the single malt seemed to have stiffened her resolve, because now she closed her eyes and laid her head back on the thick cushion. 'I need to think, I need to think!' She spat out the words, directed as much at herself as Jimmy. 'Where did I see that face before? Where! Come on, think!'

He could see that she did not need a response from him, did not want him to break her fierce concentration. But if she could force herself into the zone, why the hell couldn't he? Because for some reason, he was thinking about photographs. That photograph of Benjamin David and the kid that he'd found in the diary of his sister Allegra, the one she'd kept hidden under her mattress. The photograph set in those picture-perfect gardens, gardens he was sure he had seen before. And of the celebrity magazine shots that Maggie had shown him of the Grants and the Lawrences and the van Durens, the glossy airbrushed images capturing the perfect family life.

And at that instant, he had worked it all out.

***

Over at Paddington Green, Frank too was fortifying himself with a whisky, his a smoky Islay malt that he swigged straight from his hip-flask. Normally he turned to it when things were going badly, but tonight it was the exact opposite. Tonight things couldn't be going better. This was a celebration, albeit perhaps a premature one. What the hell.

It was the call from Eleanor and Dr Jansen that had done it. *We've found a match.* A suspect's statement from three years ago, a routine investigation into a robbery at a warehouse just off the Bath Road, an investigation that had gone nowhere because they couldn't place the accused at the scene of the crime.

I'm not joking you when I says it, I've never been near the place in my whole life.

He punched a few keys on his laptop and pulled up that interview report from the Jamie Grant case. Old Mrs what's-her-name was eighty-four, half-blind and a bit hard of hearing. Yes, he thought he had read it correctly before. *'He called out a name,'* she had told the interviewing officer. *'What was it again? Began with an 'H' I think. 'enry, that's what it was.'*

'But it wasn't Henry, was it my love?' Frank said, smiling to himself. 'It was Harry, wasn't it?' The same Harry who'd never been near the place in his whole life. He took his ruler and carefully underlined a name on his list. 'And we know who you are, don't we Harry mate? You and Vince, that son of yours.'

Back in Hampstead their individual moments of epiphany had emerged at the exact same moment, as if by some weird celestial decree. Simultaneously they had leapt to their feet, even Maggie in her condition, and screamed and shouted at the top of their voices, and when they shared their revelations and they turned out to be identical, they hugged joyously, as if they would never let go. Three minutes later they were back in the Vectra preparing to head south-west.

Chapter 28

He pretty much knew the way, but just to be sure he punched the address into Google maps, steering with his knees as they raced along the Dunston Road. Glancing at the phone, he saw the sat-nav was directing him up on to the North Circular rather than the shorter route across town. Good, he would be able to put his foot down along there, with three lanes to play with and hopefully not much traffic at this time of night. Plenty of traffic lights and speed cameras of course, but that would be a discussion he could have with the police after the fact. As long as they didn't get stopped on the way that is.

Thirteen-point-six miles and thirty-five minutes, that's what it was saying, but he reckoned he could half that. He kept it in third, the engine screaming from the strain of operating right up at its rev limit. Ten minutes later, they were across Kew Bridge and skirting the high wall of the famous horticultural gardens, and only three red lights jumped on the way, his indiscretions no doubt caught on the traffic cameras. Nine points, three hundred quid fine, maybe a ban. But worth it.

On the way he had got Maggie to message Frank with their destination postcode and a terse note. *Get here fast and bring an armed response team.* He knew that they shouldn't be doing this, that they should wait for the professionals, but this wasn't any ordinary situation. Ollie's life depended on them getting there fast and he wasn't going to wait for anyone.

Now his mission head had kicked in and he was barking out instructions. 'Look Maggie, in your state you shouldn't be on this jamboree in the first place, but since against my better judgement you are, then it's role-reversal time for us. I'm in charge, I'm the officer, and you obey orders, understand? You do everything I say, without questions or arguments, and you *don't* do anything unless I tell you, ok?'

She nodded silently.

'So, I've got a bit of a half-arsed plan worked out. There's some stuff in my old hold-all in the back seat there. Could you drag it over and see if you can find the masks? We'll need them at some point so best to have them to hand.'

'Masks?'

'Aye, look, I'll explain later. Just dig them out and then put one round your neck so you've got it handy if we need it. And there's a wee back-pack in there too. Pull that out if you can.'

She spun round, straining against the tension of her seat-belt to reach the old canvas bag and drag it onto her lap. Pulling open the zip, she started to search inside, struggling to focus under the inadequate glow of the street lights shining through the windscreen. With both hands in the bag, he knew she was relying on feel rather than sight to find what she was looking for. And then he heard her gasp as she felt it. Cold, hard, metallic, the shape unmistakeable.

'Jimmy, a gun? Is that a gun?'

'Aye, it's a wee souvenir from my time in the army. Most of the boys kept one when they went back to civvy street.'

'I'm scared Jimmy. If you think we need guns.'

'I don't know if we do. But we've had four murders and Jamie and Kitty still haven't been found, dead or alive. These are dangerous people we are dealing with.' Which is why of course they should wait for the professionals. Except that the last thing they wanted here was some big Hollywood-style shit-storm. With these armed response guys, it was all battering rams and shouting and teams of trigger-happy hard men with automatics rampaging around the crime scene. He'd seen plenty of these operations in Helmand and the problem was, they had a nasty propensity to go arse over tit. Collateral damage, that's what they called it, but they couldn't afford collateral damage on this mission. No, what he had in mind was altogether more subtle. Employing stealth not strength. Well, sort-of, if you didn't count the smoke grenade.

'The gun's just a precaution,' he soothed. 'We won't be shooting anyone, don't worry.' As long as nobody shoots at us first, he thought.

He turned off the engine as they approached the house, coasting to a halt just alongside its perimeter wall. No more than six feet high, he estimated, not hard to get over and an easy drop on the other side. There would be security cameras of course, but he guessed they would be mainly focussed around the gates and driveway. There might be one mounted on a high mast or something, doing a sweep across the garden on a two or three-minute cycle, but they could time their entry to avoid that with little difficulty.

He reached over and took her hand. 'You can wait here if you want. Until Frank and his mates arrive. I'd prefer it if you did.' He knew before he said it what her answer would be.

'Ok, so you've got your mask, good.' Rummaging in the holdall, he took out the Glock-17, slid back the safety catch and slipped it into his pocket. 'Right, just need to get the ladder and we're good to go. Ready?'

She hesitated for a second, took a deep breath and then nodded. 'Ready.'

He slung on the back-pack and pulled a jumble of orange-coloured nylon cord out of the holdall. 'Rope ladder,' he explained. 'Ever climbed one before? It's easy.'

The short ladder was equipped with two sturdy grappling hooks. A deft throw and they were attached to the top of the wall. He gave the ladder a firm tug to confirm that it was securely attached. 'First time,' he said, smiling at Maggie. 'Not lost my touch, eh? Right, so I'm going up first. Just going to check the lie of the land with regard to any cameras, and then I'll jump down into the garden. Then it's your turn. So you don't do anything until I shout the all clear, and then you've got to move as fast as you can. Got that?'

'Got it,' she replied, without hesitation.

With one final pull to check it was secure, he began to climb. On the journey, he had been mentally assessing the risks, as you did on every mission of this type. Security lights and cameras, they were a given, but what if they had dogs, or even guards patrolling the grounds? Hopefully it wouldn't be needed, but the Glock provided an element of reassurance, the only problem being you couldn't just order a dog to stop or you would shoot it. You just had to shoot first and say sorry afterwards. But then again, maybe he could just pat it on the head and say 'good boy'.

He paused on the fourth rung, gingerly bobbing his head just far enough above the wall to allow him a clear view, scanning left and right to assess the situation. Yes, as he had predicted, there was one CCTV camera, mounted on a swivel bracket on the wall of the house, conducting a leisurely one hundred and eighty-degree sweep of the perimeter wall. But that would allow plenty of time for them to get up and over undetected. He waited until it had reached the furthest extremity of its cycle, climbed the last couple of rungs of the ladder then swung his legs over the wall and jumped down. With a swift glance in each direction, he sprinted the few steps across a short section of lawn until he stood with his back up against the wall of the house and directly under the camera. *In its blind-spot.*

'Maggie, can you hear me?' He had to shout louder than he would have liked since the garden wall formed an effective sound barrier, but he didn't think anyone in the house would hear.

Her voice was faint but clear. 'Yes.'

'Ok, start climbing now, but don't stick your head above the wall until I say go. Then swing yourself over and then run to where I'm standing. Fast as you can. You'll be fine.'

The wait seemed interminable as she stood on the fourth rung, awaiting his signal. But finally it came. Mimicking Jimmy's actions, she managed to pull one leg over the wall until she was straddling it. A second later she was picking herself off the ground and dashing over to where he stood.

'Nice work,' he said, squeezing her hand, 'ok?'

'Yeah, apart from the crashing headache and only being able to see out of one eye. Oh, and I think I've just sprained my ankle. Both ankles in fact.'

'So you're fine then,' he grinned. 'Well at least you got here in more or less one piece. So here's the plan. We're just going to edge our way around this wall and then round that corner. We should if I remember rightly then come to a set of patio doors that open outwards. That's how we are going to effect our entry, if you'll pardon the military jargon.'

'Yeah, ok.'

The doors were of traditional style in keeping with the beautiful Arts & Crafts house, multi-paned and constructed in white-painted hardwood, opening out from the kitchen onto the block-paved patio area.

'Right,' Jimmy said, 'you need to be ready to pull your mask on in case I have to use this,' waving the object he had taken out of the backpack. He doubted if she could make it out clearly in the dark, the cylinder about the size of a baked bean can, attached to what looked rather like a skipping rope handle. 'Oh aye, and I nearly forgot, you'd better stick these in,' handing her a pack of tiny foam ear defenders. 'It can be a wee bit noisy when these things go off.'

'Hell Jimmy, how long have you been planning this?' Maggie said disbelievingly. 'What else have you got in that bag?'

He smiled. 'Fail to prepare, prepare to fail, that's what I was taught in the army. I always knew this op was a possibility so I started tucking things away in my hold-all a couple of weeks ago. Now, will you just shut up for a minute and stand back a bit whilst I get this door unlocked.'

He took the Glock from his pocket, stepped back a metre or so and aimed the pistol at the keyhole.

'Just a minute,' Maggie said, reaching over to the door handle. It yielded to her gentle pull. She smiled apologetically. 'I'm always forgetting to lock mine too.'

'Ah, right,' he said, momentarily nonplussed. 'Saves a bullet at least.'

'Pleased to be of assistance,' she grinned. 'So I assume we are going in? Because won't they have an alarm?'

'Yes, and yes. But let me qualify that. *I'm* going in, *you're* staying here. And yes they will definitely have an alarm. And that's what we want. Right, here we go.'

Taking a deep breath, he opened the left-hand door and took a step in. A second later he heard from somewhere in the house the faint beep-beep-beep as the alarm system prepared to unleash its full repertoire. And when it kicked off, it was everything he hoped for and more. The siren was deafening, even more so than the one at Allegra

David's place, and the kitchen was instantly flooded with blinding white light from the ceiling-mounted floodlights, causing him to screw up his eyes so that he could barely see. *Excellent, that's job number one done.* He stepped back out into the garden.

There shouldn't be long to wait now, because no-one was sleeping through that din. He assumed she would have some on-site security, but the really heavy squad would be on standby but off-site, at that very moment mobilising their forces in response to the automated alert triggered by his intrusion. He just hoped that Frank's wee army would get here before them. They bloody ought to, considering they had at least a ten-minute start. But that assumed Frank had a proper case number and had filled in the right forms. Terry and Harry Kemp wouldn't be bothering with any of that.

A moment later, the door from the hall was flung open and a figure charged into the kitchen. Gregor, the shaven-headed Latvian gardener, carrying a semi-automatic assault weapon.

Jimmy whispered to Maggie. 'Right, so get the mask and earplugs on and wait here with your back tight against this wall until I tell you otherwise.'

She nodded, pulling it up over her face, the built-in goggles clamped tightly against her cheeks and forehead, the lower mask causing her to gasp for breath as she adjusted to the restricted airflow. He gave her a quick look over to make sure she was prepared, and then removing the firing pin, tossed the grenade into the middle of the room. There was a muffled *doof* as the charge went off, the powerful shock wave blowing Gregor off his feet. Seconds later the room was filled with an acrid smoke that burned the eyes and made breathing impossible. With a barked 'Stay here,' Jimmy leapt back into the kitchen and sprinted across to the Latvian, who was still on his knees, retching loudly and rubbing his eyes furiously. And quite oblivious to Jimmy's approach. 'Sorry pal,' he mouthed to himself as he administered a savage blow to the side of his head with the butt of his pistol. As the guard crumpled to the ground, Jimmy snatched his assault gun and ran back to the door, thrusting the Glock into Maggie's hand, shouting above the deafening noise of the alarm.

'Look, I need you to cover this guy for a while, ok? Just stand here by the patio doors and keep the gun pointed at him. Don't get any closer, we don't want him making a grab for you. And if he wakes up, make sure he sees the gun is on him. Then shout for me as loud as you can. But whatever you do, don't pull that trigger.' Not the most helpful advice, he knew that, but he didn't want Maggie Bainbridge up on another murder charge. With a brief backward glance, he charged back into the kitchen. Hell, it was impossible to think straight above that bloody noise. Smoke was still swirling around the room, and although sporadically infiltrated by shafts of light from the ceiling lamps, it was difficult to make out any distinguishing features. Now whereabouts was that door into the hall? Suddenly, his question was answered, as the door was flung open and silhouetted in the doorway stood Gregor's wife Bridget. With a gun. And she looked as if she was about to use it.

'Get out now Maggie!' he screamed at the top of his voice, gesticulating wildly towards the patio doors. 'Now!' He reached her in a second and bundled her towards the exit, both of them making it to the garden just as the first shot rang out. And then another and another and another, the crack of Bridget's automatic echoing around the room.

'Christ sake, she's just firing off at random! There's no way she can see a thing in that damn smoke.'

Then suddenly the shooting stopped and they heard it, so loud that it penetrated the air even above the satanic noise of the alarm. A scream of utter horror and anguish, the likes of which they had never in their lives heard before. And now lying prostrate on the kitchen floor was Gregor, a torrent of blood spurting from the three bullet wounds in his chest. It took Jimmy a few seconds to work out what had happened and a second more to make his decision. He threw down the automatic then took his pistol from Maggie, checking again that the safety was off. Cautiously he peered into the room. Through the smoke he could just about make out the kneeling figure of the maid, her hands pressed against her husband's chest in a futile attempt to arrest the flow from the bullet wounds that she had caused. Which meant she wasn't holding her gun now.

He ran across to them, scanning the tiled floor for the discarded weapon. There it was, tight against the kick board of one of the kitchen units. He stretched out a foot and dragged it towards him, then with a firm kick sent it spinning across the floor. 'Grab that!' he shouted to Maggie.

Bridget was now sobbing, pleading. 'Help me, help me please.' There had been quite a few of the lads out in Afghanistan who would have helped her by putting a bullet in her skull, and sod the Geneva convention. He'd witnessed a few of those incidents, and it left bitter memories that never quite faded. It was one for all, all for one in time if war and you had to turn a blind eye and just make sure everyone stuck to the same story. But this wasn't war. He knelt down beside her and placed a hand on her shoulder.

'The police will be here in a moment and they'll call an ambulance. Keep the pressure on his chest. He'll pull through.' There was no chance of that, but it didn't cost anything to give her a little hope.

He ran back to the patio doors, and grabbing Maggie by the hand, dragged her across the kitchen and out into the hall. Slamming the door behind them, he helped her pull off her mask before removing his own, both grateful for the ability to breath properly again. Now they could do what they had come here to do.

First though, he needed to do something about that bloody alarm. He ran towards the front entrance, on the assumption that she would have a cloakroom in the hall, and that would be the logical place to keep the control unit. He slid open the first door to find the cupboard stuffed tight with coats and jackets suspended from an aluminium hanging rail. Grabbing a dozen or so in both arms, he threw them onto the floor behind him, pushing the remaining items aside so that the back wall of the cupboard became visible. There it was, a small white box with a keypad and digital display panel, which was flashing the message 'activated,' as if they didn't know that already. Of course, all these systems were tamper-proof, he knew that. But there was tampering, and then there was *proper* tampering. He smiled at

Maggie, took a step backwards and aimed the Glock at the middle of the unit. A gentle squeeze on the trigger and the box was blown to bits, momentarily bursting into flames as the state of the art electronics tried in vain to cope with a catastrophic re-wiring of its circuits. And then silence. Total, blissful silence. Now they were ready.

'She pointed it out to me when I was here for the garden party,' Maggie shouted. 'The door to the basement. I'm sure it was off this hall somewhere.' And then she remembered, her voice urgent. 'That one. Next to the kitchen.' It was no surprise to either that it was locked, protected by a keypad-activated combination lock. They looked at one another and exchanged a knowing smile. And then to her surprise, he handed her the pistol.

'Go on. Blow the arse off it.' He couldn't explain why, but it seemed somehow right that she should do it. 'And it probably would be a good idea if you didn't shut your eyes,' giving a faint grin as he saw her grimace. 'Just relax, and a wee squeeze will do it.'

She held the gun out in front of her, her arms rigid, squinting down the barrel to take aim, then did as he instructed. The gentlest touch on the trigger and then the deafening crack as the pistol discharged, punching a four-inch diameter hole where the lock and handle had been. He gave her a thumbs up as she thrust the pistol back into his hands, as if it was too hot to hold.

'That was brilliant,' he said, 'and I'm hoping we won't need this again. Come on.' The entrance led to a small landing with a glass-fronted elevator and to the side of that a staircase. A staircase that led down to the gymnasium and swimming pool. It took just a few seconds for them to reach the basement level, entering through a pair of satin-white doors.

But they didn't lead to a swimming pool or a gymnasium. The room looked more like the upstairs landing of an executive show-home, bathed in a beautiful natural light, warm and welcoming, the walls painted in a soothing lavender-white, the floor carpeted in a soft dusky off-grey, thick and luxuriant. Each of the two side walls had a large picture window, bordered by pretty pastel-coloured curtains held back by matching tie-backs, looking out onto a lovely sunlit garden. For a moment Jimmy was thrown, because not only were they at least three metres below ground level, but it was pitch dark outside. Until, getting closer, he saw these weren't windows but TV screens, broadcasting some weird virtual reality into this perfectly-recreated domestic paradise.

And then they saw the doors. Four of them, spaced around the room, gleaming white with delicate chrome handles, and on each of them was mounted a beautiful hand-painted enamel sign. *Kitty's Room, Jamie's Room, Lizzie's Room.*

And Ollie's Room. He leapt over and pushed at the handle but it didn't move. *Locked.* And then from behind it, he heard the sound of a child crying. *Please, please, please let him be all right. Please God.* He took Maggie's hand and squeezed it tightly. Of course it was going to be all right. He was going to make damn sure of that.

He gestured at the door. 'Right, let's get this done,' and taking two steps backward, he launched his boot at it, sending splintered wood flying in all directions.

Little Ollie Bainbridge was sitting listlessly on the edge of a bed, clutching a *Toy Story* figure and sobbing quietly to himself. For a moment he didn't react, as if unable to understand what was happening. And then, comprehension. It was his mummy, here to take him home, and he ran towards her, throwing himself into her arms. *Thank god he was all right.*

From upstairs Jimmy could hear voices, urgent barked instructions, doors being kicked open, shouts of 'clear!' Outside, a Range Rover with blacked-out windows paused for a few seconds at the front gate then after a brief weighing up of the situation, accelerated away.

'Down here,' he shouted. 'Down here Frank. It's clear.'

He could hear his brother clumping down the stairs and then a second later he emerged, trailed by two heavily-armed officers in full assault gear.

'Oh, thanks to our Lord,' Frank said as he weighed up the scene. 'He's safe. He's safe.'

'Aye, but what about the other kids?' Jimmy said, pointing at the other doors.

'Only one way to find out,' Frank said, trying the handle of Jamie Grant's room, 'but it'll be fine, I'm sure it will.'

He nodded to one of the assault squad. 'Break it down, but go easy, eh?' then winced as the burly officer took the battering ram to the door, Frank and Jimmy following him in.

It was a perfect little boys' room, wallpapered in a navy design of spaceships and stars, furnished with a single cabin bed with pull-out desk and a soft bean-bag chair in one corner. And on the bed a little boy was sleeping soundly. Little Jamie Grant, just eighteen months old when he was taken, but now nearly four.

'Let's leave him sleeping,' Frank whispered, 'until we can get his mum and dad here.'

They had already broken into Kitty's room, gently leading the little girl by the hand and entrusting her to the care of Maggie. They were sitting on the floor, Ollie on her left, snuggling up to her, and Kitty on her right, unsure at first, and then finally tilting her head and laying it against Maggie's shoulder.

Everything was going to be alright.

***

'These kids need medical attention.' Frank barked the order to his nearest armed colleague. 'Can we get the paramedics here fast, and can one of you start making some hot chocolate.'

What they really needed was to be held tightly in the comforting arms of their parents. If everything went to plan, Charles and Vivien Grant would soon be here to be reunited with their son. But Mr and Mrs Lawrence were eight hundred miles away in south-west France. He took out his phone and fired off a quick text to Inspector Marie Laurent. *Kitty Lawrence found, safe and well*. He would fill her in with the details later, and that was going to be a nice call. Afterwards, he might even invite her over to London, see the sights, take in a show, and then perhaps a little romantic dinner. It was a lovely daydream but there was no time for any of that now.

'Where is she?' he asked as his focus returned. 'Have we found the crazy bitch yet?'

'No sign,' Jimmy answered. 'I'm beginning to think she can't be at home. Nobody could have slept through that alarm.'

Maggie looked up. 'She's got a panic room. Upstairs. The door is just off her en-suite.'

Frank motioned to his two colleagues. 'Right boys, come with me. And bring that great bloody thing with you.'

'Careful Frank,' Jimmy shouted after him. His brother gave a dismissive wave as he disappeared up the stairwell.

The reinforced panic room door, strong as it was, proved no match for two burly police officers equipped with a fifty-kilogram battering ram. It took just three blows to burst the lock and they were in. Melody Montague, dressed only in a skimpy black negligee, stood motionless in the centre of the tiny room, a cigarette dangling between her fingers. She was not alone. Her companion, stark naked, cowered in a corner, his hands covering his crotch.

'Well well, caught a bit short sir?' Frank smirked. 'Very embarrassing.' He recognised the man from a photograph in the David murder file. One of the scriptwriters on Bow Road, interviewed and eliminated in the early stages of the investigation. He nodded in the direction of the door. 'Go and find yourself a towel for god's sake.'

Now he turned his attention to Melody Montague. If she knew what was coming next, it was evident from her expression that she intended to face it with defiance. At these moments he liked to get straight down to it, without messing about with any small-talk. It was a lengthy and complex charge sheet, so he had taken the trouble to put together a written copy in advance, because you didn't want any smart-arsed lawyer trying afterwards to get them off on a technicality. He took the piece of paper from his pocket, unfolded it and began to read aloud.

'Roxy Kemp, I'm arresting you for conspiracy to murder Allegra David, conspiracy to murder Benjamin David, conspiracy to murder Olivia Jane Walton, conspiracy to murder Josh Walton, three counts of child abduction and illegal imprisonment with regard to Oliver Jonathan Brooks, Jamie...'

She sneered at him. 'Spare me all that legal crap, will you? You know you can't prove any of this and if you think you can find a jury who will convict *me*...'

Frank gave a derisive snort. 'Aye, right darling. You build some weird prison in your basement and we find three wee kids locked in their bedrooms, and you say we can't prove any of it? You really think so? If you do, you're living on a different planet. And let me tell you something else. You *way* over-estimate your popularity. A second-rater like you? Lover-boy over there is already writing you out of the series. Believe me, you're history.' He gestured impatiently to one of the armed officers. 'Slap these cuffs on and make sure they're on tight. Now hold her there whilst I finish.' He glanced down at his script before continuing.

'The abduction and illegal imprisonment of Jamie Grant and the abduction and illegal imprisonment of Kitty Lawrence. You do not have to say anything...'

When he was finished, he gave a dismissive wave and Montague was led away, her face still a mask of defiance. And at the bottom of the stairs, Maggie was waiting for her. Frank guessed that ever since she had uncovered the terrible truth about her client, she would have rehearsed over and over again what she would say to her at this moment of confrontation. And now that the moment had arrived. She stood in silence, staring at her the actress, evidently unable to conjure up any words that came even close to expressing the anger and loathing she must have felt towards her.

And then, without a word of warning, she took a step forward and smashed her fist into the actress's smirking face.

***

The police had found Charles Grant at the elegant Chelsea home of his agent Edwina Fox. He had been holed up there for nearly two weeks, ever since Sharon Trent's devastating stroke. And now the cause of that stroke could be explained. It seemed that as they lay in bed together after having made love, the actress had made her feelings towards him very plain. This is just a casual thing, she had said, rather nice but it would never be anything more as far as she was concerned. And then he told her what he had done for her. *I've murdered for you.* Hadn't it proved his love for her, more than any words could say? Was it any wonder that he was now going mad, after all he had been through? But now this pretty soft-spoken policewoman seemed to be telling him Jamie had been found, alive and well, and she was there to take him to his son.

They sped through the deserted city streets, PC Green switching on the flashing blue lights and giving an occasional burst of the siren to warn any dallying vehicles of their approach. The children had been gathered in the kitchen, wrapped in blankets and sitting around the big table sipping creamy hot chocolate prepared by one of Frank's team. The paramedics had arrived together with a consultant paediatrician who had been working the nightshift at the Royal Free and had insisted on accompanying them. Still Jamie Grant and Kitty Lawrence had not uttered a single word, sitting motionless and staring at the floor. As the doctor checked their vital signs with her stethoscope, she looked at Jimmy, the sadness in her eyes confirming what they both knew. There was no physical damage, thank god, but the emotional scars would be with them for a very long time.

Ollie had not left his mother's side for a second, not that Maggie would have permitted it, but he appeared to be in good spirits as he shared some of his terrible jokes with his adopted uncle. At least the boy had only been in captivity for three days and he'd soon get over it. Jimmy placed her hand on her shoulder, causing her to look up and smile. As their eyes met he said simply, 'I think he'll be fine Maggie.' In what way he was qualified to make the statement, he could not say. He just knew it to be true, just as he knew that in one way or another, he would be bound to this little family for the rest of his life. At the other end of the table, he watched as Frank took a calming swig from his hip-flask, evidently wishing for the same thing.

***

'Mr Grant's here sir. I've left him in the car for the moment. Not sure how you wanted to play this.'

'And what about the wife?' Frank asked the young PC. 'Has she turned up yet?'

'Up north with her family. She won't be here for a few hours.'

'All right. I hope you locked the bloody car by the way. Not that he's likely to leg it again, I don't suppose.'

She nodded. 'Yes, I did lock it but no, I don't think that's likely sir. Shall I bring him in?'

'Aye, and no cuffs,' Frank said. 'I think we can risk it, don't you?'

As he was led into the kitchen, Grant saw the child. And for a heart-breaking moment Frank saw he was unable to recognise his son. It had been two years since he last saw him and then he was just a toddler, not long out of nappies, and now he was a proper little boy, chubby-cheeked and with a mop of auburn hair.

'Jamie?' Grant spoke so quietly that he was barely audible, but it was enough to make the boy look up, uncomprehending. It was clear he had no idea who this man was. Confused, he ran over to Maggie and thrust his little hand in hers.

'I'm your daddy Jamie. Your daddy.' Grant's eyes were pleading as the tears began to well up. 'Your daddy.'

'Take as much time as you need sir,' Frank said in a kindly voice. 'Why don't you take Jamie through to the sitting room so you can have some private time with him. Here, I'll take you through. There's no rush.'

It was half an hour before Frank returned to the room, this time accompanied by Jimmy and Maggie, who was still holding Ollie tightly by the hand.

'Jamie, I need to talk to your daddy for a wee while now. Will you go with this nice lady please? There's more hot chocolate in the kitchen and I think we've got some sweets too. Go on, there's a good lad.' The boy looked at his father, who gave a single nod of assent.

'Before he goes, I'd like to say something.' Grant looked at Frank enquiringly. 'If that's ok.'

'Go ahead.'

'I can never thank all of you enough,' Grant said. 'For all you've done. I never thought I would see this moment. I had given up hope, you see. Quite driven to despair. My life... it was as if I wasn't in it, but watching from outside, like a play. I know it doesn't excuse what I've done, but... well, maybe it explains it.'

Maggie smiled. 'I can't begin to imagine what it must have been like for you over the last two years. But here we are, with a happy ending.' *More or less.*

She looked at Frank as if to say, do you really need to do this? But she was a lawyer still, and she knew he must. The law was the law and it was for the courts to weigh up mitigating circumstances, such as they were, not the police.

'Jamie, come with me and Ollie please,' Maggie said in a soft voice. 'It's all going to be fine.' Reluctantly, the boy got up, not taking his eyes of his father for a second.

'Go on son,' Grant said, his voice barely audible. 'I'll be through in a minute.'

He waited until they had left then stood up and said quietly, 'I'm ready.'

Frank gave a brief nod then began to speak. And this time he didn't need the help of a script.

'Charles Grant, I am arresting you for the murder of Daniel Walker. You do not have to say anything. But, it may harm your defence if you do not mention when questioned something which you later rely on in court. Anything you do say may be given in evidence. '

'I won't say anything, if you don't mind,' Grant said, immediately contradicting himself. 'There is nothing I can say really. I did it you see, I did it, although I knew I shouldn't. It was just a moment of madness, that's all.'

Frank gave him a look of exasperation. 'Sir, sir, I did tell you that you do not have to say anything, did I not? And then when you agreed you wouldn't say anything, you did the exact opposite. So I'm going to assume that you didn't hear me properly the first time, which means I'm going to forget what you just told me. Now I advise you to get a lawyer before you say anything else to anyone, including me. *Please.*'

He took him by the arm and led him back through to the kitchen. 'Last chance sir. Just say goodbye to him, then we'll get him looked after until his mum arrives.'

'They're wanting to take the boys into hospital, keep them under observation for a few days,' Maggie said. 'Ollie too. I can go with him of course.'

'You'd better sneak in the back door then,' Jimmy laughed, 'or they'll cart you back off to your ward. Don't worry, I'll come with you and fight them off if they try it.'

'Aye, and Maggie, you'd probably better get these knuckles seen to at the same time,' Frank said. 'I wish I'd been there to see it.'

Actually he was glad he hadn't seen it. He already had about a week's worth of paperwork ahead of him and he had no desire to add to it.

'But what if Melody complains?' Maggie asked.

Frank smiled. 'Don't you worry about that. We warned her not to struggle when we took her down the stairs, but she didn't listen. Fell and bashed her wee nose as a result. Oh, and by the way Maggie, as a lawyer you didn't hear any of that.'

'I'm grateful Frank, although I know I shouldn't be.'

'Well that's all good then,' Jimmy said, stifling a yawn. 'So it's three o'clock in the morning and we've probably had enough for one day, don't you think? Time for bed.'

No-one was going to disagree with that.

Chapter 29

Maggie laughed as Frank threw down the menu in disgust. 'Sixty-six quid for a bottle of wine and the cheapest main on here's nearly forty quid. And chips are extra? You did say it was you who was paying, didn't you?'

She had gathered them once again for lunch at the *Ship* in Shoreditch, one of the capital's growing stock of achingly over-priced gastro-pubs. But since they were dining in way of celebration, it had seemed appropriate to push the boat out, no pun intended. Indeed, the celebratory post-investigation lunch was becoming somewhat of a tradition for the three of them, if just one previous occasion - the Alzahrani case - could be said to constitute a tradition.

'Actually Frank, Asvina's paying,' she said. 'The case has generated so much good publicity that she's now overwhelmed by work. She's very grateful to us.'

'She's not joining us then?' Jimmy asked, a hint of disappointment in his voice.

'No, I think she's already buried under a mountain of new cases. But DCI Smart's going to be here. She wants a full explanation of the case from start to finish, to fill in a few gaps as she puts it.'

Frank sighed. 'What, you've asked my boss along? Now I'll have to be on my best behaviour.'

'How will she be able to tell the difference?' Jimmy said, shaking his head. The single-finger gesture he got in return surely left him in little doubt of Frank's opinion of his little joke.

'Boys boys,' Maggie laughed, 'come on, let's get on with ordering. I'm starving.'

'I'm desperate for a drink,' Frank said. A stuffy middle-aged waiter glided over to their table and began to recite from memory a long list of that day's specials, each of which Maggie guessed everyone would have forgotten the second they heard it. But it seemed Frank didn't need a menu.

'Steak,' he said decisively, 'and chips. I always have steak. Medium-rare. Oh aye, and a pint of Doom Bar for starters.' The waiter made no comment as he tapped the order into his smartphone app. 'And for you madam?'

Maggie was in a playful mood and for half a second considered it might be fun to ask him to go through the specials again. But she thought better of it, settling instead for a simple dish of chicken medallions in a lemon sauce, with vegetables of the season- nine pounds extra- and sauté potatoes -thankfully included in the price. In order to keep within a reasonable budget, and since none of them knew the least bit about wine anyway, they opted for one bottle of house red and one of house white, a choice for which the waiter struggled to conceal his disdain. She noted that Frank, the detective, had detected it.

'Don't worry pal, we won't short-change you with the tip if that's what you're worried about. Not if you get that pint here sharpish.'

'Frank Stewart, ever the diplomat,' Jimmy said after the waiter had drifted away with their order.

'What?' Frank said, looking confused. 'I didn't upset him, did I?'

Jimmy smiled and shook his head but said nothing. A minute later Frank's pint arrived, ahead of schedule on a tray shared by the two bottles of wine and delivered by a pretty waitress of altogether more cheerful disposition.

'Everyone having wine?' she asked.

'Is the pope a catholic?' Frank responded. The waitress smiled politely, evidently having heard the quip a million times before.

'Red or white sir?' It seemed you weren't given the option of tasting the cheap house plonk in advance.

'Both please.'

Unfazed, she poured a generous measure into both of his glasses, before filling the glasses of the others, Jimmy opting for red, Maggie for white.

'Ah, here's Jill now,' Jimmy said, glancing across to the entrance door. Maggie shot him a suspicious look. Jill? Since when were those two on first name terms? He stood up, waving to attract her attention. Smart smiled in acknowledgement, weaving her way through the throng of lunchtime drinkers to their table. The DCI was apparently coming straight from a meeting with an Assistant Commissioner, but today she was out of uniform, looking business-like in a dark grey pinafore dress over a crisp white blouse, which Maggie thought with a hint of jealousy, suited her pencil-thin figure.

'Hi everyone,' Smart said brightly, as she took her seat. 'What have I missed?'

'Two bottles of wine ma'am,' Frank said, deadpan.

She laughed. 'Just two? I thought this was supposed to be a celebration.'

'That was just for starters Jill,' Jimmy said, beaming her one of his special smiles, which Maggie did not fail to notice. 'Anyway what can I get for you? I'll nip up to the bar, it'll be quicker since Frank's already had a bust-up with our waiter.'

'A glass of prosecco please,' she said, smiling.

'Just a glass?'

'For now, but ask me later, won't you?'

'I'll make it a large one, just in case,' he said, as he disappeared off on his mission. A moment later the waiter, contrary to Jimmy's prediction, arrived at the table to take her food order. After a cursory review of the menu, she settled on the same chicken dish as Maggie, just as Jimmy returned with her drink.

'Right then,' Smart said after taking a delicate sip from her glass, 'let's hear everything about it, omitting no detail. I get some of it, but there's a lot I don't.'

'Yes, it's pretty convoluted I must admit,' Jimmy said, 'but we'll be speaking nice and slow for Frank's benefit. Over to you Maggie.'

She smiled. 'Well, to find the start of our story we have to go right back to the marriage of Melody Montague and Patrick Hunt. She was already mid-thirties when she married him and the biological time-bomb was well and truly ticking. And believe me I know what that feels like. It happened to me at the same age.'

'Tell me about it,' Smart said, giving Jimmy a look that Maggie noticed and wasn't sure she liked.

'So of course, they talked about having children, but unknown to Melody, Hunt was sterile. That came as a massive blow to her.'

'I can imagine,' Smart said.

Maggie nodded. 'So, for a while they tried to adopt but they were turned down everywhere they went.'

'Aye, I can guess,' Frank said. 'Too old and too middle-class.'

'Probably,' Maggie agreed. 'Whatever the reason, I'm sure it was that rejection which pushed her over the edge. Because then she just lost all sense of reality.'

'That's it,' Frank said. 'She sees these happy families in the glossy magazines and says I want one of them too. It became her total obsession.'

Jimmy nodded. 'Aye, it did. So she divorces Patrick Hunt and starts pursuing this mental plan to assemble the perfect picture-postcard family. By any means she could.'

'With the help of her brothers of course,' Maggie said. 'Kidnapping was a new line for the Kemps, but when the Jamie Grant abduction netted them a cool quarter of a million, they began to see the business possibilities. A nice little earner *and* they get to make their psychotic little sister happy too.'

'And they were clever,' Jimmy said. 'That's why the abductions were spread all across Europe, so that each looked just like a one-off crime. Less police attention and less resources allocated to the crimes meant less chance of them being caught.'

'Yes, that was it,' Maggie said. 'And remember, these kids were very carefully targeted, so although the families lived in Europe, they were all what you might call of Anglo heritage. English speakers in other words.'

'Aye,' Frank said, slurping his beer, 'because I bet that Melody wouldn't have wanted a foreign kid.'

'God, she really is off her head,' Smart said, 'and I can't believe she built that weird palace under her house to keep her collection. It was like a little dolls' house only with real kids.'

A dolls' house but with real kids. For a moment everyone was silent, Maggie assuming the startling image painted by Jill was playing out in their minds. But at that point, their food arrived and the hustle and bustle around their table provided a welcome distraction. Glasses were refilled and the conversation lightened for a while, until she felt able to continue with her explanations.

'So now we need to talk about the abductions, and the ruthless planning that went into them. So what happened was the Kemps roped in their photographer mate Eddie Taylor to take some photographs and to track the routine of the victims. Then it was up to Harry Kemp and his son Vince to do a clean snatch. And because they'd left nothing to chance in the preparation, there was minimal risk of being caught.'

'Except in Ollie's case where it all went pear-shaped,' Jimmy said. 'And poor wee Josh Clark was caught in the cross-fire.'

'Look, I didn't really want to ask this question,' Smart said, her voice quiet, 'but why Ollie? Because all the other kids had parents in the public eye.'

'I can answer that,' Jimmy said. 'It was that garden party at Melody's place. That's when they took all those posed family shots with her and Danny and the kids. The thing was, because it had made great business sense for the Kemps to return the van Duren boy, there was a vacancy. And when Melody saw Ollie, she decided he was the one to replace Brandon.'

'Thank god we got to him,' Smart said, giving a shudder, 'and to all of them.'

'They'll be fine,' Maggie said. 'Kids are great, they can bounce back from anything.'

If only she could be sure the reality would match the certainty with which she said it she thought. Ollie had witnessed his father and his lover murdered in cold blood in his own home, but more than a year on, it seemed on the outside at least to have been forgotten. But she feared it had only been buried temporarily, to resurface when he was a little older, a dreadfulness that might blight his life forever. As for the other two kids, Kitty Lawrence was back with her family in France, and Jamie Grant was back with his mum in Chelsea. Would they be fine too? She hoped against hope that they would, but for quite a while she guessed it would be in the balance.

'Aye, let's raise a glass to wee Eleanor Campbell and her big Dutch pal Hanneke,' Frank said. 'Led us straight to Harry Kemp they did. She's a genius that girl.'

'Yeah, I've always been curious how you get that young woman to do all these things for you Frank,' Smart said, giving a sardonic smile.

'Natural charm and charisma ma'am. You've either got it or you haven't. Actually, the truth is she likes being tucked away out of sight in Atlee House. She can't stand all the bureaucratic crap she has to put up with at their place in Maida Vale, and I get to take advantage of that.'

They had completed their mains and were awaiting the table to be cleared. Looking at the empty wine bottles Jimmy said, 'I think I need a wee pint, don't know about anybody else? I'll take a stroll up to the bar if you shout them out.'

Smart said, 'I know I shouldn't but I'd love a G and T. What about you Maggie, the same? I'll come and help you Jimmy.'

She didn't know why, but Maggie felt a sudden tinge of resentment towards Jill Smart. Actually, she did know why. She was so ridiculously *thin* for a start, and that didn't help. And her and Jimmy, was something going on there? He was a colleague, an employee to be exact, and yes, he had become a friend too, but nothing more, and Jill was only going to the bar to help him with the drinks, for goodness sake. Glancing over her shoulder, she watched them, laughing, at ease in each other's company. As they made their way back, Jill's hand rested on Jimmy's elbow, gently guiding him to their table. You couldn't mistake that body language. With an effort, she pushed the scene to the back of her mind.

'There we go everyone,' Jimmy said, passing round the drinks. 'These should suitably refresh us I think.'

'Thanks Jimmy,' Maggie said. 'And cheers all. Shall I continue?'

Everyone signalled their assent, Smart saying, 'I hope you're going to come on to the murders now?'

Maggie nodded. 'Yes, the murders. So as you've heard, when Patrick and Melody found they couldn't have children, natural or adopted, it basically sent her crazy. And I mean *crazy* crazy, not crazy angry. She just lost all sense of reality and from that point onward, assembling her picture-postcard family became her total obsession. So she starts building her fancy nursery-cum-prison and gets her brothers to kidnap Jamie Grant.'

'And then she falls for Benjamin David,' Jimmy said.

'Exactly,' Maggie said. 'Which adds a complication, but a complication that in her crazy deranged mind is easily overcome. Because surely wonderful lovely perfect Benjamin will share her dream to build the perfect family? Why wouldn't he, after all? It's what everyone wants from their life and why should he be any different?'

'So she tells him all about it,' Jill said.

Maggie nodded. 'Worse than that. Out of the blue, she introduces him to a little boy who we now know was Jamie Grant. *This is Jamie*, she says, *he's our little boy. Jamie, come out into the garden and get a photograph with your new daddy.* Surprised and bemused in equal measure, he goes along with it until suddenly he realises what is happening. And like any sane person would be, he's totally horrified. But what should he do? He's in love with Melody and doesn't want anything bad to happen to her. But he can't share the mental burden alone so he talks to his sister, but at first stops short of telling her the full details.'

'*Everything is ruined*,' Jimmy said. 'That's what he told her.'

'And in doing so, he signs their death warrants,' Frank said, shaking his head. 'Because Melody fears he'll go the police and ruin her little plan, so she gets her brothers to take care of the problem. And then, just a few days later, just for insurance, they kill his sister too.'

'And the *Leonardo* message and the severed hands?' Jill asked. 'What was that all about.'

'That was pure diversion,' Maggie said. 'Pure theatre. Everyone knew about that incident at the Hyde Park rally, when the White British League attacked Benjamin and Allegra.'

'Especially me,' Frank said ruefully, rubbing the back of his head. 'It still bloody hurts.'

Maggie nodded. 'The severed hand thing was engineered to support the narrative that these murders were carried out by the far-right. You know, to teach all these leftie liberals a lesson. So the Kemps came up with this little cryptic puzzle which was deliberately made not too difficult to solve. Leonardo leading to da Vinci, da Vinci leading to Darren Venables.'

'And it worked,' Smart said, 'for a while, until you all saw through it. So come on, the Danny Walker murder. Where does that fit in?'

'That was all because of Charles' doomed love for Sharon Trent,' Maggie said. 'He found out his lover was going to be sidelined in the show as Melody's Patty West character took centre stage again, and in his warped mind, killing Danny so that the storyline died with him was the perfect way to demonstrate his love.'

'He was one damaged guy,' Jimmy said, 'with that self-trolling da Vinci thing and all that. Is it any wonder poor Sharon had a stroke, when he told her what he had done? *I've murdered for you and by the way I love you?* The shock must have been overwhelming.'

'Exactly,' Maggie said. 'Remember, he had been to the morgue to identify Benjamin David's body, and would have seen the severed hand and the message written on it. Rather clever, and he would have got away with it too if Frank hadn't seen through it.'

Frank gave a rueful smile. 'Copy-cat, eh? I realised that Charles Grant was the only person outside of the media who knew the MO of the original murders. And although I hate to admit it, I do believe this is the first time in his entire career that Colin Barker has actually been right about anything.'

'Yes, and he's not stopped telling anybody who'll listen about it since,' Jill said, laughing. 'Although naturally he's not mentioning that it was you who worked it all out.'

'Well Grant's going to pay the price for it,' Maggie said. 'He's looking at twenty-five years minimum, despite everything he's been through.'

Jimmy nodded. 'I feel sorry for him in some ways. But murder's murder. You can't be allowed to get away with it, can you?'

They were silent for a moment, as if the thought of Charles Grant's spiralling descent into despair had caused each one of them to reflect on how life could take a sudden turn for the worse. And then Smart said,

'But come on, how did you manage to work it all out? That it was Melody behind it all I mean?'

'A big team effort,' Maggie said, smiling at Frank. 'But mainly Jimmy. He recognised the garden, you know in that photograph of the kid and Benjamin David.'

'Aye that photograph,' Frank said. 'So presumably Allegra must have found it in the house after her brother died and knew that something wasn't right about it?'

Jimmy nodded. 'Aye, that's exactly it. And I knew I had seen the location before but my old brain just didn't make the connection. Then I went to see Melody to talk about the pre-nup and it all suddenly clicked.'

'So what about that pre-nup?' Smart asked. 'Was it important?'

Maggie shook her head. 'No, it was just a side-show in the big scheme of things. It all kicked off with the sad death of one of the witnesses to the agreement, an Italian girl called Sabrina Fellini. She was killed a couple of years ago in a hit-and-run incident.'

Smart nodded. 'And that definitely was an accident?'

'It was ma'am,' Frank said. 'We checked and that's all it was. A tragic accident, but nothing else.'

'Aye,' Jimmy said, 'but it gave Melody's ex-husband Patrick Hunt the idea that he could turn the tragedy to his advantage. He guessed that the dodgy solicitor McCartney could be bought and that his friend Charles Grant could be persuaded to go along with the scheme for a cut of the profits.'

Maggie nodded. 'And it might have succeeded had not the Kemps found out from their sources in the nick that McCartney had been visited on more than one occasion by Charles Grant. So they put two and two together, McCartney takes a beating and miraculously Melody's problem goes away. Her original document had long been lost, but it didn't take much for the Kemps to draw up a replica.'

Jill sighed. 'It corrupts, doesn't it? Money I mean.'

'I wouldn't know ma'am,' Frank said, flashing her a sardonic smile. 'You don't pay me enough for that.'

'More than you're worth mate, more than you're worth,' Jimmy said, laughing.

'But it wasn't about the money, was it?' Maggie said quietly. 'Not for Melody. It was about love and her fanatical desire to create the family life she'd only ever experienced in magazines. She was evil I know, but in some ways I feel sorry for her. And now she will never have any of it.'

***

The waiter arrived with the bill, enquiring, as dictated by his management, whether they had enjoyed their lunch, not bothering to disguise that he really didn't give a stuff whether they had or they hadn't. He listened to their eulogies with indifference then said, 'Who wants this?'

Frank raised his hand and took the bill from him, theatrically unfolding it to unveil the total. With a mock grimace, he quickly pushed it across to Maggie, who glanced at it and gave a real grimace.

Out of the blue, Smart said, 'The Assistant Commissioner mentioned you by name Frank, in my meeting this morning. Said you'd done a damn good job and asked why you were wasting your time in Department 12B. We talked about my next role too and he wondered if I was going to find a place for you in my new team.'

Maggie saw Frank give her a suspicious look, and smiled to herself. She knew that talk of new roles and places on teams and everything that went with the grubby business of climbing the career ladder would be anathema to him.

'I didn't know you were moving ma'am,' he said, his voice betraying concern.

'Frank, you know I didn't want to be stuck in godforsaken Atlee House for longer than necessary,' Smart said. 'I've been offered the job of heading up the Met's serious fraud team. It's a fantastic role and I'm going to take it.'

'Congratulations ma'am, you deserve it.' It sounded sincere, but Maggie couldn't help notice a sliver of disappointment in his tone.

'Thank you Frank. But the good news, for me at least, is that the AC still wants me to oversee 12B. He was kind enough to say it's made great progress under my leadership and that he didn't want to lose that. Of course I told him that most of the success was down to you, and *he* said, and this is his exact words, why don't you get your Scottish nutter to head up the Atlee House team? And I said I would ask you. So here I am, asking you. It wouldn't be a promotion, not at first at least, but well... what do you think?'

***

So Frank thought about it. He grimaced when he thought of the cast of casts-offs and ne'er-do-wells that would be under his command. He groaned when he thought of the endless reports he would have to write and the complicated forms he would doubtless be forced to fill in and the dull meetings he would be mandated to attend. But on the other hand, he might be able to swing an upgrade to Atlee House's vending facilities as a condition of taking on the job, *and* he would ask for them to at least give the place a lick of paint. And when he'd finished thinking about all of that, the conclusion was, to his mind, a no-brainer.

Beaming her a huge smile he said, 'That ma'am, would be bloody brilliant.' Then as much to his surprise as hers, he wrapped his arms around her and kissed her full on the lips. He was even more surprised when she made no attempt to free herself from his embrace.

Furtively, Jimmy shot a downward glance. Ten minutes earlier as they stood waiting to be served at the bar, DCI Jill Smart had scribbled her phone number on the back of his hand. Quickly, he moistened his fingertips with his tongue and began to erase it, hoping to be unobserved. But Maggie had witnessed him in the act, and suddenly, for her, everything felt right with the world.

A BIG THANK YOU FROM AUTHOR ROB WYLLIE

Dear Reader,

A huge thank you for reading *The Leonardo Murders* and I do hope you enjoyed it! For indie authors like myself, reviews are our lifeblood so it would be great if you could take the trouble to post a star rating on Amazon.

If you did enjoy this book, I'm sure you would also like the other books in the series -you can find them all (at very reasonable prices!) on Amazon. Also, take a look at my webpage - that's robwyllie.com.

Oh yes, and if you took advantage of downloading this book for free, why not buy the first book in the series, *A Matter of Disclosure*? It's a cracking stand-alone read, and you'll also find out exactly how Maggie met Jimmy and Frank. And it's just 99p/$0.99 on Amazon.

Thank you for your support!

Regards
Rob

Printed in Great Britain
by Amazon